The Fish Wife

ALSO BY KIM ANTIEAU

NOVELS

The Blue Tale • Broken Moon • Butch

Church of the Old Mermaids

Coyote Cowgirl • Deathmark

The Desert Siren • The Gaia Websters

Her Frozen Wild • Jewelweed Station

The Jigsaw Woman • Mercy, Unbound

The Monster's Daughter • Ruby's Imagine

Swans in Winter • The Rift • Whackadoodle Times

NONFICTION

Counting on Wildflowers: An Entanglement

The Old Mermaids Book of Days and Nights

The Salmon Mysteries: A Guidebook to a
Reimagining of the Eleusinian Mysteries

Under the Tucson Moon

SHORT STORIES

The Entangled Realities (with Mario Milosevic)

First Book of Old Mermaids Tales

Tales Fabulous and Fairy, Volume 1

Trudging to Eden

CHAPBOOK

Blossoms

BLOG

www.kimantieau.com

THE FISH WIFE

AN OLD MERMAIDS NOVEL

KIM ANTIEAU

Ruby Rose's Fairy Tale Emporium • 2011

The Fish Wife: an Old Mermaids Novel
by Kim Antieau

Copyright © 2011 by Kim Antieau

ISBN-13: 978-0692216101
ISBN-10: 0692216103

Cover photo by Kim Antieau.
Book design by Mario Milosevic.
Special thanks to Nancy Milosevic.

Electronic editions of this book
are available at most ebook stores.

A production of
Ruby Rose's Fairy Tale Emporium
Published by Green Snake Publishing
www.greensnakepublishing.com

www.kimantieau.com

For
the Old Mermaids
and everyone who loves them

ONE

Sara heard Ian McLaughlin whisper her name as she stood on Far Cliff and looked down at a dark green ocean. She smiled. When Ian said her name it sounded like the whisper of sea spray over rock or the beginning of a siren song.

The other villagers said her name as though it was a lament: "Sar-ow." "Where is sorrow?" they'd ask. "She's not far behind," her mother would say. "Sorrow is never far behind."

Sara did not turn from the stormy sea, even for Ian. The O'Broin women came from the sea and a tempest stirred up all that remained wild inside each of them. Sara was no exception.

"Have you seen a sign of these times yet, Sara my girl?" Ian's arms went around her waist from behind and she felt his breath on her neck. "I'm waiting for you to leave your red cap on the beach so I can steal it and you'll be mine forever."

Sara turned around so that she was facing Ian. He grinned. His eyes were the color of blue ice and his hair was as black as the raven on Muiraugh Hill.

"That is a silly story, Ian McLaughlin," Sara said. "We don't have red caps you can steal. I would let ya. But there's no need. I am already yours and you are mine."

They kissed. Then they held hands and ran down the hill toward a place where the green skin of the Earth split open and spilled out a river of rocks. They climbed down this crevice and went into an open cave that would protect them from the coming storm. Ian McLaughlin dropped his coat onto the sandy floor of the cave, and the couple lay on the cloth and made love.

"When are you going to marry me, Sara girl?" Ian whispered as he leaned over her. She reached up and wrapped a black curl around her fingers.

"In all good time," she said. "When the auld ma of the sea whispers her approval. Or when the moon is blue. Or maybe next full moon, up by the Cailleach Stone."

"Is that a promise then?" he asked.

"It is," she said. "Can you wait that long?"

"That's not far off," he said. "Don't let anyone steal you until then."

"And you keep your boat close to here until then," Sara said. "I won't have the auld ma or anyone else taking you to the world below. My sisters are very enticing."

Ian laughed. "I've known your sisters since they came out of your ma's womb," he said. "They have nothing I want except you!"

Sara smiled. "I'm talking about my sisters down below."

Ian kissed her.

"This might be the time to tell ya," she said, "that we'll be feeding three of us by end of spring."

Ian jumped up and nearly knocked his head on the ceiling of the cave. He clapped and laughed out loud. Sara smiled.

She reached for his hand and pulled him down beside her.

"Can I tell the world, darlin'?" he asked.

"Not this world," she said. "Not 'til the druid handfasts us and the priest blesses us."

Ian took Sara's face between his hands. "I've loved you forever. It'll be a grand life."

"It will," she said, "unless I decide to swim back into the ocean and leave you and the babe on your own. So you best treat me well, Ian McLaughlin."

"May the strength of a thousand old oaks be on you," Ian said.

"May the sight of the raven be on you," Sara said. She kissed Ian's lips.

"May my love be on you all the days of your life," Ian said.

"Aye," Sara said.

The next day, the sky was bird-egg blue. Ian went out fishing with his father and brothers. Sara watched them get into the boat, and then she turned and headed home. It was bad luck to watch a loved one leave; everyone knew that. But it was difficult not to look back and see Ian's face one more time. They could be gone a week or more, depending upon the weather. Sara would think of him tonight before she went to sleep and imagine him up on the shores of one of the islands. She had promised to sing for him before she fell to sleep; the great auld wind would bring her siren song to him to keep him safe and help him sleep.

Sara hurried away from the water and up the road to her mother's cottage where she lived with her mother and sisters Fiona and Aine. Her brothers, Sean and Dylan, had left for the north with her father several years ago, so now only the four women lived in the cottage. Her mother liked it better that way. She never lived easily with her husband. But she was a good wife, he always said, and she did what was expected of her.

Sara did not want to do what was expected of her. She knew, as all O'Broin women did, how to keep a child from her womb until she wanted it. Her father said the O'Broin women were still too close to the animal kingdom, still wild, and like wild dogs, they knew when it was safe to have pups and when it wasn't. Sara's mother, Maire, bristled any time her father talked about them being like wolves—or dogs.

Her Uncle Ruarc said her father did not understand the wild. Or the history of things. The O'Broin women came from the sea. The Ryan men came from the forest. Uncle Ruarc and her father were Ryan men.

"We understand wolves and bears," Uncle Ruarc told Sara once when she was a child and crying because her father had struck her. "We even know how to avoid being captured by the fey. But we do not understand the sea." He held Sara close to him as she sat on his lap. "You and your mother are sea fairies, sea goddesses, and as such, you must find your own way home again."

Sara didn't understand what her uncle was talking about then—or now—yet she was grateful for his words. She missed her uncle and wished he had not gone to the other world.

But Sara was glad her father and brothers were gone up north.

Sara heard a whistle and she looked off to the north. Cormac MacDougal stood on one of the hills watching her. She turned away and kept walking. They had once been childhood friends, but now she could hardly bear to be near him.

When they were children they used to lie on the beach together, stare up at the sky, and watch the clouds pass overhead. She had liked him then. On her twelfth birthday, Cormac kissed her and told her he wanted to marry her. It was already too late, she told him: She was in love with Ian. Cormac didn't say a word after that. He turned and walked away: From then on, they were no longer friends.

Now Sara hurried toward home.

When she came into the cottage, Maire was standing near

the fire, stirring a pot that hung on a hook over gold flames. She looked up at Sara. Fiona and Aine stood next to their mother, their faces as white as the milk that came from Neasa's cow.

"What has happened?" Sara asked.

"There's gonna be a bad storm," Aine said. "Ma heard it in the wind."

"But Ian and his da just went out," Sara said. "It looked as peaceful as can be."

"The wind knows what the sea does," Maire said, "and it has told me right. It comes from roundabout but it comes. We're down to the sea then."

Sara glanced at her sisters.

"Careful not to touch your hair," Maire said, "in case one of the villagers is watching us. You know they think we bewitchin' them every time we unbraid our hair." Her mother reached up to the bonnet on her head and pulled from underneath first one red cap and then another and another; she handed one to each girl.

"It's been a long time, since you were bairns. You probably don't remember them. I wove them with the hair of a sister mermaid, the wool from the Witch McClarny's sheep, and your own precious hair while whispering the fath fith. These will keep you protected and invisible. Keep them close always. If someone steals it, you will be obliged to do whatever you can to retrieve it again. And if it be a man that steals it, then you are his sea wife, then and there. That is the way these spells work."

"I thought that was only a fairy tale," Sara said.

"And don't the fairies know a sight more than we do," Maire said.

"Just yesterday Ian said he'd like to steal my red cap and I said I'd let him."

"Don't give yourself away to any man," Maire said. "You should know that by now. If I had found what your da stole from me, I would have left you all behind long ago."

"You wouldn't have taken us with you?" Fiona asked. "You wouldn't have taken us to the place beneath the waves."

"I hardly remember it at all," Maire said.

"I remember," Sara whispered. "I remember how it feels. Like every part of me is alive and connected to every part of the world. I remember."

"How can you, my sorrow?" Maire said. "You were so young last time you heard the siren songs."

"I hear them every night before I sleep," Sara said. "I hear them in my womb where my baby sleeps. I hear them. I sing them."

Maire nodded. "You're all old enough now, past old enough, to know your heritage and your responsibilities. The O'Broin women have always kept this village safe, despite what they have done to us. It's down to the sea we go to see if this tempest we can rest."

The sisters put on their caps and followed their mother outside. The sky was overcast now, suddenly, and Sara wondered if it was magic that made it so. She whispered the fath fith, the ancient charm to make her invisible and keep her from harm. Her mother had taught the fath fith to them when they were young. Sara used it to walk amongst the deer in the forest and swim in the cove with the seals. She also whispered it when she walked down to the cove, mostly so none of the village boys could see her and follow.

Especially Cormac MacDougal. Something wrong about the way he looked at her these days. And he was always trying to start a fight with Ian. Cormac had asked Sara to dance at Winter Solstice last. Sara told him then and there she would rather walk a foggy moor alone with a banshee than have a dance with him. She shouldn't have said it, but she was angry with him for hitting Ian when he wasn't looking. Had she a sword, she told Ian, she would have sliced off his head and used his skull as a flower pot.

Ian said, "I thought the O'Broin girls had the mer in their blood, not Boudica's! I won't make the mistake of making you angry."

Now Sara squinted at the sky and wondered why she was thinking of Cormac MacDougal. Just then three ravens flew over their heads.

"Ah, they've come to help us then," Maire said as she watched the ravens. "It'll be all right, I'm sure."

The women followed the path around the village and down to the beach. They met no one. The air grew colder and the wind began to whistle.

"The storm is calling her friends," Maire said.

Sara's breathing quickened. She felt strangely happy. She remembered other times when her mother had gone down to the beach without Sara and her sisters, times before a storm. Even then, Sara had felt as though she should be with her—her place was with her mother singing to the sea.

The tide was out, so some of the beach was exposed in spite of the waves and wind. It had grown dark, too, the way it sometimes did when a big storm was coming ashore. The wind was so strong and loud now that Sara couldn't hear her mother, or anything else except the wind. She saw other women on the beach—in a kind of line that she and her sisters and mother were now a part of— walking toward the water. The women's lips moved, and Sara heard something coming from her own mouth. It was a song, a chant, a prayer. It was a plea.

They sang, "We ask those of the Sidhe and those of the sea, calm this storm before it forms, clouds part before it starts, waves calm like a summer's balm, blessings of the sea, blessings from ye, blessings of the Sidhe. Remember us who were once you, sisters, mothers, daughters all, heed our call."

The women got closer to the water or the water got closer to them. In the semi-darkness, a wave of light filtered through the storm, and the beach shuddered and shimmered. Suddenly Sara saw the women for what they truly were, saw their tails gleam and glimmer, and she looked down and saw her own true self. Yes, yes, yes. This was how it was supposed to be. This was her place in the world. For a moment she was balanced between both worlds: She could chose. She could dive into the ocean and feel the freedom within or she could stay on land and live the life she had known for so long. She began to lose her senses. It wasn't a true choice. There was only one way. One wave.

A gust of wind unsteadied her and snatched the cap from her head. She broke from the line of sea women and tried to run after her hat; only she couldn't run at first, so she shook off the part of her that was of the sea, as though it was a skirt she no longer needed. And she ran to catch the cap.

But something happened. The wind stirred up the sand at the same time it began to rain. Sara turned to go back to her mother and sisters, but she couldn't see them.

"What enchantment is this?" she called to the storm.

She saw the red of the cap bouncing down the beach and she ran after it. Every time she almost had it, the wind snatched it up and carried it away again. She couldn't lose the hat, especially not minutes after her mother entrusted it to her.

It was so dark and the rain was so thick—like fog and rain had become one thing. Someone grabbed her arm and pulled her toward something and away from the roar of the ocean. She didn't shake loose. She should have shaken loose. She was disoriented, afraid, lost. She wasn't quite here or there, so she let the stranger drag her into one of the cliff caves, out of the storm and into total darkness.

"He's dead." The stranger said those words, and Sara recognized the man's voice. She started to run back into the storm, but he jerked her into the cave. She tried to pull away again.

"Let me go, Cormac MacDougal," she said.

"I have your red cap," he said. "I know what that means."

"It means nothing," she said. He was stronger than she would have imagined. She tried to pry his fingers off of her arm.

"He's dead," he said again. "He will never come back to you. That bairn of yours will be a bastard child."

"You use such words?" Sara said. "You do not honor your ancestors. What do I care what some old priest says about my child? And Ian is not dead. He will return to me." Her heart raced. She could feel Cormac MacDougal smiling in the darkness.

Sara sucked in her breath. "You conjured this storm, didn't you?"

"I have no knowledge of such things," he said. "But I am acquainted with those people who do. And I knew if a bad storm came, your mother and all you witches would try and stop it. I knew I could find you here."

"Make it stop," Sara said. "Let Ian come home safely. I beg of you, Cormac MacDougal."

"You'll need those banshees now, won't you?" he said.

"I am sorry for saying that to you," Sara said. "I was angry with you because you were making such a fuss. You know my heart has always belonged to Ian. Any other girl in the village would be happy to have you."

"You can't get out of this," Cormac said. "You are my sea wife now."

"I will kill you when I can," she said.

"I fear I am already dead," he whispered. "I think of nothing but you. Now that I have the cap, now that I have you, I will have some peace. That has always been the way of it."

"You will have peace," Sara said, "but what of me?"

"You will have me," he said.

And then despite everything, despite her own strength, despite her whispering the fath fith and calling on the faeries to save her, despite her screams, Cormac MacDougal ripped off Sara's clothes, and he raped her. As she struggled to get away, she whispered to her baby that all would be well. The baby's father would come home and he would save them.

"You belong to me now," Cormac said when he finished. "There's no stopping it now."

"I belong to no one," she said. "And I will tell everyone what you have done here today."

As Sara searched the darkness for her clothes, the storm eased outside and the sky lightened. She could see Cormac for the first time. He looked uglier now than he ever had, especially since his left cheek bled where Sara had dragged a rock down his face.

"I hope you tell everyone," he said. "That will make my claim on you even stronger. I will see you in the church three days hence. You must marry me. You have no choice now."

He left the cave and walked down the beach away from her. Sara put on her clothes and then tried to find her red cap in the dark cave. It was not there. She staggered out onto the sand. She could barely stand, but when she was able, she began running. She called out for her mother and sisters. The wind died, the sand settled onto the beach again, and the way was clear. She saw the other women walking away from the water. Her mother and sisters called out when they saw her and ran toward her.

"We stopped the storm," Maire said. "What has happened to you, daughter?" She put her arms around Sara.

"The storm was conjured so Cormac MacDougal could get me—get the red cap. He raped me, mammy, he raped me!"

Her sisters gasped.

"Where is the red cap?" Maire asked.

"Cormac MacDougal has it," Sara said.

Her mother dropped her hands from Sara and stepped away from her.

"Mammy," Sara said. "Did you hear what I said? He raped me. We must tell everyone. He must be punished."

Her mother started walking away. Fiona and Aine stared after her. Sara felt as though she was going to fall over. Her sisters steadied her. "Mam!"

"There's nothing I can do," Maire said.

"Ma!" Aine said. "He hurt her!"

"It has always been this way," Maire said. "I told you not to lose the red cap."

"I had no choice," Sara said. "He planned this. He conjured the storm."

Maire turned around. "And so it was meant to be. The day I return the cap to you is the day it is stolen. Cormac is your husband now. That is the way of us. It is a bargain we made, an enchantment we agreed to."

"I never agreed to it," Sara said. "I will not go with him whether he has my red cap or not! I will be with Ian McLaughlin. He is my child's father."

Maire shook her head. "No, Cormac MacDougal is the bairn's da now. You cannot change this."

"I won't do it," Sara said.

"Then you will die," Maire said, "and the baby will die with you."

TWO

Sara ran after her mother. Her sisters followed her; both of them wept and kept their red caps close.

"You should never have given them to us if you knew what could happen," Sara said.

"It was past time," Maire said. "If your da had wanted, he could have found the caps himself long ago and sold you off to one of his cronies. We had to save the town. That is the way it has always been."

"Stop saying that, Ma!" Sara said. "That is not an answer: To keep doing things the way they have always been because they have always been that way!"

"Your sisters and I will go home and prepare for the wedding," Maire said. "We will get a message to your da and brothers. We'll make it a celebration."

"I will not marry him," Sara said. She walked past her mother and started up the hill.

"You do not understand, daughter," Maire said. "You are already married to him."

Sara ran up the hill. At the top she had to stop for breath. Her legs hurt and her chest was bruised where Cormac MacDougal had struck her. She put her hand over her belly. She would wait for Ian. He would help her fight this.

She ran into town and then down to the wharf. She stood along the stone quay and looked out to sea along with the other women and children who were waiting to see if their men outlasted the storm. The clouds moved away, but the air stayed heavy with storm. Past the bay, seals stretched out on the rocks to sun themselves.

"Those are the mermaids who started this trouble." Iffy Connolly nodded toward the seals.

"I see nothing but seals," Sara said.

Iffy glanced at her. Sara knew that look. "You're one of them," Iffy was saying. "You did it, too."

"You shouldn't be talkin' if you don't know nuthin." That was Patty O'Reilly. "Them mermaids protected this village long before the likes of you came here. Kept your daddy from drowning last Lughnasadh past. You ask him, girl."

Iffy looked back to sea. "I will if I see him again."

Late in the day, some of the men returned to the village. Most of them had seen the storm coming and had sheltered on one of the islands. One by one as the men rowed home, the villagers cheered.

Sara watched the sea. Fiona and Aine came and brought her a hot pasty and a bit of drink. They leaned against the quay and watched. It grew dark. Sara glanced behind her and up the hill and saw Cormac MacDougal standing there. Her legs shook. And then she felt the fiercest anger she had ever known. She jumped up and ran into the pub. She went behind the bar before a one of them could say a thing and she grabbed the Deaglán sword hanging on the wall. It came easily to her even though it had been hanging in that same place for as long as anyone could remember.

The sword seemed light as a cloud in Sara's hand as she ran outside and stormed up the hill. Sparks shot out from her heels as they hit stone. The three ravens flew overhead again. Some say lightning struck the ground between Sara O'Broin and Cormac MacDougal just before she reached him. She raised the sword up. Cormac did not flinch.

"You cannot hurt me," Cormac said. "I am the father of your child."

"Better women than me have killed their husbands as they slept," Sara said. "I see you wide awake with my heart spilling over with hatred and I will have your blood on my face before this is done."

She cut the air with the sword and swung it toward Cormac. Suddenly someone put their hand on her arm and stayed its motion. The hand was so firm that the sword fell out of her hand and Cormac stepped back from it so that it would miss him.

"You cannot do this," the man said.

Sara screamed in anger and pulled her arm away.

It was the Catholic priest.

"You have no sway here, Father. I am not one of your flock. This man raped me. I am now taking my revenge."

"Is this true, lad?" the priest asked.

Others had followed Sara up the hill, and now they surrounded the priest, Cormac, and Sara.

Cormac reached his hand behind him. When he brought his hand around again, it was full of the red cap. The crowd gasped. Sara's eyes widened. The red cap seemed alive now, glittery, as though it was made of scarlet fish scales rather than mermaid hair, wool, and her own hair. Sara tried to grab the cap. Cormac stepped back and the priest put his hand on her again. Sara slapped his hand away.

"He has stolen what is mine," Sara said, "and he has raped me."

"She is my sea wife," Cormac said.

The priest nodded.

"Ian and I are promised to one another," Sara said. "I will birth our child in the spring."

"I must marry you and Cormac in three days time," the priest said.

"Won't anyone speak for me?" Sara asked. She looked around at the people she had known all her life.

"It's just the way of it, Sorcha," someone said her birth name, clipping off the last syllable, SUR-a-ka, so that it sounded as though a door was closing on her entire life.

"Where is the druid?" Sara asked. "He will tell you Ian and I are promised to one another."

The crowd parted, and the old druid walked up toward them. He leaned on his stick; his brown robes looked threadbare. Sara glanced at the priest. His clothes appeared new and clean. She had not realized before that the druid was getting old. And where were his followers?

When the druid reached them, Sara looked into his eyes and said, "Tell them Ian and I were to be handfasted at the next moon."

"It is true," the druid said. "I have started preparations."

Cormac held up the red cap again. This time it was more orange-red than scarlet. Sara tried to grab it.

"Is this yours?" the druid asked Sara.

"It was," Sara said. "My mother only gave it to me this morning. I have no attachment to it."

"But it has an attachment to you," the druid said. "There is nothing I can do here, Sorcha. You are already married to Cormac MacDougal."

"I do not accept this," Sara said. "I divorce him. Here in front of the entire village. He attacked me and abused me without cause. You are all witness to our divorce."

The druid shook his head. "This will not work for you, child. You are his now. It was a bargain the sea folk made with the villagers long ago."

"It is a poor bargain," Sara said. "What did we get in return?"

"You got to live with us," one of the villagers said.

"No, they got to raise their children here," another said.

"They got to take our men," still another.

"It was so long ago," the druid said. "No one knows."

"These are all just stories," Sara said. "I will not live with this man. I will not go with him. If he touches me again, I will kill him. And you are all fools and cowards for letting him get away with this violence done to me and my bairn."

Sara pushed the priest aside—and everyone else who stood near her—and she went down the hill again to wait for Ian.

She stayed the night by the water. She listened to the waves breaking and then rolling across the sand. The stars twinkled above her. She heard singing off the rocks and wondered what trick of wind did this.

In the morning, her mother and sisters came to the beach and brought her home. She ate and slept, and then she went down to the sea again. Other women waited, too. Some of the fishing boats returned. Sara watched as the men picked up their girls or wives and swung them around. It was a joyful scene. Sara smiled. That would be her and Ian soon.

At night again, the voices called to her. She stood at the water's edge. The foam of the waves touched her feet. She felt herself shifting again—felt herself in complete connection with the world. She could feel the heartbeat of her baby—and the heartbeat of the sea, the ground beneath her, the villagers behind her asleep in their beds. All was as it should be.

And then she backed away from the water. She was no one's

sea wife. She was not a fish wife with no will of her own, forced to obey a man she did not love.

The next day, Sara felt unwell. She sat on the sand and began singing, calling out to Ian.

"You have to return to me," she whispered to the wind. "I cannot live in this world without you." He had to know what happened. He had to be at her side and they would fight this together. He could not be dead.

He could not.

On the second night, Sara slept in her bed. Her mother brought her soup and her sisters tried to chill the fever out of her with cold socks on her feet that they then wrapped in wool. Sara slept and dreamed. In the morning, she felt as though her life was slipping away from her. It was like watching water drain out of a tipped tureen.

The druid and the priest came. They each said she must marry Cormac and live with him.

"I will only go with Ian," Sara said.

"Your child dies with you," the priest said.

"I have the ability to create life," Sara said. "And I have the ability to end it."

Her mother and sisters wept. Sara was not certain any more what day or night it was. Her da was suddenly sitting next to her.

"Daughter," he said, "I know you take no stock in my words. I was a bad husband and a horrible da. I strayed into a magic I did not understand and I took your ma with me. And now there's no goin' back. Same with you. This is a deep enchantment. Even the druid cannot break it. If you die, you will curse all the O'Broin women from now and into the past. You cannot break this bargain."

Sara turned from her father and whispered, "I must hear from Ian first."

"Ian is dead, daughter," her da said. "Or he surely would have returned by now. You will be dead next sunset if you do not go with your husband."

"He ain't my husband," Sara said. And she closed her eyes.

She dreamed her child was crying. When she opened her eyes, Ian was there.

"Am I dreaming? Is it the fever?" she asked.

"No, darlin'," Ian said. "I am here. Our boat was wrecked and we've been waiting for someone to come by, and now here I am. They told me what happened while I was gone. I am so sorry."

Sara started to cry. "It'll be good now," she said. "You are here. You can help me. Let us get handfasted now and leave this all behind."

"I would do it in an instant," Ian said. "I would kill the man dead if that would help. But the druid said it wouldn't. And the priest said they would hang me for sure and the village would be cursed forever and back."

"Let it be cursed then," Sara said. "We can kill him, get the red cap, and be away."

"The druid said you and the bairn belong to Cormac now," Ian said, "and nothing can be done. If you don't marry him, you will die."

"Aye, they tell me the same," Sara said. "I'd rather die then."

"You have to marry him in the church," Ian said. "That is the only way. That is our way. I've known it all my life. You must have known it too."

"I didn't!" Sara said. "I don't believe it now even as my life washes away. Take me to the sea, Ian. Throw me in. If I am a sea wife, let me go to the sea."

Ian stood and looked down at her. "I won't do it, Sara. You are his now, you and the bairn. There is nothing I can do."

"There is nothing you will do!" Sara said. She tried to push herself up on her elbows as he walked away. "You said you would love me forever! What kind of love is this?"

Ian stopped for a moment, but he did not look back. Sara sank down into the bed and wept.

They say she wept so long and so hard that the bed became her bath and when her mother and sisters came to check on her, her legs had turned into tails again and they were this close to losing her. But they took off her clothes and dried her off, and then they put on her wedding dress, the same one her mother had worn all those years before. And somehow her da and brothers and sisters and mother took her to the little chapel where Cormac MacDougal waited for her. It seemed the whole village attended her wedding. Sara looked for Ian, but she did not see him. Maybe he was there. She was still sick with fever. She felt her child moving in her womb like a fish out of water.

The priest said words. Cormac kissed her cheek. The baby settled down and fell to sleep. Together Cormac and Sara walked out of the chapel. The fever began lifting and she could see more clearly again. Cormac reached for her hand and she did not pull away. She wanted to, but she could not.

"I will take you home now," Cormac said. "You'll see. It will all be good."

Sara looked to the west, toward the cliff above the sea, and she saw Ian there. He watched them. She wanted to run to him, to be with him, but she did nothing. She followed Cormac down the path to his cottage.

They celebrated through the night. Sara remembered later that her ma and da danced together. Her brothers and sisters laughed and danced and drank. The priest and druid stayed near each other and watched her; they smiled when she looked their way.

Sara no longer felt ill, but she did not feel like herself. Her mother came and sat with her for a time.

"You are a fish wife," Maire said. "You will be a good wife. It's just the way it is."

Sara wanted to scream. She smiled at her mother.

"Dance with your husband," her mother Maire said.

Cormac came and helped her up. Then they danced together while everyone watched. Sara smiled. Cormac kissed her cheek.

Before the sun came up again, Maire took aside her daughter and handed her a small wooden box.

"It looks tiny," Maire said, "but it will do you good. Every one of the O'Broin women have had one just the same, only different. Before the time of land, they were made from seashells and seal bladders. Or so my ma told me. This one is carved from driftwood found in the auld sea."

Sara ran her hand over the smooth gray lid and the blood red hinges. Were the hinges made from wood too? Her fingers touched the mother-of-pearl clasp shaped like a mermaid; the "s" of the mermaid's tail fit over a tiny piece of shell to hold the lid to the bottom of the box. Sara carefully moved the mermaid and opened the lid.

The small box was filled with treasures.

Sara put her fingers on a small ball of yarn.

"The good neighbors helped your great great grandmother as far back as forever weave this yarn," Maire said. "It is woven from sunshine and ocean waves, spider webs and mermaid hair, hopes and dreams. It's sprinkled with faery dust, too, it's rumored, so you best be careful what magic you do with it."

Sara nodded. She had seen her mother's own ball of faery yarn many times since she was a baby. Maire used a little of it in every blanket she made, in every dress she sewed. Tonight the yarn in Sara's box was the color of white sheep's wool, but Sara knew it could take on any color, just like a rainbow.

Tears burned Sara's eyes. She blinked them away. If the yarn had so much magic, why hadn't her mother used it to save her from this fate?

Next to the yarn were several needles carefully tied together with a ribbon. Underneath them was a tiny pair of scissors.

"Needles for sewing and knitting," her mother said. "One is new and the others are from your grandmother's sewing basket. She got them from her grandmother. They've stayed sharp all these years. The story goes they were made by a smithy who was trying to protect his children from one of the folk who kept stealing the children away. As long as they sewed or kept a needle in their clothes, they were safe from all kinds of thievery, including the faery kind.

"The scissors are new to the family," Maire said. "My ma told me they were a gift to one of the sea sisters from one of the Fates herself. I give 'em to you so that you can have some control of your own fate."

Sara stared at the scissors. Could she take them out now and cut this strand of her life away so she wouldn't have to live it?

Sara moved her hand away from the yarn and touched a sea shell. She picked it up and brought it to her ear. She could hear the sea. It sounded as though a storm was brewing.

"So you won't ever forget the auld ma or the auld sea," her mother said.

Sara gently returned the shell to the box. She picked up three small vials wrapped in wool.

"Those are herbs from our land," Maire said, "and salt from our sea. And this last contains the rich dark earth from the hollow hills where the Tuatha De Danaan went when they left us; it's mixed with sand from our beaches."

"Ma," Sara whispered. "You can't be giving me this."

Maire shook her head. "Of course I can. The earth was given to me for you from back at the beginning of time. It's not just ground I'm giving ya. The earth has everything in it that has lived and will live again. The flowers, the trees, the faeries. My mother gave it to me long ago and said it was a gift for she who would be needing it. She thought it was me, but I never used it. Not once. Maybe you'll know what to do with it."

Sara embraced her mother. Then mother and daughter looked at one another.

"I'm so sad this happened to you," Maire said, "but I'm glad we're fish wives together. Now you will understand the life I've had more than your sisters ever can."

Sara looked at her mother. She had no words for her. She put her hand on her belly and hoped her daughter would never be cursed so.

"May the joy of a thousand children be on you," Maire said.

Sara wanted to say, "But that's never gonna happen now." She bit her lip. Then she said, "And on you, Ma."

It was sunrise when everyone left. Sara sat at their table. Cormac got on his knees before her.

"I promise I will make up for what I did to you," he said. "I will be a good husband. I will never go to sea and leave you like Ian did. I have plenty of sheep. We will have a good life. I will be a good father to your children."

Sara looked at him. He seemed sincere. She could feel the enchantment working its way into every part of her body, the way she used to feel her connection to the world weaving its way into every part of her—only this did not feel good. She wanted to cry.

"You mustn't cry," he said. "It'll only remind you of the sea. Come, let us go to bed."

"If you touch me again, I will kill you," Sara said. It took all her energy to say these words. She felt exhausted as she said them. She saw something flicker across Cormac's face and she knew he would hurt her again.

"You will forget all of this soon," Cormac said. "Your mother told me so. I will be patient. You'll see."

Cormac did not try to touch her that night, or for many nights after. Sara cooked for him and went out with him sometimes when he took the sheep into the hills. She sat beside her husband and looked at the sheep and rocks and trees and she felt nothing. All was gray.

She and Cormac never went down into the village proper because it was too close to the water. He feared she would return to the sea. She wanted to tell him she had never been to the sea, except in her dreams, except in the stories her mother had told her, about how she was born with a tail, unlike her brothers. She was born a mermaid through and through. So her ma took her to the sea and offered her to the dark water, to the old mother within. Maire put Sara in the water and she was sure the waves would take her away; instead, the waves turned her over and brought her back as a human child. The same thing happened to Fiona and Aine. Her ma said she had birthed ten other girls but when she took them down to the sea, they swam away to be with the auld ma. Maire called them Sara's sea sisters; she had some of her own, too.

Sara shivered whenever her mother whispered this story to her. She thought she remembered feeling the sea all around her. Thought she remembered being in the womb or in the ocean. And she had felt full of her wild self.

Now she felt no wildness. No peace. Nothing.

The baby grew within her.

Sometimes she sat at the cottage window and hoped she would see Ian. But she never did. After a while she stopped looking. Then one night her husband wanted to make love with her, so Sara told him he could if he was kind to her and did not hurt her or the baby again. He asked her to teach him, so she did.

One day her sisters came to visit her while Cormac was out with the sheep.

"They say Ian is in a bad way," Fiona said. "He wants to kill Cormac. He's been drinking and cursing the village. He swears he will take you away. He's seen you. He knows you're different now. He blames himself."

"It is not he who made the enchantment," Sara said. "But it is he who didn't fight for me, with me. We could have stood up to it."

"You were dying," Aine said. "We could all see it. There weren't nothing he could do."

"Then tell him to get peace with it," Sara said. "What's done is done."

Her sisters exchanged glances.

"Yes, this is it, sisters," Sara said. "This is what I've become. Hold true to yourselves and your red cap. Let me be a warnin' to ya."

THREE

The villagers prepared for the Samhain fires. The priest said prayers in the chapel and exhorted the villagers to pledge to build a church that would put Donegal Village to shame. At least that was what Maire told Sara. She laughed as she said it.

"We be more interested in drinkin' and lightin' the fire than puttin' anyone to shame," Maire said. "That man knows nuthin about us, even after all these years."

Fiona and Aine came running into the cottage, their faces bright red from the cold rain that swept in from the sea.

"Ian McLaughlin says he'll kill Cormac MacDougal before the fires are lit," Fiona said. "Everyone is talking about it."

"He's drunker than Da ever was," Aine said. "It is a sad thing."

Sara felt the blood rise to her cheeks. She closed her eyes for an instant and saw Ian's face there, as she did every time her husband pushed himself into her. She would hear the sea and Ian's voice in her ear. "It's only us, luv," he'd say. And then Cormac would tell her to open her eyes. "I want you to see me," he said. And she would see that streak of cruelty there, wanting to come out as he pushed harder against her.

"You'll hurt the bairn," Sara would tell him and she'd imagine the sword in her hand again, only this time she would not drop it to the Earth. This time Cormac's head would come off as easily as she sliced the green off the purple carrots growing in her ma's garden.

She hoped Ian would kill Cormac.

Sara looked at her mother. Her mother shook her head.

"Cormac's brothers are waiting for Ian," Aine said. "They'll kill him first, for certain. Can't we do something?"

"Ma, you can't let them kill Ian," Sara said.

"You still care for the boy?" she asked.

"It's been barely a moon," Sara said. "I cannot hurt Cormac or leave him, but I swear if Ian dies, I will die, too. And I'll take the bairn with me."

"I told you never to give yourself to a man like that," Maire said. "I never seen it so hard on a girl as it has been on you."

"I hear them calling to me day and night," Sara said.

"Who's calling ya?" Fiona asked.

"The auld ma," Maire said. "And the sisters of the sea. You cannot go, luv. You'd drown fer sure. Ian will take care of himself. He has his family. He will find a woman of his own."

Sara wanted to go to sleep. Right then and there. Yet part of her still wanted to run into the rain and find Ian.

"Is there no way to lift this enchantment?" Sara whispered to her mother.

"What enchantment, Sorcha?" her mother said. "You're a married woman and Cormac is your life now."

When her mother left, Sara took her sisters' hands in her own.

"I cannot move for my own good," she said. "I am bewitched. You must help me. Find some fey woman or druid who can break this spell. I cannot live in this nightmare another day."

Fiona and Aine nodded.

"We will do what we can, sister," Fiona said.

Then they left her. Sara closed her eyes and imagined them running into the forest. They would sing to the flowers and the trees. They would whisper secrets to the wind and ask for help for their sister. They would climb the rocks that led out to sea and beg the sea sisters for relief.

Sara rose from the bench and began cleaning the cottage as she did every day. While she cleaned, she looked for the red cap, just as she did every day.

When Cormac came back to the cottage that day, he said, "You look unwell, wife. What has come over ye?"

"Nothing that some sunshine and goat's milk wouldn't cure," Sara said. She did not look at him. She feared she might blush and he would guess her sisters were visiting the fey folk. She would be released from this spell soon enough.

"I saw your sisters afield today," he said, "and later they were talkin' with the druid. It's not to be done. You have to forget your life afore."

"Then why did you love me," Sara said, "if that's what you call it, if you want me to be a slave to ya?"

"I wanted peace," he said. "I knew you'd give me peace."

"And have I?"

"Not a minute of it," he said.

"Then let me go," she said.

"I will not," he said.

"At least call your brothers off of Ian," she said. "He's done nothing wrong."

"I will do," he said, "if you agree to go away with me."

"You're always bargainin'," she said. "I'm not the devil who has your soul. It's the other way around."

"We'll go away from this sea," he said. "I hear their wailing every night. It sounds like you. I cannot bear it. If I take you away, all will be good again. I'm certain of it."

"I cannot leave my ma and sisters," Sara said. "And you with your family."

"It's Ian you don't want to leave," he said. "I see it in your eyes. I feel it in your body. You are not the fish wife your ma was or my ma is."

Sara turned and looked at her husband. "This was done to your ma? And still you do it to me?"

"We leave here in three days time," he said. "There ain't nothing you can do."

"I can throw myself into the sea," she said.

"Do it," he said. "The sea will throw you back. You don't belong to the auld ma. You belong to me."

The next day, Fiona and Aine came to tell her they had found no good neighbors to listen to their songs.

"The druid said he would ask that an answer come on the wind to you," Aine said. "But that was all."

Fiona wept.

"Cormac wants to take me away from here," Sara said. "I have chains on my soul and cannot go against him."

"You leaving could be the answer, sister," Aine said. "Then Ian would be safe from harm."

"And I, your sister, would be dead to you all?"

"But you are not like our sister Sorcha," Aine said.

She was already dead to them all.

When it grew dark, Sara stepped outside and looked about her. In the distance, a spot of gold blossomed on a hillside. And then another fire flower bloomed, and another. She could hear the shouts from the villagers. The revelry was beginning. Sara listened for her husband's voice. Since she had married him, she could hear his whisper from a mile away. It was as though some part of him had become some part of her. She did not hear him now.

She smiled. It was the first time she had smiled since Cormac took her down on the beach. It was not a happy smile. She was wondering if maybe Ian had killed Cormac and now she was free.

Something was happening. She could feel it in the air.

Maybe it was freedom?

She put her hand on her belly and felt the child down below push back on her hand. Then she started to run. She could see better in the dark than almost any O'Broin woman and they were known for their vision. It came from their travels with the Old Mother—the auld mother—in the deep dark sea.

Sara heard the revelers laughing at the pub. And some were down at the quay. She didn't see or hear Ian. But she knew where he'd be: at the cave where they met last. It was at the cave last Beltane that they had first made love. It was there they had woven together their hearts forever.

Sara felt strength in her body for the first time in weeks. She ran up the hill in the dark. She skirted the edge of one bonfire and then she ran down the hill and headed for the crevice. She saw a small fire in front of the cave. Her heart quickened. *Ian was there. Ian was there.* They would break this spell together.

Sara hurried over the rocks. She slipped once but caught herself before she fell. And then she was at the cave.

"Ian," she called.

Then she saw Ian. He was half-naked on top of a woman. In his hand, he held a red cap. The woman turned her face to the light and saw Sara.

Aine.

"My own sister," Sara said. Her voice was more of a hiss than a sound.

Ian turned to look at her. He seemed surprised. He looked down at Aine. Then he quickly moved off of her. He rubbed his eyes. He looked confused. Drunk.

"I thought she was you," Ian said.

"It was the only way," Aine said. She sat up and covered her legs with her dress. "I'm Ian's fish wife now. Cormac's brothers will leave him alone."

Sara felt rage rise up in her. She could not see straight. She could not think. She roared. The cave shook with the sound. The fire went out.

She turned and ran up the rocks and was out of the crevice in two steps. She was a giant. Her rage made her as big as the beach. As large as the ocean. She ran until she was on the white part of the beach. The sand glittered as though someone had spilled a pail full of stars on the beach.

Sara saw none of it. She planted her feet in the ground and she roared. "Old Mother, hear my call! Come and make it all fall! Big and tall! Tiny and small! Bring on the flood and the blood! Wind and rain! Bring the pain! Wash away this sin done to me by my kin!"

The words tumbled out of her mouth, old and new, ancient and rebirthed. Water washed across her feet. The babe in her womb twisted and turned, a fish out of water again.

The rage seeped out of Sara and drained into the sea.

She began to cry.

"With harm to none," she whispered as she tried to take the spell back. "With harm to none."

Sara returned to Cormac's cottage. She went straight to their bed and fell to sleep. She had never slept so deeply. She dreamed of a monster storm. The winds shook her dream house and tore off part of the roof. The dream storm mixed with the cries of the revelers and became screams.

When Sara awakened, it was light out, barely. She sat up. Where was Cormac? The cottage was cold. She pushed herself up out of bed and went to the fire and stirred the embers.

The door opened and Cormac came inside. His eyes widened when he saw her.

"What is it?" she asked.

"I saw you," he said. "I saw you with Ian last night in the cave."

She shook her head. "That was me darlin' sister Aine. She's Ian's fish wife now."

"Naw," he said. "A storm came last night. Didn't ya hear it? It was so bad I couldn't get back here. I thought you'd drowned in the cave. It came on so fast. Put out the Samhain fires like that." He snapped his fingers.

"What do you mean the caves were flooded?" Sara's heart began racing.

"The whole village is gone, Sorcha," Cormac said. "We have to go now."

Cormac looked pale. He was shaking. He grabbed a bag and began shoving clothes and things into it.

Sara ran past him and went outside. Some of the thatch was off Cormac's roof. Next door, the house of his parents looked untouched. She ran up the hill, toward her ma's cottage. She looked over where the chapel had been. It was gone. She ran to her mother's house. Several people were gathered around Maire. Fiona was crying.

Maire sobbed when she saw Sara. The crowd parted and Sara went into her mother's arms.

"Aine is drowned," Maire said. "Several people saw her down in the cave with Ian. All the caves were flooded and everything inside was washed away. They found this." Maire held up Aine's red cap. "Whole families were lost down near the quay. It came on so sudden. They're certain it was sorcery. Oh my poor daughter, gone to join her sea sisters."

Sara felt sick. She pulled away from her mother and began running down the hill toward the town. The path curved and she was in the place where the whole of the village would have been visible to her. Only it was gone. Hardly a piece of timber left.

"No," Sara whispered. "I couldn't have done this. The Old Mother wouldn't have done this."

Cormac was suddenly beside her.

"We've got to go," he said.

"My sister is dead," Sara said. "And Ian, too. I saw them, Cormac. I saw him on top of her. I was so angry, I called to the Old Mother. I called to the sea."

"All the more reason we have to leave now," he said. "They'll hang you fer sure. The ship is leaving in four days time. We can be on it. No one will ever find us."

Sara couldn't think. The whole world seemed to be spinning. She let Cormac take her back to the cottage. They put what they had into the two bags, one for Sara, one for Cormac. Cormac went next door to his parents' house to sell his sheep to his father. Sara retrieved the treasure box her mother had given her from its hiding spot. She wrapped it up in a shawl and put it in her bag. She looked around the cottage that had been her home for such a short while. She was surprised that she didn't hate it. It was only a place; it couldn't help that Cormac had kept her a prisoner in it.

When Cormac returned, he adjusted the bag on his shoulder and said, "It's time, wife."

Sara looked at Cormac's bag. The red cap had to be there. She wondered if she could grab the bag now and run. He would be too surprised to hold on for dear life. And then she would be free.

Free.

To do what? To raise another storm and kill her whole family?

She didn't deserve freedom.

"I need to say goodbye to my ma and sister," Sara said. "They need to know."

"I told my ma and da to tell your family we had to leave," he said. "We need to go before they start looking for someone to blame. With Ian dead and gone, you'll be the first they will accuse."

"Or you," Sara said.

And so Sara O'Broin left the Village by the Sea with Cormac MacDougal without a word to her people. She and Cormac travelled for three days together. Sara cried most of the way. She cried so much a river grew up beside her. To this day, they call it the River Sorcha.

When she stopped crying, Sara decided she should return to the village and face her accusers.

"I will confess to it all," Sara said. "I deserve to be hanged. I killed my own flesh and blood." She counted Ian as her flesh and blood, as dear to her as her own kin.

"And what of the baby?" Cormac said. "She would die too."

"They would wait to hang me until after she was born," Sara said. "And then I'd give her to my mam to bring her up."

"Aye, you're liking this pretty picture," he said. "You dead along with your lost lover. You've forgotten he betrayed you with your sister. I'd say that is pretty evil."

"You speak to me about evil?" Sara said.

"I am your husband," Cormac said. "You must do what I say."

Cormac was right. Sara's grief had not released her from the enchantment. She followed Cormac over the beautiful green hills. Once or twice she thought she saw a flash of light in the forest or a curl of mist near to her and she whispered, "Good neighbors, can you unravel this thing that has happened to me?" Nothing changed. She was still with this man she hated while her true love lay dead at the bottom of the sea with her sister.

It seemed like years before they reached another village by the sea, this one much bigger, with ships the size of the moon moored out to sea. Cormac bought passage for the two of them on a ship called Temperance. Then they bought food and beer for the trip.

Before long, they got into a small boat and a man ferried them out to Temperance. Another man checked their names off a manifest and they followed other people like themselves down deep into the ship's hold. It was crowded and smelled worse than anything Sara had ever experienced. At first she wasn't certain what the smell was from, but then she realized it was the stench of rotting people.

When the ship left port, the smell got worse. Everything got worse as people became seasick.

Cormac was one of the first to become ill. Sara made him broth and tried to feed it to him. He curled up into a ball and didn't move, except to throw up. After a while he stopped doing that. All the time he kept hold of his bag like it was his dearest child.

Sara didn't get sick. She helped where she could, making soup or telling stories to the children.

"What'd you put in that soup, darlin'?" one man asked her. "It cured me within the hour."

"Just tears, auld one," Sara said. "Laugh or cry, your tears have got the old sea in them. That'll cure anything."

She didn't tell him or anyone that she sang to the soup, too. Something her mother had taught her. You sang to the spirits of the food always. Especially soup.

When Cormac was healthy again, he told Sara to stay away from the other people.

"Please, husband," she said. "It helps me." When she was with the others, she didn't think so much about sneaking out of steerage and throwing herself overboard. "And it'll benefit us once we get to the new world. These people might be able to help us out."

Cormac snorted. "They're poorer than we are." But she had called him husband, so he let her go.

Sometimes at night, the captain's men came down and let those who were well enough go up top. Sara loved these times. She counted a million stars. And the air tasted so clean and fresh. Sometimes she got too close to the railing and she thought she might slip under it into the water—or dive into the great old sea— but Cormac was always near and he kept his hand on her arm.

One night, one of the captain's men asked her if she was Sara O'Broin.

"I am," she said. "Do we know someone in common?"

"No," he said. "But they've been talking about your soup and your ability to charm away the sea sicknesses."

"My wife is no charmer," Cormac said. "I won't have ye insulting her."

"I mean no disrespect," the man said. "I only meant—the captain asked if you could come and feed one of the passengers. She's been quite ill."

"I'll do what I can," Sara said. She did not look at Cormac so she could not see if he said no.

"You will be rewarded," the man said.

"Good is its own reward," Sara said.

Sara followed the captain's man. She glanced back once and saw Cormac watching them. He looked helpless again, like he had when he was seasick, and she was glad for it. The man took her to the ship's galley. It was a sight cleaner than anything in steerage. And it smelled of food. The cook was a tall man with dark weathered skin and blue eyes that shone in the near darkness like tiny lighthouses. Sara only got a glance at him because he took one look at her and turned away.

"You give her whatever she needs," the captain's man said to the cook. He suddenly had a slight Irish accent, leaving behind his clipped Anglo-speak.

"Aye," the cook said. He turned around to face Sara.

"I'm Sara O'Broin," she said. She reached her hand out to the man.

"Murphy," he said. He shook her hand.

"Is that an Irish name then?"

"It was," he said. "What can you do that I haven't done? This woman hasn't liked anything I've made her."

"I dunno," Sara said. "We'll make a bit of broth."

And so she asked Murphy for this ingredient and that. His annoyance seemed to give way to interest after a while.

"Soup is the blood of the old sea, my ma used to tell me," Sara said, "prettied up some so the people will be fooled into drinking it. Ya need to sing to it, talk to it, so it can remember what it is. You're calling on its true nature. That's how everything heals."

They made the broth from a few root vegetables and a chicken Murphy butchered.

"Do you have some salt from the sea, brother?" she asked him.

When he brought the salt to her, Sara crumbled some into the broth. "We take this salt from the sea," she chanted, "and offer it as the key. It is the mermaid's kiss that will take them to healing bliss."

"Blessed sea," Murphy said.

"Blessed sea," she repeated.

After a while, Sara dipped a cup into the broth and took a drink. Then she passed the cup over to Murphy and he gulped it down. Sara laughed. "You were hungry then?"

"For the auld sea," he said. "For certain."

Murphy put a tureen of the soup on a tray, and he carried it out of the galley. Sara looked around the kitchen and waited for Murphy's return. She was in no hurry to return to steerage—or to Cormac.

FOUR

The broth did the work of the Old Sea. The woman asked that Sara O'Broin be kept nearby, in case she had a relapse. The captain's man asked Sara if she would help Murphy with his cooking. The three of them stood in the galley together.

"Only if Mr. O'Murphy will have me," Sara said. "I won't be interfering."

"Mr. Murphy does what the captain orders him to do," the captain's man said.

"Aye," Sara said. "And I do what my conscience tells me." She flinched as she remembered the storm, remembered that she and Cormac were running from what she had done to her whole village. "It's a small place, this kitchen. And he's the man in charge here."

"I could use the help," Murphy said. "My mate went sick before we left last port."

"I will do it then," Sara said. "And Cormac MacDougal, can you find him some work up in the air and the sunshine?" Sara knew that was the only way Cormac would not complain about her being gone most of the time. The captain's man agreed.

So Sara O'Broin became the cook's mate.

Sara was accustomed to hard work, but she was also used to running over hills and into the forest and down to the sea in-between cooking, spinning, weaving, and harvesting. She had times betwixt and between when she whispered to the fey folk or made love in the heath. During the feasts and celebrations, Sara had helped her ma and the others cook for all the villagers, but they were always laughing, teasing one another, or talking to the spirits of the food.

In the beginning, Murphy told Sara to shadow him so they wouldn't keep knocking into one another.

Sara was good at shadowing. She had done it with her ma most of her life. That was how Maire taught Sara almost everything she knew. Now she and Murphy made mostly stews and something he called gruel. The meals would start out one way, but almost always they turned out looking the same. Tasting the same. Sara whispered to the food and asked for blessings for the ingredients, but she wasn't sure it did any good. At first she didn't want to eat anything they cooked, but Murphy handed her a bowl with two generous scoops of gruel. What could she do? She ate it.

It didn't taste any better than it looked.

The captain's man found a place for Cormac and Sara to bunk out of steerage. Sara wasn't quite sure what part of the ship it was in. She learned her way to and from it and steerage and to the galley. Cormac swore at her whenever she returned to steerage, but he didn't forbid her from going. She tried to go once a day to see the children and tell them stories.

Most of the stories were ones she remembered from her uncle Ruarc. Sometimes she brought hardtack she had dipped in milk and the children ate it quietly and secretly while she told a tale or two.

One day the ship was rocking and tilting from the backside of a storm; the children were sick and afraid. Sara sat amongst them and said, "Close your eyes, every one of you. You're doing too much seeing with your eyes. You've forgotten the ways of the fey folk and you've only been gone such a short while. Don't you remember running in the woods and hearing the trees creaking and moaning as they danced with the wind? Ahhh. Ya hear that sound again, don't you? Aye.

"You're in that forest again. Say hello to the auld men and the auld women. That's all this ship is and that's a big and mighty thing to be. We're inside the belly of the forest. We're invisible to all those who don't know to look. Just like the good neighbors are invisible to all those who don't know to look. But they've come with us, too, along with the auld people of the forest. Good neighbors, can you let the children know you're here with them? Children, see if you can feel them here with us. A warm breath on your face. A cool hand on your arm. The sound of music in the distance. Or a twinkling. Colors behind your eyes. Do you feel them here with us?"

She was silent for a moment and it seemed the whole ship was quiet then, as though everyone was listening, everyone was in that forest that had disappeared from the land and now floated on the auld sea.

"I do feel them," one of the girls whispered. "As though one of them kissed my cheek."

"I bet they did, Rose," Sara said. "It sounds like they will let themselves be known to you by brushing up against you now and again."

"I hear the tinkling of bells," a boy said. "I do."

"I'm so glad, Peter," Sara said. "So it may be they'll let you know they're around by sending you a sound. You never know except sometimes you do."

The children laughed.

And so it went for a time. Sara O'Broin felt the rhythm of the sea and the ship and the people aboard it. She worked hard when she was in the galley. Cormac did not like her being alone with another man all day, but she knew he was glad to be out of steerage so he didn't complain. Murphy seemed to enjoy her company and she enjoyed his. He sang when he cooked. Sara wondered how someone so affable could cook food that tasted so dead. After a while, Murphy let Sara add this herb or that spice to the food from the treasure box her ma had given her. Then she would whisper enchantments over it all. It still looked the same, but it tasted better, and everyone was happier, including Murphy.

After they finished cooking for the day, she and Murphy sometimes sat and talked. He told her about his travels.

"I like it where it's warm," he said. "Couldn't stand the rain and clouds at home. Yeah, it was green. But I swear on my mother's grave, I would trade the green for the gold of sunshine any time."

"Couldn't you have both?" she asked.

"I have been to some islands where it is warm all year," he said, "and it is green all year. And the women they are comely and willing."

"And the men? Are they the same?"

"I wasn't asking," he said. "But next time I go, I will. I'll say, 'Sara O'Broin wants to know if you're willing.'"

Sara laughed. "No! Are they beautiful, too?"

"They are," Murphy said. "You'd like them fine. Don't know what your husband would say."

Sara didn't care what Cormac had to say—about anything.

She looked away from Murphy. She wasn't going to tell him her sad tale.

"Don't you want to settle down to a place and call it home?" Sara asked.

"I should be asking you the same thing," he said.

"It's true, I left my home," she said. "I cannot return there. I'm thinking I won't find another home ever."

"I found home for a time," Murphy said. "I'll go back one day. Have you ever been to a desert?"

"I never been anywhere beyond my village and parts of the auld sea," Sara said. "And those places where the stories take me. But I don't think I know what a desert is. When I think of one, it sounds lonely, with nothing there."

"Oh no, darlin'," Murphy said. "It's not like that at all. There's life everywhere. Especially your own life. In the desert, you can hide out from almost everyone but yourself."

"I swear, O'Murphy, sometimes you sound like a poet instead of the auld sea dog you claim to be."

Murphy smiled.

"How did a sailor get to the desert?" Sara asked.

"Let me tell you," he said. "I spent some years in the desert when I was sick of the ocean. I got off a ship once and I kept walking for a year or more, taking rides and getting work where I could. And then I stopped in a place south where the Native people and the Spanish lived. The first thing I encountered were these things they call cacti. Have you ever heard of them? They're plants with spines that'll prick you if you're not careful. No leaves. And once a year, these cacti grow beautiful flowers. Some are so tall: Giants that only walk around at night. They're part plant and part animal, I'm here to tell ya. And lions. This desert had lions and tigers. Snakes that will kill ya. Rabbits with ears so big and legs so long you'd swear they could leap over a mountain. The sky is so big and blue. This place I went, where I stayed for a while, was filled with magic. I never believed before.

"I've had a hard life, Sara O'Broin. I had seen a lot of things, but magic wasn't one of them. And then I went to this desert—far from any ocean or any faery folk—and I found seashells in the sand. I swear I heard mermaids singing. I followed the sound one night to a spring coming out of the sand. Nearby was part of an old wall and on it was a faded painting of a group of mermaids, it looked like. In the middle of them was a black mermaid with a beautiful red tail. And none of them looked like those pictures you've seen of mermaids—all young and pale. These were women, some of them older, and their bodies were all different. Some thin, some voluptuous, some dark, some light."

"You saw all this from a faded painting?" she asked.

"I did," he said. "As I looked at it, it seemed to get brighter and then I realized I'd been standing there a long while and the sun had moved and the dusk made the painting more visible."

Sara laughed, and then she said, "The auld sea was following you."

"It soothed my soul this place," he said. "But I couldn't stay long. I don't care much for the Spanish. Let's just say I didn't have an appreciation of their fervor for their religion and they didn't have an appreciation of my fervor for liquor and women. What they didn't understand—like singing springs, giants in the desert, or jackrabbits that could bound over mountains—they destroyed. I didn't care for that."

"Did they destroy the mermaid spring?"

Murphy shook his head. "Naw. I didn't tell them and none of them went very far into the desert. Every part of it scared every part of them. Someday I'll go back. Maybe they'll all be gone. And you, Sara, if you ever need a port in the storm, that's the place to go. No one would ever find you."

Murphy looked at Sara. She met his gaze for a moment before turning away. Perhaps Murphy understood more about her life than she had ever let on.

"How could I ever find a place like that?" she asked.

"Maybe I'll take you there one day," he said. "But you could go yerself. If it was meant to be, it would draw you to it, as it drew me to it. It's in a place called Sonora in New Spain. It's way south of a speck of a village called Wayward."

"I like that name," Sara said. "I've always been a bit wayward myself."

Sara didn't see Cormac often. He spent most of his time with the crew, working when he had to and drinking when he could. Cormac had never been much of a drinker, so this new drunkenness surprised Sara. She didn't care as long as he kept his hands off of her. She couldn't close her eyes and pretend it was Ian any more when Cormac tried to make love to her—she'd see Ian and her sister together—together and drowned.

When she could, Sara stood at the railing and watched the water below. Sometimes dolphins followed the ship. The sailors seemed happiest when the dolphins swam with them. They cheered and sang. They were less happy when an albatross flew over the ship. They would whisper little enchantments and spit into the wind; if they were hit with their own spittle, they would survive any bad luck that might befall the ship.

Sara stared into the water and wondered if any of her sea sisters swam with the ship. And the Old Mother, was she there? If she leapt into the water would she instantly grow a tail again? Or would she drown? She no longer wished to drown. At least for the moment, her melancholy had lifted.

Then one day, the winds stopped and the current deadened. The ship hardly moved. This continued for days. One night a fog covered the ship like a dead man's shroud. The crew began whispering about bad omens and death coming on the next wind. It felt as though the world was holding its breath. Everyone was holding their breath, waiting. Then they exhaled, the fog moved away, and the sickness began.

No one was certain what caused the illness. Maybe the water had gone bad. Or maybe someone had brought the sickness on board and it was only just now going around. The ship's doctor did what he knew how, but that wasn't much. He had leeches and he did some bloodletting. Sara's mother and the local witch sometimes nicked her finger when she was sick—to get the body to wake up and fix itself, they said—but the ship's doctor did more than nick people. When that didn't seem to help, they started bringing people out onto the deck for fresh air.

Sara made broth, sang to it, and then served it to the ill. It didn't seem to help. Still, she nursed those she could. The children were the sickest. She fed them broth and bathed them as their bodies shook with fever.

The winds picked up and the captain looked for a quicker route to a port of call. If the water was bad, they needed fresh supplies immediately.

One of the children died. Little Rose. Her mother's screams rose up into the night sky and scattered the birds following the ship. The crew quickly wrapped up the little girl in a muslin sheet and slid her body into the sea with only a brief blessing. Sara leaned over the railing and called, "Take care of her, auld ma. May she swim with her many sea sisters."

The crew began getting sick.

Two more people died.

Then Sara felt a fog come over her. Murphy took her to her bed. She lay with her eyes closed as the fever burned into her. She remembered what it had felt like when she refused to marry Cormac. How her life had begun seeping away. This time, it felt as though her life was burning away. She opened her eyes once and Murphy tried to smile. She started to laugh and it turned into a cough.

"Don't look so worried, auld man," she said. "What could happen that could be worse?"

When she opened her eyes again, Cormac was there.

"You need to come back," Cormac said. "For me. For the child."

She turned away.

She dreamed. Or was she awake? Later when she thought about it, she was never sure. Her daughter stood next to her.

"Mammy," she said. "You need to wake up. The flowers are speaking to you. You need to listen." Her daughter opened her hands. White flowers bloomed from her palms. Then they withered to brown powder that dusted her palms. "It's from the auld sea and the land of the Tuatha de Danaan. It will fix what ails ya." Her daughter opened the barrel of water next to her and slapped her hands together. The brown dust fell into the water. Her daughter's legs fused into a tail and she dove into the barrel. "It's the only way," she said. And she was gone.

Sara tried to drag herself from her bed. She needed to save her daughter. But she couldn't move. She opened her eyes. Murphy was there.

She told him where she had hid her bag and her treasure box. "Take a little of the powder and put it in the water."

"They'll kill me if they catch me," Murphy said, although his lips did not move. "They'll think I'm poisoning it."

"Please," she pleaded. "It's the only way."

Sara fell to sleep again, or slipped into unconsciousness. She did not remember much after, except maybe Murphy getting her to drink some liquid. She knew later that Murphy had done what she asked and soon people began recovering.

For some reason, Sara O'Broin was the last to wake up.

"I dreamed I was swimming in the auld sea," Sara said when she opened her eyes. Murphy sat beside her. "With my sister Aine and Ian McLaughlin and my daughter. It was a beautiful thing to see. We all had the most beautiful tails." She looked around. "Where is Cormac?"

"He's been here right along," Murphy said. "Even when you were calling out for Ian McLaughlin."

"Aye," Sara said. Tears began streaming down her face. "Ian's the father of my daughter. Cormac stole my red cap and claimed me and the babe for his own."

"It still works that way?" Murphy asked.

"It does," Sara said. "I fought it but it is more powerful than I am."

Suddenly she felt a cramp. Pain seared through every part of her body.

Sara screamed. The whole ship shuddered.

And Sara's daughter slipped from her womb.

They say Sara O'Broin's daughter was curled up like a spiral seashell and her blue-green tail glittered in the lantern light. Maybe that all was true. Or maybe her precious legs were cold and blue because she never took in a breath of air. She had one thumb in her mouth. Her eyes were closed. She was so tiny she fit in both of Murphy's hands. He held the bairn and wiped the blood from her face.

She did not breathe.

Sara screamed again and birthed the placenta. Or whatever it was. Some stories say she birthed another dead baby then, or something evil that had planted itself inside her when Cormac MacDougal assaulted her that day on the beach. Sara heard the stories later. She knew she had given birth to something besides her dead baby. But it was dead, too.

When Sara stopped screaming, when the pain was done and over with and she had more grief to feel, Sara took her daughter from Murphy, she took all that she had birthed, and she wrapped it up in a shirt Murphy brought her.

Sara got up from the bed and staggered out to the deck. Bloody and battered, she went to the railing. She did not see the other people on deck watching her. She felt Murphy's steady hand on her back. She went to the railing and held her bairn over the sea.

"Swim strong, sea daughter, swim strong."

And she dropped her baby into the sea.

They say the dolphins rode up beside the ship then. When the bundle reached the water, the shirt melted away and Sara's daughter found her sea legs. She shimmied and shivered and swam alongside the dolphins. And then the mermaids began singing. Everyone heard it. Everyone was certain it was a siren song they heard. Sara's daughter's siren song.

Everyone but Sara. She heard nothing but the roar in her ears as she collapsed into Murphy's arms.

FIVE

Sara stayed in her dreams for a long while. They weren't happy dreams; she was calling on the forces of nature, drowning her own people, traveling forever inside a forest floating on the ocean. Sometimes the dreams changed and Cormac was raping her again and then it was Ian. She flailed against both of them, but it did no good. Her daughter kept calling for her, but she couldn't find her. Sometimes she wandered to the edge of the sea, and then someone pulled her away. She wasn't sure if she was dreaming or if it was the real time. Sometimes she heard Cormac's voice, and she slapped him away and he'd turn into a fly that she chased out of her house.

Sara had always been a strong girl, a practical girl, but she couldn't seem to wake up from these dreams.

Then one day she did.

She sat up and looked around. Cormac was watching her.

"Are you done with this now?" he asked her. "I've got work ta do."

"You're asking me this?" she said. "You are the one who put me here. You are the one. I will never forgive you. Unless you give me back what belongs to me right here and now."

"I belong to you," he said, "and you belong to me. We have since we were children. We pledged ourselves to one another."

"We didn't," Sara said. "I loved Ian since I was a girl. I pledged myself to him and no other."

"You don't remember all the days we spent together?" Cormac asked. "You have forgotten all the good times."

"We were children," Sara said. "You wanted me and I didn't want you. It happens all the time. You need to carry on."

"It is you who need to carry on," he said. "You are my wife now in the eyes of the church."

"It's not my church," Sara said.

He stared at her.

"One day I'll figure it out," Sara said. "I cannot believe my relations were so cruel that they agreed to this enchantment. As every spell is cast, so may it be broken. In the meantime, I have to do what you say. But if you want me to stop hating you, you need to be different."

"Like Ian?" he said.

"Like you were when we were children, maybe," Sara said. "Then at least we could start to remember why we were friends."

Cormac shook his head.

"Since you seized me," Sara said, "my true love has died, my sister has died, my bairn has died, and my village has been destroyed. I am trying—"

"You destroyed the village," Cormac said. "I saved your life by taking you away. Be grateful, wife. I have been protecting you all along. That Murphy person could have hurt you, but I turned him in. You won't have to deal with him any longer."

"What are you talking about?" Sara asked.

"Someone saw Murphy put something in the drinking water," Cormac said. "They think he's the reason so many people got sick. He poisoned the water."

"He put that in after everyone was sick," Sara said.

Cormac stood and looked down at her.

"What do you know of this?" he asked.

"I asked him to do it," Sara said. "Why did you tell anyone?"

"Because I thought he was the reason you were ill," Cormac said.

Sara pushed herself up off the small bed. She ran her hands through her hair and looked down at herself. She still wore the nightgown she had on when her daughter was stillborn. She pressed her hands over the bloody stains. Her breasts hurt.

"Where is he?" Sara asked. She took off the nightgown and put on her dress.

"They've got him locked up," Cormac said. "They'll probably hang him tomorrow."

"Cormac," Sara said. "Why must you be so small? Why did you have to interfere?"

"Where are you going?"

"To see the captain," she said. "I have to tell him that Murphy was only doing what I asked him to do."

"They'll hang you then!" Cormac said.

"I won't let Murphy hang for this," Sara said. "I will help him."

"Wait," Cormac said. "I didn't know you were involved. Let's figure this out. It was the boy, Peter, who told me. And then I told the first mate. Maybe we can get him to recant."

"Peter was telling you the truth," Sara said. "Why would he take it back?"

"Maybe he saw it wrong," Cormac said. "We'll ask him."

Sara hesitated, and then she followed Cormac down to steerage. Peter ran to Sara as soon as he saw her and put his arms around her waist.

"You're all well? I was afraid that man had poisoned you, too," Peter said.

"What man?" Sara asked.

"I saw that man they call Murphy put something in the water," Peter said.

"What were you doing back there?" Cormac asked. "Maybe it was you who did it."

"What?" Peter looked frightened. "No, miss, it wasn't. I saw him do it."

Sara put her hand on Peter's shoulder. "We know you didn't do anything wrong," she said. She glanced at Cormac. "But Mr. Murphy didn't do anything wrong either. If you'll think back, didn't you see him after the sickness started?"

Peter was quiet for a moment; he looked up as he tried to remember.

"Yeah, it was," Peter said. "Because I went over by the water to get away from all the sickness. My ma told me to play there. And later I saw him. I saw other men before him. I saw them pull out some rats. They was dead. Later I saw Mr. Murphy put something in the water."

"Thank you, Peter," Sara said. She looked at Cormac. "I will go speak to the captain now."

"It won't do any good," Cormac said. "Peter still says he saw Murphy put something in the water."

"I'm going to talk to the captain," Sara said.

"I forbid it," Cormac said.

"I'm goin' anyway," Sara said.

"You'll get sick again," he said, "for disobeying me."

"So be it," she said.

"Go on then," he said. "But it'll come to no good." He walked away from her.

Sara found the first mate and told him it was urgent she see the captain. He wanted Sara to tell him why, but she said it was private and urgent—and it concerned Murphy. The first mate finally instructed one of men to take her to the captain's cabin.

The captain got up from behind his desk when Sara walked into the cabin.

"Good day, Mrs. MacDougal," he said. "I am Captain Beale. What is it I can do for you?"

"It's Sara O'Broin," she said. "And I wanted to talk about Mr. Murphy." She was silent for a moment; she suddenly realized she was standing in a grand place and she was still wet with tears and her hands were stained bloody from her miscarriage. She blinked. None of that mattered now.

"I talked to young Peter," Sara said. "He told me he saw Mr. Murphy after everyone had fallen ill. It couldn't have been him who did anything wrong."

"But he did see him put something in the water," the captain said. He sat at his desk again.

Sara chewed her lip. What could she say? How could she save Murphy?

"It was me," Sara said. "I asked him to put something in the water. But it wasn't poison. I'll get it for you. I'll taste it myself in front of you. It was a gift from my ma when I got married. Dirt from the land of the Tuatha de Danaan and the beach near my home."

"Pardon me?"

"I had a dream," Sara said, "during my sickness. My daughter came to me and showed me that the dirt could fix what was wrong with the water. I was too sick to do it myself. So I asked Mr. Murphy to do it, and he did it because he is a friend. He knew I meant no harm. And no harm came. That was when everyone started to get healthy again. And Peter said he saw men come and clean the water, take out the rats. Murphy put the dirt in after that."

"She is a cunning woman."

Sara turned around to see who had spoken. An older woman sat near the small oval window, knitting.

"I wish I was a cunning woman, ma'am," Sara said. "I don't know much. But my daughter came to me in a dream and asked me to do this. I figured it was a message from the fair folk."

The older woman nodded. "I would have done the same."

The captain cleared his throat.

"This is my mother, Elizabeth Beale," he said. "Mother, this is Sara O'Broin. She's the one who made your broth."

"I guessed as much," she said. She glanced at Sara. She looked at her son. "Can you release this man Murphy now? It's obvious he didn't do anything wrong."

"I can release him," he said, "but I can't keep him on the ship. He should have told me what happened. He didn't say a word about you, Sara."

"He was protecting me," Sara said. "Should he be punished for that?"

"Yes," the captain said. "On this ship, the crew must be loyal only to me, and I look out for the welfare of all. Murphy will have to be put off at the next port. And you with him, you and your husband. We can't have rumors of witchcraft. No good will come of that."

"Please don't do that, sir," Sara said. "We are already so far from home. With no money. We haven't done any harm. And I helped your ma."

"You could argue she saved your entire ship," Mrs. Beale said.

"I understand what you believe," he said. "And I do appreciate everything you've done. But a ship is a country of its own while we're at sea, and sailors are very superstitious. If they caught wind of any of this, I might not be able to protect you."

The old woman sighed.

"Richard, can you arrange for that man's release," Mrs. Beale asked, "and let me speak with Sara alone for a moment?"

The captain stood again. "All right, Mrs. Beale." He nodded to Sara, and then he left them alone.

Mrs. Beale patted the space next to her. Sara went and sat near her.

"I heard about your child," she said. "I am so sorry. I have lost three children, and it never gets easier. Lost. I didn't lose them! Why do we hide the truth behind such useless words? They died, and they're gone and buried. I am not from the sea as you are, but my people come from the woods. Sometimes at night I think I hear the dryads still trapped in the timber of this ship. I know an enchantment when I see one. You are sick with one."

"Aye," Sara said. "I don't know how to be released from it. The druid couldn't help me. He said he would ask for the answer to come on the wind to me. So far, I haven't heard anything, except my own screams as my baby died."

"I think the answer is in you," she said. "In what you know."

Sara shook her head. "No. I mean no disrespect. But I didn't believe in it, this curse. I almost died and I saw the truth of it. And now . . . now I couldn't go back any way. You wouldn't believe the destruction I've left in my wake."

"I still believe the answer will come to you," she said. "Like the dream came to you and you saved us all. Or maybe on the wind. For now, this is your destiny. You must go with it."

"I don't believe in destiny," Sara said. "Or else destiny is cruel. This man who calls himself my husband raped me. While the child was in me. That's probably why she died. I can't wait to see him die, too."

"Remember he's under the same enchantment you are," Mrs. Beale said. "You are locked in this together."

Sara shook her head. "Will you give me the key then, so I

can unlock us? You know the auld ways, but you're on this ship with your boy?"

"Yes, we're everywhere, dear," she said. "You only have to look."

"How did you survive in your world?"

"I learned to be invisible," she said. "And then my husband started treating me as though I was invisible. While he wasn't looking, I got to know other people who became my allies. After a while I was able to do what I wanted. And I wanted to be here."

"I don't want to be invisible," Sara said.

"There were times in your life when you did want to be invisible," Mrs. Beale said.

Sara remembered the fath fith.

"For sure," Sara said. "But now I wish I could scream or run away. Do something. I haven't the strength for any of it."

"Try to remember everything your mother taught you before you went under the enchantment," Mrs. Beale said. "That will put you right."

"She was under one, too," Sara said. "I don't know that I can trust anything she told me, now can I?"

"You are harsh on your auld ma," she said, imitating Sara's accent.

"I don't mean to be," Sara said. "I don't trust myself most of all. You wouldn't believe the harm I've done."

"You can't do anything about the past," Mrs. Beale said. "And I'm not sure you can do anything about the future. It's only the here and now."

"My people believe we can change the past," Sara said, "and shape the future. They always have. I need to learn how."

"I can't help you with that," Mrs. Beale said. "Will you help me with something?"

"Anything."

"May I have a strand of your hair?" she asked.

"You won't use it against me?" Sara asked.

"I will not," Mrs. Beale said.

"Then do it," Sara said. "Take whatever one you want."

Mrs. Beale reached over and plucked a strand of Sara O'Broin's hair.

"I'm making this sweater for my grandson," she said. "He's going into the army. Everyone knows hair from a live mermaid's head will protect you. If I had enough of your hair, I could make my grandson invisible and he would be protected from harm from his enemies. But I don't want to make you bald."

"I doubt my hair has any such power," Sara said, "or I'd be using it myself. But I'm glad to help. You can take a few more if you like."

And so Mrs. Beale did. Later when Sara was gone, Mrs. Beale wove the strands into the sweater which still later came to be put on her grandson. They say he survived many a battle because he wore the sweater beneath his uniform. Years later, he asked a woman to take apart the sweater and sew five more sweaters from it to give to his own children when they went away to war.

Captain Beale eventually returned to his cabin.

"Mr. Murphy has been released," Beale said. "We'll put you off at the next island. We'll be there in a day or two if the winds hold."

Sara tried to get the captain to reconsider, but he would have none of it. She tried to convince him to leave her on the island and let Murphy and Cormac continue without her. Finally the captain called in the boy outside his door and told him to escort Sara back to her quarters.

Cormac was waiting for her, his face red with fury.

"I told you to keep out of it!" he said. "Now look what's happened! We're going to be put off the ship in some forsaken place where they use Irishmen as slaves! We'll never get off the island."

"The captain said ships come there all the time," Sara said. "We can get passage. You can get passage. You can leave me there and you can go on without me."

Cormac raised his hand as though he was going to hit her. Sara stepped back. Then she said, "If you strike me, I'll never let you near me again."

He started to laugh and dropped his hand. "I can do whatever I like." He looked around their tiny space. "Clean this up. It smells like something died in here."

He walked away.

Sara's face burned with anger and humiliation. She wanted to kill Cormac. She wanted to hurt him. Of course it smelled like something had died. Her baby had died. She had died.

"You can't do whatever you like either," she shouted after him. "You can't stay on this ship!"

She shook her head. Someday when it was safe, she would kill him and take back her life.

A nd so the following day, the captain and his men anchored the ship off shore of one of the islands. Sara said good-bye to the children, and then she got into the rowboat, along with Murphy, Cormac, and several members of the crew. She looked back once to see if Mrs. Beale or the captain had come out to see them off, but she didn't see either.

The men slowly rowed the boat toward the beach. Murphy looked up at the bright blue sky and then down at the pale blue water.

"Ain't this beautiful?" he said. "What more could a man want?" He smiled at Sara.

"I'm sorry I got you into this," Sara said.

He shrugged. "I told you I'd rather be someplace warm any day. Now that I'm looking at those white beaches, I'm asking myself why I ever got back on any ship in the first place."

Cormac sat behind them. Sara did not look at him, but she could feel his stare on the back of her neck.

When the boat went aground, the men got out and pulled it up onto the beach. The first mate reached for Sara's hand and helped her out.

"There's a place up through there where you can spend a few nights," he said. "And where you can book passage on another ship." He handed Sara a small bag. She took it from him. She could feel the weight of coins. "This is from the captain. Payment for your work."

Sara glanced at Murphy. He nodded slightly, and she knew he had been given his pay, too.

"Tell the captain I hold no grudge," Sara said.

Cormac snatched the bag of coins from her. The first mate looked at Sara. She pressed her lips together. Then she reached over and took the coins from Cormac. The first mate moved forward slightly, as though he was preparing to stand between them. Cormac didn't move.

The first mate reached inside his coat and pulled out two folded pieces of paper. He handed one each to Murphy and Cormac.

"Letters of reference so you can get work on another ship," he said.

He nodded to Sara, and then he turned away and began shouting orders to his men.

Sara looked up and down the beach. It was good to feel land under her feet again, although her legs felt a bit shaky.

Murphy squinted at the sun.

"Have you been here before?" Sara asked.

"I have," he said. "It's a goodly place."

Cormac grasped Sara's arm. "We have no more business with you, Murphy," he said. "You're the reason we were put off the ship, so I'm warning you now to stay away from my wife and me. You're nothing but trouble."

Cormac tried to pull Sara up the beach. She jerked away from him.

"I may be your fish wife," she said, "and I'll go where you say, but you need to treat me with respect. I'm not a piece of baggage you can drag from here to there whenever you want."

Cormac grabbed the bag of coins from her again and walked up away from the beach toward the village buildings. Sara looked back at Murphy. He sighed and shrugged. She followed Cormac.

They walked toward a big long white building that shone like a white flower amongst the tall strange trees. The trees had no branches or leaves except way up at the top. Other buildings were scattered here and there. Some looked more like paper shacks than anything else and Sara realized they were partially made from the fronds of the tall trees.

People with different skin tones and in various states of dress walked around them. Some wore only a piece of cloth wrapped around their waist. Others—Europeans, Sara guessed—had almost every part of their bodies covered in clothes. As Sara and Cormac walked toward the white building, Sara suddenly remembered being a child running down the beach, naked. Years later, all grown up, she and Ian danced on the beach skyclad.

Sara breathed deeply. She did not want to think about Ian. The fragrance of some kind of flower tickled her nose.

"Mammy, the flowers are speaking to you. You need to listen."

Sara stopped. Had she heard her daughter's voice just then in her imagination or had the wind brought it to her from the land of the ancestors?

Cormac continued into the building. Murphy walked up next to Sara.

"Are you all right, luv?" he asked.

"I am," Sara said. "I'm tired to the bone, though. I'd like to rest on that beach over there for a while, until the waves come in and roll over me."

"I'll follow and save ye," he said.

Sara put her hand on his arm. "You cannot. Don't even try."

Murphy squeezed her hand, and then he went into the building.

Cormac got him and Sara a room. He looked tired and angry when he told Sara the innkeeper didn't expect another ship for weeks. Their room was large with beds enough for two other couples, but no one else was there.

Cormac tossed his bag on the end of one of the beds and then sat next to it. He put his head in his hands.

"It's possible no ship will come at all," he said, "and we'll be stuck here until the spring."

Sara looked out the window. The pale blue water lapped on white beaches.

"That wouldn't be so bad," she said. "It's beautiful here."

He reached for her hand. She let him have it.

"You shouldn't get close to the water," he said. "I hear it calling to you all the time."

Sara laughed and pulled her hand away. "We've been on a ship surrounded by water for weeks. I've come to no harm."

He looked at her. "You don't know then how many times I brought you back from the edge of the railing. You don't know how many nights I was with you while you moaned and cried for Ian and your sister and your dead bairn. I'm so tired from watching you. From keeping you from diving into the auld sea."

Sara sat next to him. "If you won't let me go—"

"I can't let you go!" he said. "Don't you understand? It's impossible now. It would be like cutting off my own arm."

In that moment, Sara realized what Mrs. Beale had told her was true: Cormac was under the same enchantment as she.

"Then cut it off," she said. "Or cut off mine. That's the only way you'll have peace."

"I wish it were that easy," he said.

"It is," she said.

She knew that was a lie. It wasn't easy. Ian and Aine and her baby were dead. Her village was destroyed. None of that could be undone.

"I want to love ya," he said. "That's all I want."

Sara didn't say anything for a while. She didn't believe he loved her. She didn't believe anything he said. But sometimes she did feel sorry for him. She wished he had lived his life differently.

"We're on an island," Sara finally said. "It's a small island. There's nowhere I can go even if I could run, which I can't. I'm bound to you body and—" She stopped. "I'm bound to you. I'm not going anywhere, so I plan on enjoying the sun while I'm here."

Sara left Cormac in the room and went down the hall. She could feel his panic and fear as she walked away, but he did not call her back, so she kept going until she was outside. She laughed a little when her feet slipped in the sand. She leaned over and put her fingers in it. It felt drier than any at home, but still the same: the holy earth. She held some of it up to her cheeks and pressed it against her skin.

Then she ran to the beach, took off her shoes, and began walking. The cool wet sand felt nice on her soles. The blue water seemed to stretch out away from her forever. She walked and walked, following the curve of the beach as it went away from the village.

After she had been walking for some time, she turned and went toward the water. She stood on the tideline for a minute. Every time the wave gently rolled onto shore, she moved away from it. She did this for some time. Eventually she let the wave cover her feet. She stood that way for a time, and then she walked a few feet into the sea.

Nothing happened. She didn't feel her soul shift. She didn't feel herself connecting to the universe. She felt the cool water embrace her calves. It felt nice, but that was all.

She turned and walked out of the water. She wasn't sure if she felt relief or sadness. She wasn't sure any longer what she felt about anything. She wasn't even certain if she felt anything at all.

SIX

Sara spent the next few days wandering the island. Sometimes she stopped and talked with the people she met, but mostly she was silent. She saw some of the crew. The captain allowed them to stay on the island most of the time, in-between loading the ship. They often sat on the beach carousing. Some of the island women stayed with them. Sara watched them from afar. She had always loved a celebration, but now something about it frightened her. Sometimes Murphy joined the crew, Cormac, too, although they never sat near one another. The men drank and laughed.

At night Sara slept on a bed on the other side of the room from Cormac. He didn't argue with her. He didn't seem to care. He spent most of the day drinking and most of the night too. She didn't mind his drunkenness as long as he stayed away from her and let her do what she wanted.

Some days when Sara was sure Cormac was off drinking or sleeping, she and Murphy walked the beach together. She liked Murphy's company more than most people she had known. She was surprised. She had met strangers in her village; she had gotten along with them just fine, but they remained strangers to her. Except for their first few awkward minutes together, she and Murphy got on as though they had known each other all of their lives.

"What will you do now?" Sara asked him one day as they sat together in a secluded lagoon. They dangled their feet in the warm water.

"I was thinking I could put an end to Cormac's life," Murphy said, "and spend the rest of my days here making love with you."

Sara laughed. "I can't have you talking about my husband that way," she said. "Someone might overhear and think we're conspiring. Besides, I think of you more like an uncle."

"Oh that hurts, girl," he said. "I'm not old enough to be your uncle am I?"

"You're auld enough to be my granddaddy," she said.

"Hush," he said. "This auld man's heart will break."

"Quit avoiding the question," she said. "What will you do then?"

"Find me a girl and have some babies," he said. "Wouldn't that be something?"

"You could have done that years ago," she said. "Why didn't ya?"

"I was in love once," he said, "when I was too young to know better. I was working in the Sea of Cortez and our ship went aground. We went to land for a time. I wandered around just as you have been and I met one of the local girls. She was beautiful. But it was more than that. Something about her eyes and the way she was in the world. I can't explain it. I loved her the moment I saw her. How does anyone explain these things? I didn't see her often. She would come and be with me and then disappear for days at a time. So one day I followed her."

"Without her knowing?"

"Without her knowing," he said. "I lost sight of her for a moment and then I saw her swimming away from shore. I stayed there, waiting for her for a long time, but she didn't come back. I fell to sleep. When I woke up, I saw her and her sisters on the beach up a ways from me. I got closer to them, without them seeing. They were naked, you understand, so it was only natural I'd want to see more of them."

Sara laughed.

"In the sand I saw their clothes," he said. "At least that's what I thought they were. They were shiny and glittery. Like nothing I had seen up to then—and only once since. When the women had their backs to me, I grabbed the cloth that was nearest my lady love. This gave me away. The other women cried out and grabbed their dresses. Only they weren't dresses. They wrapped them around their waists, and I can't be certain, luv, but it seemed I saw a flash of tails as they each dove into the water. Every one of them except my love. I knew the stories of the red cap. I knew about the sealskin women. I knew that if I kept a hold of this beautiful thing I held in my hands, my love would be mine forever."

Sara looked over at him.

He nodded. "Yes, I knew what would happen. I wanted her so much, Sara. I thought my life depended upon her being a part of my life."

"What did you do, O'Murphy?"

"She held out her hand to me," Murphy said. "And I returned to her what was hers. She kissed me. Then she bent over and picked up the most beautiful shell I've ever seen—tiny and shaped in a spiral—and she said, 'You know what this means, don't you?' I shook my head. She pressed the seashell into my hand. 'Whenever you find a seashell it means a mermaid has found her tail and is free again.' And then she dove back to the sea and swam away. I never saw her again."

"You acted honorably," Sara said. "I wish it was you who

had stolen me away from my home and my people instead of Cormac."

He shook his head. "No, you don't, darlin'. Stealing is stealing, no matter who does it to ya."

"Were you sorry?" Sara asked.

Murphy shook his head. "No. But I missed her. Missed her so my heart was breaking. And then I grew up and never fell that hard again. I went back to the sea. Years later, I left again and walked into the desert, like I told you. I think in a way, I was looking for her. I don't really know."

"You said you'd seen something that looked like the mermaid dresses—or tails—twice, once on the beach. When was the other time."

"You know when," Murphy said. "I was with you."

"When my baby was stillborn," Sara said. "Is that when?"

"Yes."

"It's all a blur to me," Sara said. "I don't know what was true and what wasn't. I only know the heartache is real. I keep hearing my daughter's voice. She tells me to listen to the flowers. I'll discover what that means, I suppose, soon enough."

Murphy and Sara kept talking and eventually the sun made them drowsy and they fell to sleep on the sand. The story goes that someone was working magic somewhere that day. Sara dreamed of flowers. A tall black woman held out a bouquet to her. When Sara reached for it, the bouquet disappeared, and the woman laughed.

When Sara awakened, it was dark night. She shook Murphy awake. It was so dark Sara wondered how they would ever find their way back to the village. Murphy took her hand.

"Keep the sea at our right and we'll be all right," he said. "It's an old sailor's motto."

"That doesn't make any sense, Murphy," Sara said. "When

you're on a ship the sea is always on your right and on your left. You're surrounded by the auld sea."

"Now you know why so many sailors get lost at sea," he said.

"Look at the stars," Sara said. "There are millions of them. They're so beautiful. I wonder if my ma and sister are looking up at them."

Murphy squeezed her hand.

"Right now, I can imagine that I'm walking home," Sara said, "with my best friend in the world. I'm taking you home to meet Ian and our daughter. My ma might be there, too, along with Fiona and Aine, my sisters. We'd have a fine meal, and you'd stay with Ian and me until you were ready to move on."

"That's a pretty picture, luv," he said. "You asked me what I was going to do. Before all this happened, what did you want to do with your life?"

"I wanted to be with Ian and our children," she said. "I wanted to live near our village alongside the people I'd known all my life. I was good at knowing the signs of the woods and the seasons. I was good with those who were needing care. The witch wanted me to apprentice with her, and I wanted to know all my ma knew because I thought she was the wisest woman in the world. I didn't know then that she was cursed, too. But that was all I was wanting for my life. What more is there then to be with the people you love, living on the land you love? It's all I've ever wanted."

"Why didn't you and Cormac stay there and live, like your mother did when she married your da?"

"The night before we left, I ran away from Cormac," she said. "I knew something bad could happen but I wanted to go to Ian, I wanted to make certain he was safe. I went down to the cave where we used to meet and he was there. He was there on top of me own sister. It looked like she had gotten him drunk and then gave him her red cap. I was so angry about everything that had happened to me that I went down to the sea and I called on the powers of the sea, the powers of the storm, the powers of my sea sisters and the auld ma. I wanted to bring vengeance down on the people who had harmed me. I wanted Ian and my sister punished."

Sara shivered. Murphy put his arm across her shoulders and rubbed her right arm.

"I went to sleep that night, the deepest sleep of my life," she said. "When I awakened, the village was gone and Ian and my sister were dead. Cormac took me away to protect me from the villagers. I should have stayed and faced them all. I haven't been myself since Cormac stole my red cap and took me as his property."

"I'm sorry that happened to you," Murphy said.

"But you can see I deserve whatever happens to me from now on," she said. "I brought that storm down on the people I loved."

"I don't believe it for a second," he said.

"I was there," she said. "I can tell you that."

"Things are not always what they seem, luv," Murphy said.

"Aye," Sara answered.

"Sara." Her husband was calling her.

"Cormac is looking for me," she said. "I can hear him."

"I don't hear him," Murphy said.

They stopped walking and stared into the darkness. After a few moments, Sara saw a light coming toward them. She hoped it was a faery ball bouncing down the beach, but she knew it was a lantern and Cormac was holding it.

"It's him," she said.

Murphy let go of her hand.

"If he sees us together," she said, "he'll think something was going on between us."

"There was," he said. "We were talking with each other like civilized human beings do."

"Murphy," she said.

"I'm not afraid of that little weasel," Murphy said.

"Please," Sara said. "Stay here. I'll walk ahead. There's been enough bloodshed on account of me."

"Are you sure?" he said.

"Yes!"

"I will then, for you."

Sara hurried forward in the darkness. Murphy stayed behind. Soon enough she saw that the man with the lantern was Cormac MacDougal.

"I'm so glad you've come," Sara said. "I fell to sleep on the beach and when I woke it was dark and I wasn't sure how I'd get back."

Cormac did not say a word. He held the lantern up to her face. His eyes were watery with drink. He stared at her. She smiled uneasily. He turned around and began walking back. Sara followed. He stumbled several times and Sara thought he would fall. She wanted to push him down and let him smother in the sand. She looked back once in the darkness and could not see Murphy, or anyone. In the sky, the stars twinkled.

When they were back at the inn and inside their room, Cormac grabbed Sara and pushed her up against the door.

"You're hurting me," Sara said. "And you stink."

"You were with Murphy all day again," he said. "The other men saw you and told me. They were laughing about it."

Sara tried to push Cormac away.

"I saw Murphy today, of course," she said. "I used to work with him every day. That never bothered you then."

"Now I know what you were doing all that time in the galley," he said.

"Yes, that's right," she said. "We were having sex day and night. We couldn't stop ourselves."

Cormac smashed his hand across her face, hard. She was so startled she didn't even call out. A moment later, she felt blood trickle down over her lips.

"I'm your fish wife," she said. "How could I have sex with another man?"

"They said they saw you," he said. "Both of you. You can't keep doing this to me."

He balled up his fist to punch her. She moved her head so the blow grazed her, but it still hurt. She felt dizzy. She tried to knee Cormac, but he leaned against her and she could barely move.

"You won't make a fool of me," he said.

"You've done that yourself," Sara said. "Let me go. You said you wanted to love me. This isn't love. Remember when we were children together. You never hurt me then. Cormac, you're acting crazy now. It's the liquor. You don't want to do this."

He began lifting up her dress with his free hand.

"Please, Cormac, don't do this again," she said. "You're killing me. You're killing yourself."

He put his hand over Sara's mouth, and then he raped her again.

When Cormac was finished with Sara, he stumbled over to the bed, fell on it, and passed out. With her hands shaking, Sara lit the lantern. Then she began looking everywhere in the room for the red cap. She opened up Cormac's bag and threw the contents on the floor. She didn't find the cap there, so she went over to Cormac and checked his pockets. It wasn't there, but her bag of coins were. She jerked it out of his pocket, opened it, and dumped all but a few coins on her bed. She closed the bag back up and put it in Cormac's pocket again. Then she dropped the coins into the pocket of her dress. She would hide them later.

Her face throbbed where he had struck her. She put her hand

on her belly. She wanted no child from this encounter. She had to stop it, but she wasn't sure she remembered the old ways. The wild ways. She wasn't sure she could stop it. It was so soon after the baby's death, so maybe she was safe.

She looked around the room one more time, but she did not find the cap. She kicked Cormac in the leg, and then she ran out of the room, went down the hallway, and out into the night. When her eyes had adjusted to the darkness, she started walking away from the building. Before she had gone far, she began limping. Her leg hurt in the same place she had kicked Cormac.

She headed for Murphy's place. He had rented a back room in a house that belonged to an English family who lived on the island. Sara tiptoed to his window and knocked on it softly. Murphy's face appeared in the window briefly. A moment later, she heard the back door open. Murphy came out to her.

"What's wrong, luv?"

She was glad he couldn't see much of her face in the darkness.

"Can I come in?" she asked. "Are you alone?"

"Come on," he said. He took her hand and led her through the open door, down a few steps of the hall, and then into his room. He closed the door. She heard him strike a match to light a lantern.

"Don't do that, Murphy," she said. "Let's stay in the dark."

He hesitated. She could see his hand was shaking. He blew out the candle.

She went to his bed and sat on the edge of it. Murphy sat next to her.

"I'm gonna tell you something," she said, "but you have to promise me you won't do nuthin about it. It's my business, and I won't have you hurt over it again. You've already lost your work because of me."

"You're asking me not to kill him," Murphy said. "Aren't you? He's hurt you again."

"You must promise me," she said.

He was silent. They sat together in the darkness.

"I will do as you ask," he said.

"He beat me," she said, "and he raped me again. Murphy, I think I'm forgetting the auld ways. I'm afraid I'll be pregnant with his bairn, and I can't do that. It would be like growing evil in my womb."

"What can I do?" he asked.

"Make love to me," she said. "If I'm gonna have a baby from this night, I want it to be yours."

Murphy was silent again.

"I know what you're thinking," she said. "It's so soon after my miscarriage and now he's ravished me and hurt me bad and you don't want to hurt me."

Sara could feel the warmth of Murphy's body next to hers. He was still trembling.

"That was what I was thinking," he said.

"That's because you're a poet at heart," she said, "and those are the wisest men of all, and the most tender. I know you won't hurt me. You could have taken your own true love and kept her for yourself, but you didn't. And it's that man I want to make love with now and erase all the evil of this night."

"Sorcha," he whispered her name. "The first mate was waiting for me when I returned. They can't find a cook. They thought they could get one here, but they couldn't. They've ordered me back. When I said I wouldn't go, he said I had a contract and they'd bring me back in chains. It doesn't matter that they nearly hanged me and tossed me off the ship themselves. They're leaving tomorrow and I have to go with them. Come with me."

"I can't," she said. "Every time I try to leave Cormac or defy the enchantment, someone is hurt or someone dies. I won't put you in harm's way again."

"It's my choice," he said.

"I will figure out a way to leave him without me or anyone else dying," Sara said. "I feel some of my strength returning. Until then, I want those I love safe. I don't have many I do love left. Besides the whole world."

"Can I kiss you?" he asked.

"Aye," she said. "On the right side, where he didn't hit me."

He kissed her lightly on her lips. She tasted her tears or his. She began to sob.

He unbuttoned her dress and carefully took it off. She winced slightly. Then he helped her out of her undergarments. She lay on the bed. He went over to the washstand and dipped a cloth into the water. Then he sat on the bed and gently washed her.

"The auld sea is washing away the blood," he said, "and his seed. It is washing away the pain and the misery. Imagine your sea sisters here with you. They are singing to you. They are telling you all will be well."

He washed all parts of her, and he did it with care, as though he were washing a baby. He carefully turned her over and washed her back.

"There are slaves on this island, Sorcha," he said. "Our people were sent here and to the New World as slaves. Did you know that? I come from people who were slaves in the New World. Some of my ancestors worked on tobacco plantations. And they would sing and dance and worship with the black people on the plantations. Our people didn't live as long. We aren't made for the sun, you know. We're made for the dreary wet weather. But they would dance along the beach if they could, or along a river bank, and they would carry seashells and dance and call out to Yemaya. She had known great suffering herself, and she always came to those who asked for her. When I was on one of these islands some years ago, I came upon one of these celebrations. And I swear as the moon rose up over the water, this dark beautiful giant woman with a tail the color of emeralds and rubies rose up out of the water. She reminded me of the auld mermaids I had seen in New Spain. As she came up out of the water, I could feel her power and love radiate to everyone there. It was only for an instant, and I will admit I had been drinking a wee bit. At the end of the night and the celebration, those people were still slaves and I was still a lonely sailor, yet we all felt something—as though we could do what we needed to do to get through our lives."

Sara had stopped crying and now she turned over and looked up at Murphy in the darkness. "She sounds like the auld ma," Sara said, "and I'm glad for those people, I suppose, but I don't want to just get through my life. I want to *live* it."

She reached up and put her hand on Murphy's cheek.

"Your hand feels so soft against my grizzled skin," Murphy said. "How can you bear to touch it?"

"I feel only tenderness," Sara said. "You're shaking, Murphy. What's that all about?"

"I'm shaking, darlin'," he said, "because I've really only loved two women in my life and I'm looking down at one of them now."

"How can you tell?" she said. "It's so dark. I could be someone you don't know at all."

"I know you," he whispered.

Sara smiled.

"Come lay beside me," Sara said.

Murphy took off his clothes and lay next to Sara.

"What is your true name?" Sara asked.

"Termain O'Murchadha," he said. "Me ma told me Termain meant sanctuary, but I don't know Gaelic. She called me Terry."

"You're living up to your name tonight, Terry O'Murphy," Sara said.

Murphy kissed Sara then. He kissed and touched her until he could move into her easily. When that happened, the story goes,

Sara and Murphy made love all night and all day and all night again. They say Sorcha O'Broin and Termain O'Murchadha were guarded by a giant old African woman who wore a dress so colorful and long it looked like a mermaid's tail and if anyone came near, she moved her hands just so and they disappeared. And the whole time, she sat knitting or weaving or some such. They say Sorcha and Termain were together until the New Moon went Full and came around New again.

Sara only knew she felt as though she was swimming in Murphy and he was swimming in her. For a heart-stopping moment, she thought, "If I had never had my troubles, I would never have met Murphy and we would have never had this night of nights," and then she stopped thinking and pressed herself against Murphy's skin.

As the air began to lighten outside, Murphy and Sara lay in each other's arms.

"I can see where he hit you now," Murphy said. "I'm sorry I ever promised you not to hurt him."

Sara looked down at her leg. "See that bruise," she said. "I kicked Cormac. A minute later, I had this bruise."

"Does that mean his face is all bloody and battered?" he asked.

"I don't know," she said. "He's never hit me before."

"I want you to go to the mermaid wall and the singing spring when you can," Murphy said. "You'll find sanctuary there. I'm sure of it. You've got to get away from him."

"Does that mean I'll find you there?" she asked.

"I'd like to say that I will end up there," he said, "but I won't promise. You've had too many promises broken. Besides, what would you do with an auld man like me?"

She lay her head on his shoulder.

"Can we stay like this for a few years longer?" she asked.

They fell to sleep together and awakened to the sound of banging on Murphy's door.

"We're leaving within the hour," the man called. "If you're not there, we've been told to horsewhip you and drag you onto the ship."

"I'll be there," Murphy said. "Go on now!"

Sara listened. She didn't hear her husband's voice anywhere looking for her.

"I think he's still in his drunk sleep," she said.

Murphy wrapped his arms around Sara and they held onto one another for a few more minutes. Then he got out of bed and put his clothes on. He stuffed what was his into a bag. Then he helped Sara get on her clothes.

"Are you sore from the beating?" he asked.

"A little," she said.

"Sorcha," Murphy said, "Years ago I met a woman on the other side of this island. They call her May and she works on one of the plantations. She has healing salves that might help. I haven't seen her this time around, so I don't know if she's still alive. Find Daniel Martin. He can get you in touch with her. She's a slave, but they let her do what she wants. She might be able to help with other things, too."

"I'll do it," Sara said.

They stood close together.

"Did you ever wonder why I turned away that first time I met you?" he asked.

"In the galley?" Sara said. "No. I figured you were annoyed that they'd brought this stranger into your kitchen. I understood. I was glad you turned away because I thought I'd fall right into those beautiful blues eyes of yours. I remember thinking they were like little lighthouses."

He smiled. "Really? You noticed my eyes?"

Sara laughed. Tears streamed down her cheeks. "What is it you're trying to tell me?"

"I turned away because when I saw you, my knees started to buckle. I felt as though I knew you through and through and that I'd been waiting for you all this time."

He shook his head and looked down. "I don't want to leave you."

"They'll take you one way or another," Sara said. "This is the better way."

He reached into his shirt pocket and pulled something out.

"What do you have there?" she asked.

"Take it," he said.

Sara picked it up off his palm and held it up to the light.

It was a small spiral shell.

"Is this the shell your own true love gave you on the beach that day?" Sara asked.

"It is," he said.

"I can't take it," she said.

He folded her fingers around it.

"Keep it," he said. "You can give it back to me when we meet again."

SEVEN

Sara watched from afar as Murphy rejoined the crew. They got into their boat and rowed back to the ship. She sat on the white sand and curled into a ball. She felt the Earth throbbing beneath her, as though she was lying against a giant and listening to its heartbeat.

After a while, she got up and returned to the White Inn and went to the room she shared with Cormac. He was still lying on the bed in the same position he had been in when she left him. The room stank. She leaned over him to see if he was still breathing. He was. She used her foot to turn him over. His face was puffy and bruised, like hers.

"That'll teach ya," Sara said.

Cormac opened his eyes.

"What are you looking at?" he asked. He coughed and sat up.

"Look at yerself in the mirror," Sara said.

"What are you talkin' about, woman," he said. He pushed

himself up and staggered over to the small oval mirror on the washstand.

"What happened to me?" he asked. "Did I get into a brawl last night?"

"You don't remember what you did, you stupid sot?" Sara said.

"Why are you talking to me this way?" he asked.

"Look at my face," she said. "You beat me last night."

"I wouldn't hurt a hair on your head," he said. "You're lying. You were off with your Murphy friend and he probably beat ya."

"You did this," Sara said. She put her face close to his. "You did it. And what you do to me, you do to yourself."

"You hit me when I was drunk," he said. "That's what has happened."

"I never touched your face," she said. "Though I wish I could have hurt you. But what I do to you, I do to myself as well. Cormac, we are going to have to come to some peace with one another."

He pushed her away from him. "My head hurts," he said. "And I think I'm gonna be sick." He fell back on the bed again and moaned.

"Is this what you want your life to be?" she asked. "We've got to change things. Let's start treating each other better. Let's be kind to one another. And you gotta stop drinking. You said you loved me but you beat and rape me. What would you do to someone you hated?"

"Leave me alone," he said.

"I will," she said. "Get yourself cleaned up. Let's start acting like the married couple we are. You won't hurt me and I won't hurt you. And that doesn't mean I have to give in to your every whim." She started to leave the room. "The ship is leaving today, and Murphy is goin' with it, so I don't want to hear another word about him from you."

And then she left the room and closed the door. She would pretend to be nice. She would do whatever she had to do to make peace with Cormac. She had to make herself invisible to him—and then she would make her escape.

That day while Cormac slept off his drunk, Sara asked around the village for Daniel Martin. She finally found him in a shipping office a bit of a walk from the village.

"I'm Sara O'Broin," she said when she came into the office, "and I'm a friend of Termain Murphy. He said you might know where I could find a woman named May. I'm needing some salve for my face."

"I can see you've had some trouble," he said. "Sit down and I'll get you some tea." He got up from his desk as Sara sat across from him. She watched while he poured tea from an old chipped pot into a cup and then brought it over to her.

"I'm surprised Murphy didn't kill the man who done this to ya," Daniel said.

"He woulda," Sara said. She took a drink of the tea. She grimaced a little, then set the cup on the desk. "But I asked him not to. It was my husband that done this."

Daniel Martin nodded. "It's a tricky thing to get between a man and his wife."

"Yeah, that's how he takes me," Sara said, "as his property. But I won't be runnin' him down to ya. I need to find May."

He leaned back in his chair.

"How'd you get to be here?" he asked. "You off the ship? Isn't it leaving today?"

"It is," she said. "We was put off because the captain was afraid his crew would think I was a witch and hang me."

"Are you?"

Sara shrugged. "Do you think if I was, I'd let a man put his hands on me like this."

"I imagine witches get beaten, too," he said.

Sara smiled. "I can see you are a practical man," she said. "My husband wants to wait for a ship to Boston. I was wondering if any other kind of ships will be coming."

"Not to this island," Martin said. "There's not much here. Not sure why I'm here. But there are ships coming to the other islands." He leaned forward. "I could get both you and your husband to another island. Wouldn't be nuthin to do."

"What about getting me to another island," she said, "and then getting me as far away from here as I can get?"

"I could do that," he said. "The next ship will be bound for New Orleans."

"One place is as good as another," Sara said. "Isn't it?"

"If you're trying to hide," he said, "New Orleans is a better place. You'll need to get your papers, in case someone asks for them."

"I don't know anything about papers," she said. "I didn't see any when I rummaged through my husband's things."

He squinted. "You're under an enchantment, aren't you? That's how he got you through."

"I don't understand," Sara said.

Martin shrugged. "It doesn't matter," he said. "I can get you what you need. If you don't have the money for bribes and passage though, you'll have to work it off when you get to New Orleans."

Sara nodded.

"When do you want to leave?" he asked.

"I have to work something out first," she said. She looked at him. Should she explain that if she left Cormac she would probably die?

"If it's magic you need," Martin said, "you should go talk to

May. She's at the next plantation down the road. You can ask for her. She has free roam of the place. You can't miss her. She is covered in flowers. You'll know what I mean when you see her. No one quite knows how she does it, but she does it. You tell her Murphy and Daniel Martin sent you and you'll get what you need. I'll make some inquires and see what I can do. Where can I get in touch with you?"

"It'd be better if I came to you," she said.

"Come back in a couple of weeks then," he said. "And I'll see what I can do."

"Thank you," Sara said. "You will keep this to yourself, Mr. Martin?"

"I will," Daniel Martin said. "If I didn't, I know Murphy would hunt me down. If you've got him as an ally, you're doing well."

Sara left the shipping office after Martin gave her directions to the plantation. She knew she didn't have long before Cormac would come out of his stupor and wonder where she was.

When she got to the plantation, she didn't go to the big house. She went to the slave housing as Daniel Martin had instructed. It turned out she didn't have to ask anyone about May. It turned out the way these things sometimes do that May was sitting under a group of young palm trees. Sara knew it was May because she was wearing a dress with flowers all over it, and she had flowers in her hair. The fragrance from the flowers wafted over to Sara as she walked toward her.

"Mammy, the flowers are speaking to you. You need to listen."

May looked up from the sewing in her lap and smiled.

"I've been expecting you," she said. She spoke English that had a kind of lilt to it, as though she were singing. "A little girl told me you'd be coming. Was she your daughter?"

Sara nodded. "She's in the sea now," Sara said.

"She gone back to the mother," May said, "to the source of all."

Sara sat on the bench next to May.

"Did her father do that to your face?"

"No," Sara said. "Her father is at the bottom of the ocean, too."

"I didn't see him in the dream," May said. "Only the girl."

"My husband did this to me," Sara said. "He stole my red cap and now I am obligated to be his fish wife. They all say my ancestors agreed to this arrangement and I can't break the enchantment, but I don't believe it."

"You tried to leave him and you grew so ill you nearly died?"

"Yes," Sara said. "I have searched for the red cap, but I can't find it. I don't know if I will ever find it, but I'm not going to pass my life away as his fish wife."

"What was the red cap made from?" May asked.

"My ma made it with the hair of a sister mermaid, the wool from the Witch McClarny's sheep, and my hair while she whispered the fath fith."

"I don't know this word 'fafee,'" she said.

"It's a protection charm to make ya invisible," Sara said.

"It sounds as though the magic goes deeper than the cap itself," May said. "Like the magic of this place. It still exists no matter what I do. For many years I tried to destroy it, but then I had a dream. In the dream I was standing in church, and it was like this." May drew a rectangle in the air. "And I made a circle in this church. I sang my chants and lit my candles and called to Yemaya and she rose up from the chalice of wine as easily and clearly as though she was rising up from the river. From then on, I looked for what could sustain me here. And it's the flowers. My true name is Titi. But I don't mind being called May because that is the month when the most flowers bloom, at least in my head."

She tapped her forehead. "In the place where my parents came from Titi means flower. I am a child of the flowers. I speak to them and they speak to me. And they give me healing, sustenance, and magic."

"Are you saying I need to find the magic in the life I have now?" Sara asked.

May laughed. "Some things we can change," May said, "and some things we can't. I speak to the flowers to find out which is which. Who do you need to speak with?"

Sara sighed. It sounded like a riddle to her, and she had never been good with riddles.

"I am speaking with you," Sara said. "I have tried to find the answers on my own and it hasn't worked. My daughter said to listen to the flowers, and here you are, covered in flowers. Can you help me break this enchantment?"

May looked at her. "First we must get you something for those bruises," she said. "We may not be able to break the enchantment but perhaps we can make it safe for you to leave this man and travel far from him so you can live your life as you see fit."

"I will settle for that," Sara said. "Daniel Martin said he could get me to another island and then get me passage to America."

"But you'll need to get away from your husband first," May said. "You need to create something that is more powerful than the red cap. Something which will make you invisible to him."

Sara remembered Mrs. Beale plucking hair from her head to make a protective sweater for her grandson. "If I had enough of your hair, I could make my grandson invisible and he would be protected from harm from his enemies." Sara put her hand on her hair.

"Yes," Sara said. "I know what to do. I will quilt a blanket using my hair, the faery yarn my ma gave me, and whatever other cloth and words I can find to weave protection for myself."

May nodded. "And we will do what we can to cut the cord

that binds you to one another. Go home now. Ask for a dream from your ancestors. Ask for answers. Have your blanket done by the full moon. We will meet down by the lagoon as the moon rises. Now let me look at those bruises. I've got something to put on them."

They got up from the bench, and Sara followed May into a small room in one of the planation buildings. The walls were covered with paintings of flowers.

"I want to thank you for what you're doing," Sara said. "Can I do something for you for your kindness?"

"I don't need nuthin," she said. "But for the spirits, bring liquor. For the ancestors, bring flowers or other remembrances. For the land, bring your dreams. And there's one more thing you need to bring. You need three strands of hair from your husband's hair."

"I cut his hair," she said. "I could do it then."

May shook her head. "We need it plucked right from his scalp," she said.

"If I do that, he'll suspect witchcraft," Sara said. "But I will work it out."

"And then there's this," May said. She handed Sara a vial. "We'll arrange for your escape, we'll cut the cord, you'll make your quilt—and you'll give him a little sleeping potion to be doubly certain you can get away. Pour that into something he drinks and he will sleep like a baby."

Sara looked at the vial.

"Can you do it?" May asked.

"I can," she said. She wasn't sure how she was going to get hair from her husband or how she would drug him, but she would.

When May finished tending to Sara's cuts and bruises, Sara hurried away. She felt filled with purpose for the first time in a long while. She would soon be free. How would she do the quilt? She couldn't sit there making a quilt for herself. Cormac would be suspicious. She could say she had gotten sewing work to make extra money. He would approve of that.

On her way back to the White Inn, Sara knocked on doors and asked if anyone in the household needed any of their clothes repaired. She said she would do the sewing in exchange for a few pieces of old cloth. She was soon loaded down with dresses to hem, pants to repair, and shirts to mend.

She took it all back to their room at the White Inn. Cormac still slept. Sara dumped the clothes and pieces of cloth on the bed, and she organized them so she would remember which clothes went with which house. She put the pieces of cloth together and stuffed them into a bag. She got the treasure box her mother had given her and added that to the bag.

She took it all downstairs to the parlor. She put the bag behind a chair while she went into the dining room and had a meal. She talked amiably to the other guests.

Afterward she went into the parlor and began making her quilt. First she put a sweater on her lap and she mended it. When she was finished with it, she left it there. She took out the ball of faery yarn and whispered, "The spirits of here and the spirits of there I always honor thee. With this thread, I unweave the spell over me. I untie the ties that bind me to he. Oh, the spirits of here and the spirits of there. With this yarn, I weave a new spell with all my might. I tie the threads up nice and tight. I undo the magic that has been done on me so that I may be forever free."

Then she began knitting and created small square patches, one at a time. Whenever she thought she heard Cormac or saw someone coming her way, she began working on the sweater again. When the people moved away, she took out the knitting. She whispered all the time, trying to weave a new spell into the thread.

In the days and nights that followed, guests of the inn who saw Sara in the parlor noted that she was not alone. Some thought

faeries sat with her; others said they were pixies. Still others were
sure the banshees moaned next to her. The innkeeper swore later
that a little girl danced in the room—and sparks flew up from
her feet.

Cormac came downstairs the first day and asked Sara what
she was doing.

"I'm earning us some money," she said, "so when we get to
the new world, we can buy things." She glanced up at Cormac.
He looked like he had just walked out of some hellish place.
Maybe he had. Maybe he'd walked out of the terrible place he
had made for himself and her. For a moment as their eyes met,
she thought he was going to say, "Here's your cap. You're a free
woman now."

But he didn't, and she looked down at the sweater again.

They ate supper together in the dining room. Cormac had
washed himself and shaved. He didn't drink anything at dinner.
The people at the table with them hardly said a word to them.
Later, Sara realized they both looked so bruised and bloodied
that everyone must have assumed they had beaten each other up.
For some reason, Sara thought this was funny. She considered
mentioning this to Cormac but decided against it.

After the meal, she told Cormac she was going to sew for a
little while and then she would come up to their room. He sat with
her for a few minutes. Then he got up. He stood on the threshold
and looked out into the night; then he glanced up at the stairs.
Sara could see he was trying to decide if he would go out and get
drunk or go to bed.

"You'll be up soon?" he asked.

"I will," she said.

He sighed and trudged up the stairs as though he was on the
way to his execution.

Sara smiled. She wished he was on his way to his execution.

She shook her head. No, she couldn't have those thoughts. She had to weave her own way of being in the world—a way that would help her leave Cormac behind.

In the days that followed, Sara worked on the quilt all day and part of the night. She felt like she had drunk a powerful elixir that was filling her up with a strange kind of vigor. She felt focused, yet the world appeared a little fuzzy. Every once in a while she thought about Murphy and her stomach lurched. Then she'd shake her head and stop thinking of anything except the thread or yarn she was sewing or weaving. She wanted to sit by the sea and do her work, but she knew that would make Cormac nervous, and for now, she wanted to appear to be the obedient fish wife.

After she dropped off the sewing the first time, she gave Cormac one of the coins she had stolen from him, telling him that was how much she earned from her sewing.

"They're paying you a lot for what you're doing," Cormac said. He put the coin in his mouth and bit it.

"They were happy with my work," she said.

The next day she exchanged her coins for smaller change. When she gave Cormac coins that night he said, "These people are cheap bastards, aren't they?"

Cormac did not seem to suspect anything. Sara hoped she would finish with the quilt before her coins ran out.

She made an effort to be nice to Cormac. She ate meals with him. If he worked during the day, she made him tea in their room. Once a day, she walked on the beach with him. He began to relax and talk to her as though they were a true married couple.

"It'll be great when we get to the city," he told her. "There's so much work in America. We'll never go hungry; we'll always have work. We'll have a grand life. Our children will be well-cared for."

He smiled as he talked, and Sara could see he was far away in his dream future.

"We never went hungry at home," Sara said. "Did you?"

"We did," he said. "My da wasn't much of a fisher or a shepherd. He was good at beating on us and my ma."

Sara looked over at him. "I never heard of such a thing," she said.

"Aye," he said. "We were a lazy lot, he said. He was probably right."

"Naw, he wasn't," Sara said. "You can't ever strike our children, Cormac. Not ever. You must promise me."

She knew if she said something like that, he'd start trusting her even more. He'd think she was planning their future together, too.

"I won't ever hit them," he said. "I swear. And I swear I will never hurt you again."

One day when Cormac was away, Sara asked the innkeeper's wife to tell Cormac that she was taking a walk on the beach and she'd be back soon.

"I will do as you ask," the woman said. She held Sara's gaze for a moment. Sara felt like she should say something to the woman, but she did not know what that something would be. So she thanked her and hurried out of the building. She went toward the beach in case anyone was watching her. After a few minutes, she headed away from the beach and went toward Daniel Martin's office. She was glad to find him in.

He invited her into the office and then closed the door behind them.

"I've made the arrangements for you to leave," he said. "Have you seen May?"

"I have," Sara said. "I'm to meet her on the full moon. It would be easier to leave then. I don't know if I could get away twice."

"We can hide you for the night and get you away first thing in the morning," he said. "Do you have any money?"

Sara gave him most of her coins. "This won't pay for much,"

he said. "I'll give the captain of the ship this and what I can and you'll work off the rest."

"Thank you, Mr. Martin," she said. "I need to get back now."

"I'll see you soon," he said.

At night, Sara left her bag of sewing by her bed. She tucked it away casually, as though it had no meaning for her. If Cormac got suspicious, he might dig around in the bag and find the quilt; although it wasn't a quilt yet. It was only pieces of cloth—some knitted from faery yarn, some taken as payment from her customers. She wouldn't sew it all together until just before she was ready to leave.

"When will you start sleeping in our bed again?" Cormac asked her one night when the bruises were almost healed.

"When I can be sure you aren't gonna force yourself on me," she said, "or beat me."

"I told you I wouldn't do it again," he said.

"I know," she said, "but you told me that the last time."

"Come to bed then," he said, "and I won't touch you. I only want to feel you next to me, like husband and wife."

Cormac looked at her. He seemed to be pleading with her. Sara tried to see if underneath something else was going on. She didn't trust him, but she didn't want to make him angry now. She didn't want to give him any cause to doubt her.

So she lay in bed with him and he didn't touch her, except to pat her arm and tell her to have good dreams. In the middle of the night, Sara awakened to find Cormac curled up next to her, with his fingers lightly touching her arm. She looked at him in the moonlight. His face was soft, his body relaxed. It was hard to imagine he could ever hurt anyone.

She closed her eyes. What was it that happened to people that made them do evil? She didn't believe it was the devil, like the

Christians said. She wasn't sure she even believed in evil. It was just a word to explain the bad things people did to one another.

She suddenly remembered she needed to get three strands of hair from Cormac. If she reached over now, maybe she could get one before he awakened. But then how would she get the other two? She could get him drunk so that he passed out again. Then she could get whatever she wanted from him. At the risk that he would attack her again.

She had to do something. The moon was getting fuller every night. Sara turned away from Cormac. Soon, he would be out of her life forever, one way or another.

EIGHT

The time came for Sara to sew the pieces of her quilt together. She feared this was the most dangerous part of her work.

"Cormac," Sara said to her husband upon awakening one morning, "I'm feeling a little ill this morning. I'll do my sewing up here."

"Do you want me to stay with ya?" he asked. "I was going to do some work for Mr. McKean today."

"You go ahead," she said. "I just need a little rest."

"Is it a baby?" he asked.

Sara looked at him, startled. They had only had sex once since the miscarriage, and that was when he raped her. She squinted. She wanted to ask him, "Does that mean you remember raping me and beating me?" But she didn't.

"There's no baby," she said.

"We should try for another one soon," he said. "When you're ready. It'll give you something to do."

"I have plenty to do," Sara said. "I think we should wait until we are settled in our new home. You don't want the burden of a wife and child so soon."

"It's no burden," he said. "It's what I desire more than anything in the world."

Sara forced herself to smile. "It is my desire as well, husband. But I want to be a help to you and I can do that better when I'm not carrying around a baby."

He frowned. She could see he wanted to argue with her. But he didn't. He kissed the top of her head.

"I'll come by and check on you," he said.

"You'll wake me up," she said.

"All right, then," he said. He left the room.

Sara sat still for a moment and listened to his retreating footsteps. Then she wiped the top of her head with her sleeve.

"I want none of you on any of me," she said.

She got her bag and began pulling out all the pieces. She put them on the bed so she could cover them and herself quickly with the blanket if Cormac returned. She laid out the needles and thread. Now she had to sew the pieces all together using mermaid's hair as the thread—that would bind the spell and the quilt together. Hers was the only hair she had, so she began plucking hair after hair out of her scalp.

She heard footsteps in the corridor. She quickly folded the blanket over her and her work.

Someone tapped on the door.

"What is it?" Sara asked.

"Mr. MacDougal asked me to bring you up some breakfast," it was Mrs. Smith, the innkeeper's wife.

"Come in then," she said. She sat up, careful not to disturb the quilt patches.

Mrs. Smith opened the door and carried in a tray and set it on the small table at the end of the bed.

"You've got the bloom on ya," she said. "When will you be havin' the baby?"

Sara shook her head. "No child is coming. I must have eaten something."

Mrs. Smith frowned.

"Oh, nothing from here," Sara said. "Everything here is delicious." Sara smiled. She was amazed how quickly she had learned to lie about almost everything. The food in the inn was not terrible, but it had a peculiar deadness to it.

"This here is broth from a chicken killed this morning," Mrs. Smith said. "It'll heal you right up." She sat on the bed across from Sara.

Sara wanted her to leave, but she didn't want to hurry her out. She couldn't have anyone suspicious of her. Sara smiled. Mrs. Smith had hardly said a word to her since she arrived, and now she wanted to have a heart to heart?

"I read the entrails," the woman said.

Sara looked at her.

"It's something the women here taught me," she said, her voice low.

"Did they now?" Sara said. She reached over for the broth and put the bowl in her lap and began spooning the soup into her mouth. It was delicious. Sara looked up at her.

"Aye," Mrs. Smith said. Her words had a lilt to them now. "I made it for you. My husband won't let me cook so that the food is alive. He doesn't like any spice in his life." She giggled.

Sara smiled.

"The entrails told me that you're under an enchantment," Mrs. Smith whispered. "But I knew that all along. You see, I understand such things."

She leaned over, unbuttoned her left shoe, and slipped it off. She unrolled her stocking. She glanced at the door and then she took off the stocking. Sara looked at her toes. They were slightly webbed.

"Selkie," Sara whispered.

"Yes," she said. "I've been looking for what he stole from me for most of my life. I saw you a couple weeks ago. He beat you, didn't he? You got in your licks though. I wish I could do that."

"I didn't touch him," Sara said. "When he hit me, he injured himself."

"That must be part of it then," she said. "I'm Ruby McGonagle, by the way." She held out her hand to Sara. Sara took her hand in her own and squeezed it.

"I am Sara O'Broin," she said.

The two women looked at one another.

"The entrails did say you were having a baby," she said. "And that you had a rough journey ahead of you."

Sara sighed. She had hoped it wasn't true. She put her hand on her belly. It wasn't Cormac's baby. It was Murphy's. And that was what she would tell the child.

"He forced himself on you," Ruby said.

"He did," Sara said. "I wouldn't have him any other way now. It's a long sad story that I'm weary of tellin'."

Ruby nodded. "Mine as well."

"Can I do anything to help?" Sara asked.

Ruby shook her head. "Escape," she said. "It'll give me hope. When I was younger, I thought I was free as a bird. As free as the fish in the sea. I never knew what kind of prisons we can make of our lives. And now it's all I know. You can drink the soup, you know. I'm not fancy."

"I'm grateful," Sara said. She picked up the bowl and drank the liquid. "It is a marvel, this soup. I cannot thank you enough."

"I used to make it for my babies," Ruby said.

"Where are your children now?" Sara asked.

"They've grown and gone away," Ruby said. "They are all

boys. They've gone to America. That's where we were going but we got stuck here. It is a lovely place. And Mr. Smith is not a bad man. He's never struck me, never forced himself on me."

"But he won't let you go," Sara said.

"He won't," Ruby said. "When will you go?"

"I don't know," Sara said. "One day."

Ruby looked at her. She smiled. "I agree with you," she said. "Don't trust anyone. Until you can." Her lilt was gone now. She put her sock and shoe back on.

Sara suddenly said, "Do you want to come with me?"

Ruby smiled. "I would if I could," she said. "But for now, I'll read chicken entrails and make soup for kindred spirits. If you get someplace some day, get word to me. I won't tell anyone. Say hello to May. She told me to watch out after you."

"Thank you," Sara said. The two women embraced.

"May you know liberty," Ruby said, "and beauty, all the days of your life." Ruby pulled away from her. "I'll make certain no one disturbs you all day."

And so, after Ruby left the room, Sara spread out the pieces of the quilt. She braided two strands of her hair with thread from the faery yarn and then she ran them through the needle and they became the thread that wove the patches together. Sara sang softly as she sewed, "The spirits of here and the spirits of there I always honor thee. With this thread, I unweave the spell over me. I untie the ties that bind me to he. Oh, the spirits of here and the spirits of there. With this yarn, I weave a new spell with all my might. A spell of protection in the night. I say this charm to keep me from harm. I tie the threads up nice and tight. I undo the magic that has been done on me so that I may have liberty and be forever free."

Legend has it that on that day, many travelers from near and far couldn't find the White Inn. There it stood near the white beach and the blue sea in plain sight, but it was lost in the fog of whatever enchantment Sara O'Broin and Ruby McGonagle wove that day. When Cormac MacDougal walked from another side of the island to see about his wife, he got lost once or twice or plenty of times to cause him to turn around and return to his work.

And Mr. Smith couldn't find his way back either. Ruby McGonagle used this opportunity to look for the sealskin her husband had taken from her so many years ago on a faraway beach. At the time, she had thought he was a pretty boy and she saw no harm when he laughed and held the sealskin out of her reach. And his kisses were softer than any she had known before. But now on this tiny island in the middle of a sea that was not always very peaceful, she wanted her life back.

Depending upon who is telling the story, some say Ruby found what she was looking for that day. She pressed it against her heart and laughed with joy. She thought about running upstairs and telling Sara, but that thought lasted for only a second. She forgot Sara, forgot her husband, forgot her children. She ran out of the White Inn and toward the sea. As soon as her webbed feet touched the water, Ruby McGonagle disappeared. At one point during the day, Sara thought she heard someone laughing and then the sound of splashing, as though two otters were having fun in a nearby river. She listened for a moment and didn't hear anything else and she went back to sewing.

Others say Ruby McGonagle disappeared that day and was never heard from again. And still others say Ruby went to visit a friend on the other side of the island and returned a few days later.

Sara finished the quilt that day. She put it around her shoulders and pulled it close to her body. She closed her eyes. She felt as though she was being embraced by her mother, her land and sea sisters, by the faeries, by the auld mother. She felt rocked by the sea itself. She looked down at the quilt. All the patches appeared to be the same color so that the quilt looked as though it was made from one cloth, yet it glittered. She blinked and it was emerald glitter; she blinked again and it was ruby glitter.

Then she felt something in the pit of her stomach and she heard the whisper of her name from a distance. She had heard it off and on all day. Now she knew Cormac was coming closer, and he sounded angry.

She quickly folded up the quilt. She stuffed it in her bag, along with the treasure box. She hurried out into the corridor and opened the door of one of the empty rooms. She flattened out the bag as much as she could and then she put it under one of the mattresses.

She hurried back into their room. She straightened everything up and sat in the chair and waited for Cormac. She recognized his footsteps. She heard the anger in every footfall. Tomorrow night she had to meet May. Tomorrow night she was leaving this place and Cormac for good, and she had to make certain nothing happened to jeopardize that. She took a deep breath.

"Help me, sea sisters," Sara whispered. "Help me sooth his heart so that I may depart."

The door swung open. Cormac's face was red, his eyes were watery.

He was angry and drunk.

Sara looked up at him. She was not going to let this happen again.

"Cormac," she said. "How are you? I was beginning to worry. You've been gone so long."

"I couldn't find my way back," he said. "Someone has been doing sorcery. I can smell it." He looked around. "Has someone been here with you?"

"Mrs. Smith stopped by to bring me soup," Sara said. "That's all. Come sit. I have news for you."

"Did you do this sorcery to me?" Cormac asked.

"I didn't," Sara said. "Why are you angry with me? I've been waiting all day to give you this news."

"What news?" He sat on the bed.

"I didn't want to tell you this morning because I wasn't sure," she said, "but then I had a dream and I realized you were right. I am going to have a baby."

Cormac didn't say anything.

"I thought you'd be happy," she said. She pretended she was crying. "I thought this was what you wanted."

"Oh darlin'," he said. "This is what I wanted. I'm very happy. I'm just surprised. You were so sure this morning."

He came and sat next to her. He put his arm around her and pulled her close. She didn't resist.

"So now you can see what happened that night was for the best," he said. "We'll have our own little baby. It'll make everything all right again."

Sara wanted to scream, "It will not be all right 'again.' It has never been all right." She wanted to spit in his face.

She swallowed and then said, "I think we should celebrate tonight, don't you?"

"Yes!" he said. "We can tell everyone! It's a happy day."

They went downstairs for supper. Sara looked for Ruby McGonagle but didn't see her. Cormac drank a great deal and told everyone about "his" bairn. How big and strong he'd be.

"He'll be fit to be king," Cormac said. "Fit to be king!" And he raised his glass in salute and drank some more. Sara ate and watched him. She didn't want him to get so drunk he was belligerent. But she wanted him drunk enough to pass out.

Eventually they went upstairs. Sara brought up a bottle of liquor with her and gave it to Cormac.

"Come sit next to me," he said. "No, come lie with me." He giggled. "I'm feeling a little dizzy, Sorcha, my love."

"Don't call me that," she said.

"Call you what?" He laughed again.

"Why don't you lie down for a rest," Sara said.

"No, I don't want to lie down unless I'm lying on top of you," he said. "I think I should lie down here for only a minute, Sara. Why can't I call you Sorcha?" He lay back. "The whole room is spinning. Ma, do you think you could get me something to drink?" He chuckled.

He closed his eyes.

"You can't call me Sorcha because only the people I love can call me that," Sara said.

Cormac began snoring.

"And I hate you with every part of my body," Sara said. "I hate you with every part of the earth I have ever stepped upon and every part of the sea that I have ever swam in. I won't curse you, though, Cormac, because you've cursed me and I won't do to you what you done to me. But I will do this."

She bent over and pulled out several strands of hair.

"Ow," he said sleepily. Then he turned over.

Sara wrapped the hair in a kerchief and then ran next door and put the kerchief in the treasure box.

Then she went back to their room and lay down on a bed across the room from Cormac.

"Sleep well, rotten boy," she whispered, "for tomorrow I will be free or I will be dead."

She would not accept any other outcomes.

NINE

Sara opened her eyes. She had had no dreams. No messages from the ancestors, her sea sisters, or her daughter. Cormac was still sleeping across the room from her.

Sara got up and splashed her face with the cold water in the wash basin. Then she tiptoed into the empty room and got her bag. She dug out the vial with the sleeping potion and put it in her pocket. Then she took the bag downstairs and put it behind the chair where she usually worked. She sat in the dining room where she could keep an eye on it. She had to make certain nothing went wrong today.

Mr. Smith served her breakfast.

"Where's Mrs. Smith?" Sara asked.

Mr. Smith looked more distressed than he usually did. "She's gone to visit a friend," he said.

Sara hadn't seen Ruby in a day. Could it be she had found the sealskin and run away? She hoped it was so.

Sara ate slowly. She knew it was going to be a long day. When she finished breakfast, she went into the parlor. She pulled out a shirt from her bag. She had four shirts to mend today, and she would do the work slowly. The pocket was ripped on this one. It looked as though it had been torn on purpose. This was Jimmy Kennedy's shirt. He was a single man living with the Johnsons. She could tell he was sweet on her. Every time she returned to him something she had repaired, he found something else for her to do. She had repaired one shirt four times. She finally said to him, "Jimmy, you're gonna have to learn to be less clumsy or you're gonna tear something besides your poor shirt."

He had just smiled at her.

Now Sara sewed the pocket back into place and whispered blessings on him. "May you know peace and happiness all the days of your life, sweet Jimmy Kennedy."

After a while, Cormac came downstairs. He sat next to her.

"I have a headache," he said. "Do you have anything that can help it?"

"Lean over," she said. He did. She kissed the top of his head. "There. All better."

He smiled slightly.

"That worked when my ma did it," Sara said. She felt slightly giddy. Her freedom was so close.

"I'm sorry I drank so much last night," he said. "I was excited about the baby."

"That's all right," Sara said. "No harm."

"I had a dream," he said, "but I'm can't seem to remember it."

"It was probably nothing," she said. "Why don't you eat something. You'll feel better then. Are you going to McKean's today?"

"I am," he said.

"Come home before it's dark," Sara said. "I'll fix you some tea."

"Will do," he said.

Sara was relieved when Cormac finally left. She wanted to stand up and dance. She kept smiling as she sewed.

Sara finished her sewing by early afternoon. She hid her bag upstairs again. Then she returned the clothes she had repaired to their rightful owners. They all had more sewing for her to do, but she told them she was taking a break for a couple of days. Everyone accepted this except for Jimmy Kennedy.

"Oh please, Mrs. MacDougal," Jimmy said. "I put a hole in these pants." He ducked into his room and came out with a pair of trousers.

"Jimmy," Sara said as she looked at them, "these are big enough for a giant. These can't be yours."

"You could take them in then so they'd fit me better," he said.

Sara smiled at him. "All right, Jimmy. I'll take these and work on them."

She started to leave when he said, "If you ever need anything, Mrs. MacDougal, let me know."

She looked at him. "I told you to call me Sara," she said. "And I appreciate the offer."

"I mean it," he said. "I-I remember when you first came by and your face was hurt. If you ever need help, I'm your man. I know this island better than anyone."

"That's a kind thing you're offering," Sara said. He was hardly more than a boy, and she was pretty certain Cormac could crush him.

He must have guessed she was sizing him up because he said, "And I could teach you to box. I was pretty good at it back home. My da said it was always better to work at being strong than to pray to be strong. Take life into our own hands."

Sara nodded. She had underestimated him.

"I thank you, Jimmy," she said. "I'll remember what you've said."

It seemed as though he had something more to say, but Sara waited, and he didn't say anything else. So she left. She carried his trousers back to the White Inn. She went up to her room and patched them up before Cormac returned. When she was finished, she folded them up and put them on her bed. She put a bottle of liquor in her bag and laid some picked flowers on top of it all—to give to May later.

Then she sat and waited. She listened for Cormac, but he didn't come. She watched the sun fall lower in the sky. She had to be away before dark. She got her bag and took out the quilt and looked at it one last time. Then she put it away with her treasure box and the few clothes she had. She'd take the whole bag with her.

She fingered the vial in her pocket. She decided to go downstairs and get the tea anyway. He would be back any minute. She brought the tray, tea pot, and cups back up to the room. She arranged them on the table, and then she rearranged them. She couldn't wait until it was dark. She would never find her way to the lagoon then. She could get to Daniel Martin's office though. It would be all right.

Finally she heard Cormac's footsteps. Her heart started racing. He wasn't calling her name tonight. He wasn't even whispering it. Down the corridor he came. She took the vial from her pocket, took off the stopper, and poured the contents into the cup on her left. She quickly put the empty vial back into her pocket.

The door swung open.

Cormac looked at her. "Good day," he said.

"How are ya?" Sara said. She smiled. Something was off about him. He wasn't drunk. But something was wrong.

"Are you hungry?" Sara asked. "I've got some cakes here and a little tea."

She reached for the pot. She hoped her hands wouldn't shake. She carefully poured the steeped tea into first one cup and then another. She put a cake on a plate. Then she picked up the cup on her left and the plate and she set it down opposite her. "Here you are," she said.

Cormac went over to the wash basin and put his hands in it.

"This is cold," he said. "Could you get me some warm water?"

"Of course," Sara said. "I should have thought of that."

She went over to the wash basin and picked it up. She tried to move with purpose but without fear. She carried the basin over to the open window and threw the cold water out. She got the empty pitcher and hurried out of the room and down the corridor. She tried to breathe deeply to steady herself. She could hear her heart beating. Everything was fuzzy again, as if she couldn't quite concentrate on any one thing.

She went downstairs, poured hot water into the pitcher, and then carried it back upstairs. Cormac sat at the table.

Sara smiled and poured the hot water into the basin.

"Nice and hot for ya," she said.

Cormac got up and went over to the basin.

"Did you have a good day then?" she asked.

She sat down. She picked up her cup and took a sip. She set it down again. She had let it steep too long. It was bitter. She wondered if Cormac would notice.

"It's a little bitter," Sara said. "Do you want me to put sugar in it for you? Some milk?"

"I'm fine," he said. His back was still turned from her.

Sara suddenly felt a little dizzy. The room tilted a bit. She put her hands on the table to steady herself. She had gotten dizzy a couple of times when she was pregnant before. It would be all right.

She was exhausted. She looked around the room. Nothing looked right. She squinted.

She looked down at her tea.

Cormac turned around and looked at her.

"I remembered my dream," he said. "In it, you poisoned me. By serving me tea."

Sara glanced up at him. "I would never do that," she said.

She tried to stand, but she was too dizzy. She tried to breathe deeply.

Cormac was still looking down at her.

"What have you done?" Sara asked. "Did you poison me? What about the baby?"

"There is no baby," he said.

"There is!" Sara said.

She felt like she was going to throw up.

"What did you do?"

"I didn't do anything" he said, "except exchange your tea for mine."

She sighed. That was good. He hadn't poisoned her. And she had only had a sip of the tea.

"Then why am I so dizzy?" she asked. Maybe she could fool him.

He leaned down close to her. "Because you poisoned my tea."

"On the life of our child," Sara said, "I swear I didn't poison you. Do you think I'm having a miscarriage?" She gazed up at him. She hoped she appeared fearful. He stared at her. He looked hateful. She knew he wanted to beat her again, rape her.

"Cormac," she said. "Do you think I'm having another miscarriage? Is there a doctor here? Maybe if I ate something?" She reached for one of the cakes and began eating it. As she chewed she started to feel steadier. Steadier and sleepier.

"Could you go downstairs and get me something to eat?" she

asked. "Mrs. Smith made me some broth yesterday that really helped. And maybe some kind of bread and meat." She tried to think of something that would take time making.

She looked up at Cormac again. "I didn't try to poison you," she said. "You are the father of my child. I don't know why I'm sick now, but I don't want to lose our baby. Please help me."

Cormac's face shifted a bit. She saw fear in his eyes—and doubt about his certainty.

"I'll bring you something to eat," he said. "Go lie down and rest. It'll be all right."

He strode out of the room. She listened for his footsteps but only heard a couple. He was waiting outside the door.

"Oh my," she said, loud enough for Cormac to hear. "Please don't let me lose this baby too. It'll be all right, baby. Your da will take care of me."

Then she heard the footsteps again. Heard Cormac go down the stairs. She tried to get up quickly but the whole world lurched. She exchanged her tea cup for his, in case he came back and drank it. Then she stuffed another cake into her mouth and got up from her chair.

She wanted to run, but she couldn't. The world wobbled and shifted. She picked up her bag. It seemed so heavy. She would never be able to carry it now. She pulled out the quilt and her treasure box. She put the box in her pocket. Then she wrapped the quilt around her as though it were a shawl.

"By the powers of the fath fith, I say this charm to keep me from harm," Sara said. "May I be out of sight before anyone discovers my flight." She shut her eyes for a moment. "Please help me, auld ma."

She tiptoed down the corridor. At least she tried to. She wasn't certain of anything. She felt drunker than she had ever been and so giddy she could barely walk.

"Freedom," she whispered, "freedom."

Down the stairs she went. She would have to pass in view of the dining room to go out the door. She hoped Cormac was in the kitchen. She tripped near the bottom of the stairs, but she grabbed a hold of the railing and steadied herself. One of the patrons walked toward the front door.

"You can do this," she whispered.

She held the quilt tighter around her. The man opened the door. Someone called to him and he looked back.

Sara ran through the open door and out into the near night. She almost fell again. The fresh air was a tonic, but she still felt drugged. She was so glad she hadn't gulped the whole cup.

She started to run down the beach and immediately fell face down on the sand. She lay still for a moment. She wouldn't be able to get to the lagoon by dark. She needed help. Maybe Daniel Martin was still in his office.

She pushed herself up off the sand and began walking. She couldn't run. She could barely walk. She hoped the quilt and the spell would keep her hidden. She walked to one palm tree and leaned against it. Breathed. Steadied herself. Then walked to the next one. She had to hurry. Hurry. But she was not able to move quickly. Any moment Cormac would discover she was missing. She didn't hear him yet. Now even a whisper.

She staggered to the next tree and the next. The trees wobbled. They called to her. Each embraced her and then sent her on to the next one.

Soon she was at Daniel Martin's office.

But the office was closed. He was nowhere in sight. It was near dark. Where could she go? What could she do?

Someone was walking toward her. It couldn't be Cormac. Couldn't be. Wouldn't she have heard?

She moved back and pressed herself against Daniel Martin's building.

The man came closer. Walked right up to the door and didn't seem to see her.

It was Jimmy Kennedy.

"Jimmy," she whispered.

He turned and looked in her direction but didn't seem to see her.

She had forgotten the fath fith.

"Jimmy," she said again. "It's Sara O'Broin. I need your help."

He moved closer to her, blinked, and saw her.

"I had a dream," he said, "that I was to come here tonight. I thought it had something to do with you."

"It seems everyone got a dream but me," she said. "I'm running away. My husband drugged me and I can barely walk. I need to get to the lagoon. Do you know the place?"

"Sure," he said. "I'll take ya."

"He'll be coming after me soon," she said. "You might get hurt."

"I'm willin'," he said.

"I want you to hear me, Jimmy," Sara said. "There's an enchantment."

"That's plain enough for anyone to see," he said. "Come on now. Take my arm. I'll lead you through. I know a shortcut."

"Can you see in the dark then?"

"My ancestors were forest people," he said. "So I can see through the dark as well as anything living. The moon is rising. It will light the way."

And so, Sara O'Broin put her hand through Jimmy Kennedy's arm. She leaned on him, and he went forward, fast and steady. Darkness fell over the island so quickly that it felt as though the spirits had blown out the candle that was the sun. Sara was glad for it: darkness would hide her from Cormac.

It seemed she and Jimmy walked forever and not far enough.

Then the moon began its rise. It came out of the sea, round and fat. As they neared the lagoon, Sara was certain she could see a woman on the surface of the moon, dancing.

May came toward them.

"Sara," she said. "You're ill?"

"I'm sorry I didn't get here sooner," Sara said. "This is Jimmy Kennedy. He helped me good. Cormac switched cups on me and I got some of the sleeping potion. He'll be coming soon enough."

"He knows about the lagoon?" May asked.

"I don't know," Sara said. "Thank you, Jimmy."

"Jimmy has helped me before," May said. "He's one of my many Irish sons."

"I finished your trousers," Sara said. "But I left them at the inn."

Jimmy laughed softly. "It doesn't matter, Sara. I don't need them now."

"I feel tipsy," Sara said. "When will the potion wear off? Will it hurt the baby?"

"I don't know," May said. "Come. Let us begin the ceremony. Jimmy, can you keep watch when we start?"

"I will," he said.

Sara looked around the lagoon. Several women stood near the water.

"I had to leave the offerings behind," Sara said. She pulled the treasure box from her pocket. "But I have Cormac's hair." She moved the mermaid's tail and opened the lid of the box. Her hands shook. "Jimmy, could you hold up the lantern?" She took the kerchief with the hair in it and handed it to May, who carefully unfolded it. She moved out of the light. Cormac's hair glowed in the dark.

"The enchantment is strong," May said.

The scissors in the box reflected the moonlight or lantern light.

"Are those scissors meaningful to you?" May asked.

"They are," she said. "My ma gave them to me."

"Take them and use them when it's time," May said.

Sara took out the scissors. Then she closed the lid to the box and put it back in her pocket.

"And now we need strands of your hair," May said. She plucked hair from Sara's head.

"Jimmy, go watch for us but leave the lantern here," May said.

Then he was gone.

The women sang softly as they gathered around May and Sara. Sara looked at the dark faces in the moonlight.

"They're calling to Yemaya," May said. "They're asking Yemaya to find the spirits or ancestors who created this spell."

May crouched to the sand. Sara did the same. She felt clearer now, not as giddy. May took the strands of Cormac's hair and the strands of Sara's hair and began weaving them together. She whispered as her fingers moved.

"Sara!" Sara heard the urgent whisper of Cormac's voice.

"He's coming," Sara said. "I hear him."

The song of the women grew louder. The moon got brighter. The light of the moon made a path across the lagoon to them. May stood and held the braided hair across the palms of both of her hands. The tiny braid glowed. May walked toward the water and the women parted and formed a half circle behind her and around the curves of the lagoon. Sara followed her. Beneath the water, she thought she saw moving spots of green light.

"Mother of the waters," May said. "We ask your help in assisting our sister Sara to break the spell that binds her to a man she does not love."

The light of the moon quivered on the water.

May turned to Sara. She held out the braid to her. Sara took it. It throbbed in her fingers.

"Go out into the water," May said, "and cut the cord that binds you. It is your enchantment from your people. You must break it. Say what needs to be said."

Sara wasn't sure what to say or do. She heard Cormac's voice again. It sounded closer and angrier. She had to hurry.

She walked into the moonlit water. The cool water circled her ankles. She kept walking until the water was up to her knees. Something brushed against her legs. It felt like a tail. She shivered. Then she held the braid in one hand and the scissors in another. The moonlight washed the glow of the braid away.

"By all the powers of three times three, this spell unbound shall be," Sara said. She took the scissors and cut the braid in half. She felt a sharp pain in her stomach, as though someone had pricked her lightly with a needle. The water in the lagoon rippled. "By all the powers of three times three, this spell unbound shall be. To cause no harm, nor return on me, for the good of all, oh blessed sea!" She cut the braid again. The water shook and tiny waves pushed against her, as though a boat was in the water and creating a wake. The women sang louder. Or was it a hum coming from the water itself? She said again, louder, faster, as she continued to cut the braid into tiny pieces, "By all the powers of three times three, this spell unbound shall be. To cause no harm, nor return on me, for the good of all, oh blessed sea! Auld ma and all my sea sisters, hear my plea!" Sara felt a wind all around her. The water splashed her. Cormac was screaming somewhere, near or far, calling her name. She felt pinpricks all over her body. Then something blotted out the moonlight as it rose up from the water or came down from the sky. It was blacker than night, except for the part that glowed blue and green and moved in the water like a fish.

Sara trembled. Her voice shook. But she kept cutting, kept chanting.

The ground beneath her feet shook. Nothing remained of the braid in her hand except tiny bits of hair.

"Take this, auld ma," Sara said. She put the scissors in her pocket and then dipped her hands in the water. She felt dizzy again, and she could barely stand. Or see. The glowing green lights beneath the water moved toward her as the bits of hair floated down. Did the lights take the hair?

Cormac was screaming. The moonlight returned.

May tugged on her arm.

"We have to go," she said. "Daniel is here. He'll take you now."

Sara walked out of the water. She wanted to glance back, to try and see what she hadn't been able to see a moment ago. But Daniel was there. Jimmy was beside her, too. "Someone is coming," Jimmy said.

Everything happened so quickly after that. Some say that a storm cloud passed over the moon so that darkness covered the island. Others say a storm came that night and tore up trees and destroyed houses. Sara didn't remember any of that. She knew she followed Daniel. He took her to a small boat and then they followed the shore for a long while until they came to a river. Daniel rowed up the river and then steered the boat into a kind of swamp. It smelled like mud. Tall reeds surrounded them. Daniel pushed her head down several times when they thought they heard someone coming.

Sara no longer heard Cormac calling to her.

When the night turned gray, Daniel took the boat out into the open water again, and he followed the shore for a time until they came to a bigger boat. He called out to the men aboard.

"This is Sara O'Broin, lads," Daniel Martin said. "I've already contacted Captain Dunnett. He'll take her out on the next ship. Sara, these boys will take you over to the next island. I've got some food and stuff in here for ya." He handed her a duffle bag. "Take care of yourself. If you see Murphy again, send him my regards."

"I thank you, Mr. Martin," she said. "You've saved my life."

"I hope so," he said. "Be careful. I don't know this Captain Dunnett well. He'll want you to work off the passage but make certain he's fair."

The men helped Sara climb up into the new boat. Then the men pulled up anchor and they headed out to sea. Sara watched Daniel Martin for a few minutes. She waved. When she couldn't see him any longer, she turned around. She looked out at the open water and smiled. She was almost free.

The boat docked at a busy sea village. It was noisy, with more people in one place than Sara had ever seen. The men kindly took her to the ship's purser who took her to Captain Dunnett. He sat outside an eating establishment, under a clear blue sky. He looked over her papers as he ate.

The purser told the captain that Daniel Martin had sent her.

"Yes, he told me you were coming. I understand you don't have money for passage. He said you're prepared to work."

"Aye," she said. "I worked on my last ship as a cook."

He looked up at her. "That's not happening on my ship," he said. "I meant that you're prepared to work once we get to our destination."

"Yes," Sara said.

"What can you do?"

"I can sew," she said. "And cook. I have some healing skills. I can shepherd, too, and weave. I can do most anything country people do."

"This is a city I'm taking you to," he said. "But your sewing skills could come in handy. What's your name?"

She started to say Sara O'Broin, but she saw he was about to write it down on one of the papers.

"O'Connor," she said. "Catherine O'Connor."

He wrote down the name. Then he pushed the paper toward her. "This says that you will work off the amount of your passage once we reach port," he said. "If you come up with that amount, then you can pay it off before your time is up. Sign at the bottom. You can put an 'x' right down there." He pointed to the bottom of the page.

Sara put her 'x'. None of the O'Broin women had learned to read. Her mother said reading changed people's minds and they couldn't think straight any more. "They can't hear the trees whispering to 'em," she said, "or the birds singing to 'em." Sara gave the quill back to the captain and wondered if the auld sea spoke to him.

"Good," he said. "I will get you a copy of this once we're on board. Have a good journey."

Sara smiled. "Thank you, captain. I'm sure I will."

She followed the purser away from the captain. She didn't know where she was going. She didn't know what would happen next. She didn't care. She only knew she was finally free of Cormac MacDougal.

TEN

The ship was nothing like The Temperance, Captain Beale's ship. Steerage was worse than anything Sara could have imagined. It smelled. The crew didn't empty the privy often enough. The drinking water was cloudy. People all around Sara were constantly sick. They were packed into the hold as though they were cargo.

On the Temperance, Sara had helped the sick and told stories to the children. Here, she could barely move. The moaning and screaming frightened her. The unidentifiable noises frightened her even more. She positioned herself so that her back was against something solid and she wrapped her quilt around her and kept her bag close to her.

As soon as they got out to sea, Sara began to feel ill. She was nauseated all of the time. And when she fell to sleep, she had nightmares. Usually Cormac was on top of her. Or he was chasing her.

After a while, she must have gotten used to what was happening or people got used to each other, and little groups formed. People slept together, ate together, and watched out for each other's things. A woman and her husband and three other women drew Sara into their circle. She didn't say much. She felt like all the words had left her. She had been so happy to be away from Cormac, and now that she was, she felt worse.

She had left a beautiful tropical island for this? She felt panicky. What if she lived the rest of her life here? What if this sea journey never ended? She tried to shake away these disturbing ideas. But they kept getting a hold of her. She closed her eyes sometimes and felt the cool water around her legs. Ian and her family and Murphy felt far away—almost as though they had never existed.

Sometimes she would see one of the men eying her and she'd pull the quilt closer around her and whisper the fath fith. She kept the scissors in her hand most of the time. She wasn't letting anyone near her. She said this to herself again and again, but she knew she wouldn't be able to fight them off if they decided to take her. Cormac had done it more than once.

She didn't like this world. She wanted to go home.

Sometimes she felt so alone and without connections that she missed Cormac. Or something. She couldn't explain it to herself. At least when he had been with her, none of the men had looked at her. No one had approached her.

When she had lived in her village with her mother and sisters, she had known how to handle almost anything. She had been a fighter. And yet Cormac had happened to her.

How could she then wish he was still with her?

She didn't. She didn't wish that.

She missed home and her people. And once upon a time, Cormac had been one of her people.

She didn't feel like herself. She felt weak and ill and so tired. She couldn't concentrate on anything. She ached for home.

The others on the ship began to think she was mute. Even her little group began to shun her. She wrapped her quilt around her and hoped it would be over soon.

And then they came into the harbor. Sara wasn't sure if it had taken a week or a year. Once she was up top again, she felt dizzy. The light was too bright, so she closed her eyes for a moment. The noise was incredible. The only sounds she recognized were the shouts of people all around her. When she could open her eyes more fully, she saw ship after ship on either side of them. She followed the others off the ship.

"Contracts over here," the purser shouted.

Sara wondered where she would find work. How could she work? She could barely walk.

"That means you, missy." The purser was motioning to her. She stepped over to the side.

This was good, she thought. She could stop for a minute. Get her bearings.

She stood with a group of people who looked haggard and sick. She looked down at herself and knew she looked the same. Was the same. She clutched her bag to her. Several well-dressed men stood off to the side, watching them.

"Stand so they can see ya," the purser said.

"This one has a five year contract," he said. He indicated a man standing next to Sara. She wondered who the purser was talking to. "He can do carpentry. He's run cattle and sheep. This one has a three year contract. She's an excellent seamstress and cook. She can also weave and take care of farm animals." He was pointing to her. The men just beyond them were now looking at her. What did he mean a three year contract? He was on to the woman next to her. But Sara didn't hear what he was saying.

"What does he mean a three year contract?" she asked the man next to her. It felt strange to speak again.

"That's the term of your service," he said, "to pay off your passage. That's your indenture."

"I have to work for the captain for three years?" Sara asked.

"Naw, he's selling us off," the man said. "We could go anywhere."

Sara's heart raced. She couldn't stay here. She had to run. She looked around. Where would she go?

The man next to her touched her arm lightly. "If you run," he whispered, "they'll put you in jail. It won't be so bad. You might get good people."

After a few minutes, the purser went over to the group of men. When he returned to them, Sara said, "I didn't sign up to be a slave. I want to speak with the captain."

"You signed this contract," he said. "You can pay it off any time you like. Right now even. Do you have the money?"

Sara stared at him.

"Then you're going with that man there," he said. "He's got your contract. You're lucky anyone took you. You have no skills to speak of."

The purser directed her to a young man standing apart from the group of men. A boy stood next to the young man.

"Are you Catherine O'Connor?" the man asked as she approached them.

Sara didn't know who he was talking to. Then she remembered she had changed her name.

"Yes," she said.

"Come with me," he said. "You will be pleased to know that Monsieur Fontenau has purchased your contract. You will be working in the household of Marie Broussard. She is a very kind mistress." He spoke English with a strange accent, and his skin was cinnamon-colored.

"Are you Irish?" he asked.

"I was," she said.

"Good, good," he said. He began walking. She followed him reluctantly. He seemed boyishly happy. "This is my buggy. Here."

He helped her up into a small carriage drawn by one horse. The boy hopped onto a seat on the back. The young man got in next to her. Then he slapped the reins against the back of the horse and the animal pulled them forward. Sara was glad to be leaving the noisy waterfront behind.

"Madame Broussard will be happy to have you," the man said. "She has so many dresses that need help! Is it your first time in our decadent city? Of course it is. We need to get you a bath. Forgive me for saying so but you have a peculiar odor. It's not an Irish thing because Polly is from Ireland and she smells like flowers, flowers, flowers. I haven't said who I am, have I?"

Sara breathed deeply. The air smelled sweet.

"I am Renaud Broussard Fontenau," he said. "That is Pierre behind you."

"I am pleased to meet you," she said. She glanced back at the boy.

"He is mother's little runner," Renaud said a little more quietly. "He can run faster than anyone, but he doesn't say very many words. He was a field slave for years. I think they were very cruel to him." He nodded. Sara didn't know what to say.

"I know I'm supposed to be formal with you because you're going to be our servant," he said. "But I'm not that sort. Don't tell Mameau. That's what we call maman. Almost everyone calls her that. It is a name we made up when we were children. Father wants to set me up with a good job. A career! I want to go to France and study. I would make a great diplomat, wouldn't I? When Mameau is not with me, you may address me as Rey. If she is there, please say Monsieur Rey or Mameau might be cross with both of us."

Sara looked over at him. He was dressed in fancy clothes.

He smelled like some kind of perfume. And he had the kindest smile.

"I'm sorry I'm not participating in this conversation," Sara finally said. "But it has been a long trip. I can't remember when last I ate or had clean water. I didn't know I was signing up to be a slave. I didn't have the passage to get on the ship but I had to get away from my husband who beat me."

"No, no! My dear Catherine. You are not a slave!" He waved his hands around and startled the horse, who seemed to be going his own way, without any help from Renaud.

"My name is Sara," she said. "I lied about my name so that my husband couldn't find me."

Renaud looked away from her at the horse. "Ami, go the short way. I must show Mameau what I've found!"

They were traveling down a tree-lined street now with colorful buildings pressed up against one another on either side of the road. The upper stories of each building had balconies fenced in by wrought iron filigree. A dark woman dressed in a bright white cotton dress stood on one balcony holding a cat. She watched them as they passed.

"You are not a slave," Renaud said. "I would know! My mother, she was a slave. But my father fell in love with her and set her free. We are all free."

"Your father owned your mother?" Sara asked.

"Don't all husbands own their wives?" Renaud asked. He laughed. "They met at a ball. They say it was love at first sight. They have a left-handed marriage. We don't see him often enough because he has to be with his other family too."

"He has two families?" Sara asked. "I cannot imagine that working out well."

"We are French! It is our way!" Renaud laughed. "That is what my father would say. He does not understand the Spanish or the Americans who treat their women like chattel. Wait until you see my mama. She is so beautiful! And my sisters. Madeleine and Thérèse. I am the ugly one of the family and you can see how beautiful I am."

Renaud stopped the buggy in front of a house that was set close to the road and close to the other houses. Renaud got out and then helped Sara out. Pierre jumped into the front of the buggy, took the reins, and clucked the horse forward.

Renaud opened the front door and stepped inside the house. He motioned Sara into the airy, cool house. Sara breathed deeply. She liked the house instantly. Maybe she would be all right here for a time.

Colorful paintings hung on the walls. Leafy plants tickled Sara's arms as she walked past them. Renaud took Sara to a room like the parlor in the White Inn, only this room was larger—or more open. Sara had never seen anything like it before. It opened up into other parts of the house.

"Mameau! Look what I have brought you!" Renaud walked up to a woman sitting on a burgundy-colored sofa. She looked like a queen on a throne. Her black hair was piled on the back of her head, laced with what looked like tiny pearls. From her ear lobes hung tiny rubies. Around her neck was what looked like emeralds. Her gown was shiny white covered in white lace. Her feet were bare. She was lighter-skinned than her son.

"This is Sara," he said. He took a piece of paper from his pocket and handed it to his mother. Then he kissed her cheek. "She is a seamstress! The man said she can do magic with a needle and thread."

The woman read the piece of paper and then looked up at Sara. When their eyes met, Sara felt a shock go through her body.

"Renaud, you foolish boy," the woman said. She had an accent similar to her son's, only her voice was deeper, and her words had more of a lilt. "Next time have them clean up before they come into the house. And you must take this one back. She is pregnant. She won't be of much use to me soon. I shouldn't have let you go out to that foul place. Your father is so good at picking servants."

"She has such nice eyes," he said. "I thought she needed a safe place to stay. And she doesn't look pregnant."

"Did you even ask her any questions?"

"No, I did not," he said.

"It wouldn't have mattered if he had asked," Sara said. "I would have lied. The baby probably won't last. My last one died before it was time."

"The last one?" The woman pursed her lips. Then she said. "You Irish, you are so . . . prolific."

Sara felt the blood rise to her face. The woman watched her. Then she stood and came over to her.

"Good," she said. "You still have some fire in you after all that has happened. You will have this baby." The woman placed her hand on Sara's nearly flat stomach. She sighed and shook her head.

She turned to her son and put her arm around his waist.

"You cannot bring home all the orphans and strays you find," she said, "but I am glad you have brought this one. She has the kiss of Yemaya on her. There is a reason she has come to this household. We won't tell Papa she is pregnant yet. Maybe he will never notice." The woman held her hand out to Sara. "I am Marie Broussard. Welcome to my home. Renaud is correct in saying I need help with my dresses. And Polly will set you to work on other things, too. For now, Renaud will take you to the back and you can clean up, eat something, and get some rest."

"Mameau!" They all turned at the sound of another woman's voice. A tall lithe young woman bounced into the room. She was dressed in trousers, shirt, and jacket. Her long black hair was straight and loose around her shoulders. She smiled.

She was the most beautiful person Sara had ever seen.

"This is Madeleine," Marie said, "my daughter."

"Oh, a pretty new thing," Madeleine said. She came up close to Sara. Sara felt shabby next to her.

"She's not your new playmate," Renaud said.

"She could be," Madeleine said.

"Maddy, leave the poor girl alone," Marie said. "She just stepped off the ship."

"Yes, I can smell that," Madeleine said. "But she'll clean up nice."

"My children came out of my womb all mixed up," Marie said. "Renaud thought he was she and Madeleine thought she was he."

"Not true!" Madeleine said. "I am all woman."

Sara glanced at Renaud. He shrugged. "She's right about me."

"Fortunately their father is a tolerant and loving man," Marie said.

Madeleine plopped down on the sofa. "And he's got Thérèse and his other children. His very white other children. Thérèse makes up for all of us. First she wanted to be a nun. Then she decided to come out and go to the balls and find herself a white man to care for her. She had many suitors. Papa has offered a dowry and trousseau."

"That is partly why you're here," Marie said. "Thérèse will need new clothes before she sets up her new household." She smiled. "We are all very excited."

Madeleine grinned. "Oh yes, we are all very excited." She rolled her eyes.

"Your papa will be here for dinner," Marie said. "Please dress accordingly."

"I will dress according to how I would like to dress," Madeleine said.

"Renaud," Marie said. "Can't you see this poor girl is about to drop. Shall I call Polly in or will you take her back?"

Sara looked at Renaud. He motioned for her to follow him. They left the parlor and walked into a courtyard. Sara looked up and saw a skylight.

Renaud followed her gaze. "I should have had Pierre open that today," he said. "It is such a beautiful day!"

The courtyard was filled with plants. Behind the plants, the walls were swimming with mermaids. Renaud walked quickly by the fountain in the middle of the courtyard. Sara stopped and looked at it. Water flowed through a pale blue fish that a pink mermaid with a green tail was holding. The mermaid was looking up and laughing.

"What is this?" Sara asked. "What are all of these?"

Renaud stopped and turned around. "They're mermaids," he said. "Didn't I mention that Mameau is one of *Les Sirènes?* The sirens. She is one of the beauties from the island. They say she and the others like her were created to seduce white men. I don't believe it. It's her gift. We all have gifts. Hers is beauty."

Renaud kept walking. Sara looked at the fountain mermaid again, and then she followed Renaud. She glanced back once and saw Marie Broussard watching her.

ELEVEN

When Sara looked back later at the first few days at her new home, she remembered very little. She met an older woman called Polly who took her to her tiny room and then helped her with a bath. She ate in the huge kitchen and then she slept. Mostly she slept. And slept.

Then one day she woke up. She put her hands on her belly and felt the slight rise of her baby. She sat up and looked around. She saw only walls. No windows. Her dress hung from a hook on the wall. Someone must have washed it. She got out of her tiny bed and went to the wash basin and splashed her face with warm water. She washed her hands, then wiped them on the cloth hanging on the basin stand. She put on her dress and slipped on her shoes.

She wanted to see the sky. She wanted to smell the air. She vaguely remembered where the back door was. She found it and stepped outside into an enclosed area. It was green enough, with trees at one end. And the privy was over there, too, she remembered. The sky was milky white. And the air was fragrant and noisy. She could hear the sounds of the city.

She went back inside and walked to the kitchen. Polly was sitting at the big wooden table at one end of the kitchen. Behind Polly someone had painted an outdoor scene on the entire wall. Two rows of huge old trees arched over a grass-covered path. Wildflowers seemed to move in the grass. Sara felt like she could walk right into the painting.

Polly looked up when Sara came in.

"There you are," she said. "How are ya?"

"I am well," Sara said. "Thank you for your kindness." She couldn't take her eyes off of the painting.

"Monsieur Renaud did that," she said. "Isn't it beautiful? Sometimes I think I can hear the wildlife in it running around and singing, baying, barking."

"I've been here quite a few days now, haven't I?" Sara said. "It's time I get to work then?"

"The mistress wants you to start sewing," she said. "She saw what you did with the quilt—"

"The quilt!" Sara said. She had forgotten. And her treasure box.

"It's all there," Polly said. "In your bag. You needn't worry about that. There ain't a thief among them. They're good people. Not like our people, but they're good."

Polly put a pastry on the empty plate in front of her. Then she speared pieces of fruit from a platter and added them. She pushed the plate across the table toward Sara.

"There," Polly said. "Eat that." She poured coffee into one of the empty cups on the table and handed it to her.

"Are you indentured to them, too?" Sara asked.

"I was when I first come here," she said. "Not to them. Another family. They were not kind to me. Later I married and had my babies. They're all grown up now and my husband's dead, and I needed work. There's only the three of them to look after, so it's not difficult. I do the cooking. That's it. They've got other people for other things. He's a very wealthy man. What about you now, luv?"

Sara shook her head. "It's a long and sad story," she said. "The last of it is that I needed to get away from the man who claimed to be my husband. I didn't have the money. I didn't realize I was signing a contract to give away my life for the next three years."

"It'll go by like that," she said. "And you'll be safe here. He'll never find you, if he should come looking for you. You're a fish wife then?"

"How'd you know?" Sara asked.

She shrugged. "You have the look."

"I'm not any more," Sara said. "I broke the enchantment."

"But the bairn," Polly said. "That will bind you."

Sara shook her head. "No, it's not his." Sara picked up the pastry and bit into it. It melted in her mouth.

"This is good," Sara said. "You talk to the spirits of the food?"

Polly smiled. "You're noticing. That's a fine thing. Here, can I get you some more?"

When Sara finished eating, Polly took her upstairs to Marie's sitting room where her daughter Thérèse, Renaud and Madame were drinking tea together. Renaud leaned against the wardrobe.

"Here she is!" Renaud said. "I told you, Mameau. Isn't she beautiful?"

"Yes, Renaud," Marie said. "But can she sew?" Marie smiled at Sara. Today Marie was dressed in blue with pearls around her neck and in her hair. She held a string of cowrie shells in her hands in a way Sara had seen other women hold a rosary. "This is my daughter Thérèse Fontenau. This is Sara." Marie looked at her. "What is your full name?"

"Sara O'Broin," she said. Sara glanced at the daughter. She looked like the twin of her sister and mother, only she was a little smaller, dressed in a shiny brown dress. Her hair was pulled away from her face.

Thérèse nodded at Sara.

"Mameau," she said. "Can't we hire Monsieur Le Côte? He makes the best dresses in the world! I'm sure this girl is very talented, but can she compete with Monsieur Le Côte? I don't think so."

"I promise you," Marie said, "your dresses will be the envy of every woman on Rampart Street and beyond. Let Sara measure you and then you can go out and play! Monsieur LeFevre will be here for dinner tonight along with Papa. You can tell Polly what you want her to serve. It will be good practice for your own household."

Thérèse stood impatiently while Sara measured her, and then she left the room. Renaud stretched out on the divan. Marie went to the wardrobe and opened it up. She pulled out several dresses and showed them to Sara.

"I'd like this design, but in a blue satin for Thérèse," Marie said. "And this one in taffeta. A creamy color." Marie kept talking and Sara tried to concentrate on what she was saying. She had never made a dress like any of these. Her mother had never made a dress like any of these.

"What is wrong, child?" Marie asked. "Do you need to take notes?"

Sara shook her head. "I can't write," she said.

"Renaud," Marie said. "You must teach her to read and write."

"I would like that," Sara said. "I don't want to sign away my life again. I had no idea what the contract said and I trusted the captain to tell me."

"What do you mean?" Marie asked. "What contract?"

"I couldn't pay passage," Sara said, "so I thought I would have to work for the captain for a few months to work off my debt. I didn't know I would be in servitude for three years. I'm grateful it was you who found me, Mr. Renaud and Mrs. Broussard, but three years of my life were promised to someone else. I just spent a few months chained to a man against my will and that was a version of a Christian hell I don't wish to repeat."

"We are a French household," Marie said. "Please call my son Monsieur Renaud or Monsieur Fontenau. You may call me Madame Marie. Monsieur Renaud will teach you to read. And you will find that this is a good place to work."

"I'm sure it is, ma'am," Sara said. "But servitude is servitude, isn't it? It's still not freedom. I went through a great deal to obtain my liberty. And then it was snatched away from me."

"We are all in servitude to something or someone," Marie said. "We have to make the best of what we are given."

Sara pressed her lips together. This wasn't the time to argue.

"And to be honest, Madame," Sara said, "I've never sewed anything fancy before. I'm good with a needle, it's true, but I wouldn't want to disappoint the young miss."

Marie laughed. "Thérèse is in a constant state of disappointment. I could retain the services of many great dressmakers in this city, but I want you to make her dresses because I saw the quilt."

"We all saw the quilt," Renaud said. "We didn't open the box though. We were all tempted, except Mameau. We loved the sweet mermaid that doubles as a latch. We didn't want to pry into your private life. Besides, we thought we might be cursed if we opened it without your permission."

"I don't understand," Sara said.

"Mameau can conjure many things," Renaud said. "People come for her protection and her gris-gris bags."

"Renaud," Marie said. "You must learn some decorum. You can't go around telling everyone our business."

"I don't tell everyone," Renaud said. "I am telling Mademoiselle Sara." He looked at Sara. "Sometimes the way people talk around here makes me insane. They talk in circles. Not you, Mameau. I wasn't talking about you."

Marie sighed. "When you sewed that quilt, Sara, you sang to it. I can hear your siren songs when I look at it. When I touch it. Whoever uses that quilt will be protected from great harm. I can feel it. I don't think it is the material you used because most of it was scrap. I think it was your words, your songs. My daughters and I are what some call *Les Sirènes*. Many envy us and try to do us harm. I want my daughter to have as much protection as possible as she goes out into the world."

"Of course I will do that for your daughter," Sara said. "You have been very kind to me and I appreciate it."

"Bon!" Marie said. "Now we will get to work."

Sara looked carefully at each of the dresses Marie wanted her to copy. Then she figured out how much material she would need for each. She went with Marie and Renaud to a dry goods store that had bolt after bolt of colorful cloth and dozens of spools of thread and ribbons and lace. Sara had never seen anything like this store. When she thought no one was looking, she reached out and touched the red satin and then the blue satin. She rubbed a piece of silk between her fingers.

"It feels like cream tastes, doesn't it?" Renaud came up next to her. "Like cream over strawberries. Mmmm. I must be hungry."

Sara nodded. She closed her eyes and let the cloth run between her fingers like water.

They stopped at another market before they went home. Sara wanted to go back to the house. The city was overwhelming to her. She could hear her heart beating in her ears. And all the noises. She kept jumping at every bang, pop, or shout. She had trouble looking at anything for more than a few seconds. Her eyes would slide away, as though they couldn't take anything in. She broke out into a sweat. She closed her eyes and hoped none of these strangers would touch her. She imagined herself running over the green hills of home and into the arms of her mother or the waves of the auld sea. She wanted something familiar. She wanted something from the before time.

"Sara?" She opened her eyes and saw Renaud looking down at her. "You look like a ghost. Are you all right?"

"I-I'm not used to all these people," Sara said.

"I'll take you out to the buggy," he said. "Mameau knows everyone and everyone wants to know her, so she may be here for a while."

Sara glanced over at Marie. She wore a simple white cotton dress and a bonnet that covered her hair, but she still looked like a queen—a queen who was bestowing favors on her eager subjects.

It was hardly any quieter outside, but Sara followed Renaud out to the buggy. The horse whinnied, and she went to his head. He nuzzled her and she leaned against him. She could feel his breath on her chest. Renaud watched her. He was uncharacteristically quiet.

"Don't worry," Sara said after she'd caught her breath and her heartbeat slowed to normal. "I won't let you down, Monsieur Renaud."

He looked forlorn and she wanted to reach out and comfort him, but she knew that gesture might get him into trouble.

"I know what it feels like to be a stranger in a strange world," he said. "It is very lonely."

"I never was afraid of nothing," Sara said. "You could ask anyone. I was the first one to try anything. And if a boy looked at me and I didn't like it, I punched him!"

Renaud laughed. "I can see that."

Sara shook her head and patted the horse's neck. "It wasn't that long ago, but it seems forever ago."

The horse nodded. Sara smiled and let his head go.

"His name is Ami," Renaud said. "It means 'friend' or 'deeply loved' in French. When I was a boy, I was in love with everything, including this horse. I wanted to name everything 'love.' I believed everything in the world could be fixed with love."

"And now?" Sara asked.

Renaud looked down at his feet and then up at the sky. A moment later, he looked at her and smiled his radiant smile.

"Of course," he said. "Love will solve everything!" He held his arms out and bowed before her. "I best go find mother, *soeur* Sara."

"*Soeur?*"

"Sister," he said. "The moment I saw you I felt as though you were a kindred spirit. A sister spirit!" He smiled. "I hope you don't mind."

Sara leaned against the horse. "Mind? No. I could use a brother. As long as you're a good brother. My two brothers weren't worth much on a rainy day."

Renaud frowned. "*Quoi?*"

"Anyone can be a good friend on a sunny day," she said. "It's those that keep you company on a rainy day that are worth their salt."

Renaud laughed. "I like that, Sister Sara. Now for Mameau!"

He left Sara with the horse. She looked at the animal.

"You want to run away with me then?" she asked.

The horse nodded. Sara laughed. "Be ready. I'll give you the signal when it's time."

Two of the menservants—Thomas and William—cleared out a room near the courtyard to make a sewing room for Sara. It had the most light of any room in the house, Marie said. Thomas and William put the bolts of cloth on specially made shelves. The bolts brightened the room like a colorful painting. The men built drawers for the spools of thread, other drawers for the lace, still others for the ribbon, each with their own container. When Sara opened each drawer, she could see all the spools of thread or ribbon or lace. They painted the walls a pale yellow, lighter than the fuzz of a newly hatched chick.

When the room was finished, Marie, Madeleine, and Renaud stood on the threshold as Sara looked around her new room. It smelled like fresh cut wood. She walked to the long table near the back of the room. In the middle of the table was a big red pincushion filled with needles. Sara's eyes widened. She had never seen so many needles. She remembered her mother hoarding her needles: They were expensive and difficult to get. Sara sat in the chair next to the table. On the other side of the room was a sofa and a low table.

"The sofa is for us," Madeleine said. "So we can come play with you."

"Do you need anything else?" Marie asked.

"No, I'm ready to get to work," Sara said. "Thank you."

"I think she needs something on the walls," Renaud said.

"Like in the kitchen," Sara said. "I love the painting in the kitchen. It's as though you can walk right into it."

"It's called *trompe l'œil*," Renaud said. "'Trick of the eye.'"

"Oh no!" Marie said. "Not more murals!" She clapped her hands in mock horror.

"Oh Mameau, let me!" Renaud said.

"You are a great artist," Marie said. "You shouldn't hide your talent in this house."

"This house is my talent!" Renaud said.

"Let him do as he pleases or we'll never hear the end of it," Madeleine said.

"Do as you will," Marie said. "It is only my house."

"What is it you would like me to paint?" Renaud asked Sara.

"I'll let you decide," Sara said. "But now, I need to get started."

"Yes, leave her be," Marie said. "We're planning a special dinner for tonight, Sara, so Polly might need your help tonight."

"Of course, Madame Marie," she said.

They left Sara alone. She stood in the middle of the room and breathed deeply. If she looked out the door of the room, she could see the mermaid fountain. She closed her eyes. She heard the birds singing outside. Was that the caw of a crow? She imagined them flying over the open skylight. She put her hand on her belly.

"This is our home for now," she said. "And I am grateful for it."

TWELVE

Sara sewed. She cut up fabric, and then she sat in her chair and sewed.

She sang, softly, to the thread and the cloth. She sang about Thérèse's happiness, good health, and prosperity. She sang about harm never coming her way. The needle and thread moved easily through the cloth.

She brought Marie's dresses down to the sewing room, so she could examine them when she wasn't certain what she was doing. She was glad for the extra cloth because she did make a mistake or two. She tossed the mistakes into a basket. She'd figure out something to do with them later.

Sometimes she dragged her chair out of the room and sat under the skylight. Whenever she was there, birds flew down to the fountain. They drank, splashed, and bathed themselves. But mostly they watched Sara and sang with her from time to time. Three big crows perched on the open skylight windows. Some say they had come all the way from Ireland to protect an O'Broin woman. Maybe they were ravens. Some didn't know a blackbird from a crow from a raven. But everyone knew magic when they felt it. Marie sat in her parlor or in her own conjuring room and felt the hum of the whole building and she was glad—even though she was worried for the girl Sara. She knew she had more trouble coming her way.

Madeleine and Renaud spent a lot of time in the room with Sara. Sara wasn't quite certain why they came, but come they did. Madeleine usually brought something to eat for them all. Renaud brought his paints. First he drew on the wall, but Sara could not tell from the faint lines what he was creating.

"Sad Sara," Madeleine said one day, "tell us your story."

Sara glanced up at her. Then she shrugged. "My story is no different from anyone else's."

"Let's see if that's true," Madeleine said. "My mother was bred like a cow to be some white man's own true love, so in a sense you could say I was bred the same. *Les Sirènes.* Only I had the good luck of being freed once I was born. I started out a slave, but I've shaken all that off." She dusted off her pant legs as though something was there. "I was supposed to follow in *ma mere's* footsteps, but I couldn't do it. Fortunately too many people are afraid of Mameau and Papa to do anything about Renaud and me."

"If that's your story," Sara said, "it isn't much of one. It's got no beginning. No middle. No end. No *fadó.*"

"What's *fadó*?" Renaud asked. He painted a streak of green across part of the wall.

"It's how we start our stories," she said, "so that you know something strange and fabulous is about to come. Otherwise it's only words, isn't it? It's like reciting your letters, like you've been having me do, Renaud."

"Are you criticizing my life?" Madeleine asked.

"Is that how you're takin' it?" Sara made a face. "I didn't really hear anything about your life."

"She's got you there, sister," Renaud said.

"Then tell us your story," Madeleine said, "so I can get an idea."

"I'll tell you some of it," she said, "although it pains me to say it. *Fadó*. My da stole my ma's red cap, and she let him. She had ten baby girls and she took every one of them out to the auld sea and the auld sea took every one of them. Then I was born with a tail the color of salmon and my ma took me down to the auld sea as she had the others. She put me in the water. This time the auld mother turned a daughter back to my ma.

"I spent my days on the rolling hills and in the mighty forests and along the auld sea. I knew the smell of the air when winter was coming or when spring was trying to break through. I learned all I could from the Winds, the faeries, the trees, and all the flowers and animals who would speak with me. And I learned tales from my uncle Ruarc. I learned to sew from my ma. I learned love from my two sisters, Aine and Fiona. I learned to hate from my da and brothers.

"I loved Ian McLaughlin without any learning. I loved him. That was it. We made love on the beach and in the caves. And I was going to have our baby. We told the druid we wanted to be handfasted on the next full moon. I said goodbye to Ian McLaughlin as he went out to sea. I learned a great storm was coming. My ma said we had to do what all O'Broin women had done before us: We had to save the village. She gave us our red caps that day after hiding them from us until then. She warned us to keep them close. We would have to marry any man who stole them from us. And as we were calling upon the auld sea, the wind snatched away my cap and put it into the hands of Cormac MacDougal. He took me and the red cap into the cave and he raped me. I went to the village and asked for help. Everyone said the enchantment was set and nothing could be done. I was Cormac's fish wife. I refused, but the spell worked its way on me and I almost died. Ian McLaughlin returned. I knew he would help me."

Sara stopped sewing. She looked at Renaud and Madeleine.

"He didn't help me," she said. "Later I found him making love to my sister. I called the waters and wind down on the village, and the weather spirits listened to my biding and sent a storm to destroy my village. It took my sister and Ian with it."

She suddenly felt exhausted.

"I can't tell any more," she said.

"There's more?" Madeleine asked.

"There's more," she said.

"Tell us something good," Renaud said. "Something that will cheer you."

Sara wiped her hand across her eyes.

"Not the part where Cormac raped me again," she said. "Or when he beat me. Or when I huddled in the stinkin' hold of a ship for weeks or years. There is one thing. I met a man named Termain Murphy. He is the father of my child. He told me about a place where I could go and be safe and live a life of beauty and happiness. He said it's in New Spain. It's in a place where they have cacti that are as tall as giants and they walk around the desert when no one's looking. And they have rabbits that are as big as giants, too. And there's a place in the desert where the mermaids sing. A place where he found shells in the desert and a mermaid wall. It's sunny all the time and not like anything I've ever seen."

"Where is Murphy now?" Madeleine asked.

"I don't know," she said. "I'd like to go to the mermaid springs and see if he's there. And even if he's not, I'd like to go. He said you can hide from everyone there."

"Like the Wayward Ranch," Renaud said. He spread more colors on the wall. "That's where I'd like to go."

"Not that place again," Madeleine said. "Please don't talk about it. It's not going to happen."

"I met this very nice gentleman some time ago," Renaud said. "He told me he had a place called the Wayward Ranch where I would be welcome."

"This man is an Englishman," Madeleine said. "You can't believe anything they say."

"He wanted me to paint the entire ranch," Renaud said. "I don't even know what a ranch is. But it sounded beautiful. Out in the desert."

"He is in love with this man," Madeleine said. "So you can't believe a word he says either."

"Papa says if the man sends part of the commission," Renaud said, "he will let me go. Maybe it's near your desert."

"It's not my desert," Sara said. "I've never been there."

"Wouldn't it be nice, though," Renaud said, "to have a place in this world where you were always welcomed and loved for who you are?"

"That's here," Sara said. "You are loved and welcomed here, aren't you?"

Renaud nodded. "Yes, I am. But we're not really free to do as we please. My papa can go anywhere and do anything."

"But you have this house," Sara said. "And you have each other. You seem prosperous and healthy. What more could you want?"

"There are all kinds of prisons, Sara," Madeleine said. "All sorts of ways we are kept in chains."

Sara nodded. Hadn't someone else said that to her not long ago? Yes, Ruby from the White Inn. Sara wondered what had happened to Ruby. She hoped she was free and happy.

Sara enjoyed the days with Renaud and Madeleine. Sometimes they brought over friends and they all gathered in the sewing room. Or they lounged in the courtyard while Sara sewed. She always sewed. And she sang softly. She watched Renaud and Madeleine with their friends. How easy and affectionate they were with them. She liked seeing the different shades of people. Where she came from, they were all the same shade: pale.

When she wasn't sewing, she helped Polly in the kitchen. Polly was easy company. She talked about home, or her children, and she never asked Sara any questions about her life.

Sara didn't like the nights. She didn't sleep well. When she did sleep, she dreamed too much. Sometimes she dreamed of Cormac who became Ian who became Murphy. Sometimes she spent the night walking from one part of the house to the other.

She finished first the blue dress and then the cinnamon-colored one. Marie encouraged her to design her own particular dress for Thérèse, so she did. She worked on it when she took a break from the other dresses.

One afternoon when Monsieur Fontenau came to the house he asked to see Thérèse's new dresses. Sara helped her on with the blue dress, and then Thérèse hurried out of the sewing room. Sara could hear Fontenau's booming voice coming from the parlor where Thérèse was showing off her new dress. The house always seemed even more lively when he was around. When Fontenau was at home, the family mostly spoke French together, so Sara didn't understand what they said to each other. She didn't mind. She liked listening to their voices; it was like listening to music.

A few minutes later, Thérèse returned to the sewing room, and Sara helped her out of the blue dress and into the cinnamon-colored one.

"Papa wants to see you," Thérèse said.

"Me?" Sara asked.

"Yes, you," Thérèse said. "He wants to meet the one who has created my beautiful dresses."

Sara followed Thérèse into the sitting room. The whole family was there. Madeleine sat cross-legged on one sofa with her brother. Marie and Monsieur Fontenau sat next to each other on another sofa. He was a tall man with dark hair and dark eyes. Sara had seen him in the house before. This was the first time she had been this close to him. His hair was graying around the temples. It appeared he was a bit older than Marie.

"There she is, my beautiful *petit-fille!*" he said to Thérèse. "*Magnifique!*"

Thérèse spun around in front of her father.

"This is as beautiful as the first," he said in English. His accent was thicker than Marie's or his children's. "And this is the woman who is responsible for these creations, *non?*" He looked at Sara.

"Madame Broussard is the woman responsible," Sara said. "I only followed her instructions."

Monsieur Fontenau laughed. He glanced at Marie.

"You should keep this one," he said.

Sara looked at Renaud and Madeleine. They both smiled.

"I hope you are comfortable in Madame Broussard's house," he said. He kept his gaze on her, as though he was trying to learn something about her by looking at her. He glanced at her belly.

"Everyone has been very kind," Sara said. "Thank you."

"She doesn't look like she is carrying a baby," Fontenau said.

"She isn't far along," Marie said.

"I look forward to seeing the rest of the dresses," he said, and he turned away from her.

Sara left the family and went back to the sewing room. A few minutes later, Thérèse returned with Madeleine. Sara took the dress off of Thérèse. Thérèse put on her frock and hurried out of the room. Madeleine crossed her arms.

"Don't mind my father," Madeleine said. "He talks frankly

about everyone's personal lives. The good thing is that you've passed the first test."

"What do you mean?" Sara asked.

"Papa looked you over," she said. "You can stay because he didn't bite."

Sara sat in her chair and pulled the dress she was working on to her lap. Sara shook her head. She had no idea what Madeleine was talking about.

Madeleine whispered, "Papa has a roving eye. But even he stays away from pregnant women." She smiled and shrugged. "But who knows what will happen once you have the baby. What belongs to Mameau belongs to Papa. Although Papa actually owns your contract; he could take you any time he wants. I better get back to our happy little family!"

Madeleine left. Sara leaned back in her chair. The baby was kicking up a storm.

"We don't need any more storms, darlin'," Sara said. She put her hand on her belly. She was sick to her stomach. She had thought Marie held her contract, and that fact had brought her some small comfort: Marie was a good woman who would keep her from harm.

Sara did not want to be owned by another man.

That night Sara couldn't sleep. She wandered around the house. She stood in the parlor for a few moments. She could hear Renaud snoring upstairs. He must have left his door open. It was one of the few nights he was actually home asleep. She breathed deeply. She did not feel comfortable in this room. It was not her room.

She left the parlor and walked toward her sewing room. Perhaps she could get some work done. She noticed light coming from Marie's private room. Renaud and Madeleine called it her conjure room. Sara had never been there. Mameau must have left a candle burning.

Sara heard whispers coming from the room. Maybe not whispers. It sounded more like wind blowing through trees. The light flickered beneath the door. The whispers grew louder.

Sara walked over to the door and opened it. Inside, light flickered from dozens of candles on the tables and countertops. Madame Marie stood at one end of the room. She glanced back at Sara.

"I'm sorry," Sara said. "I thought someone had left a candle burning."

"As you can see, many candles are burning," Marie said. "I asked Papa Legba to open the door to the spirits and then you came to me. It is a sign. Step in. You can help me."

Sara glanced around the room. She didn't see anyone who looked like a Papa Legba. The room was lined with shelves filled with various sized jars. Renaud had been teaching Sara to read English, and she was picking it up quickly, but she could not read these labels. On a small table were several colored candles, beads, rocks, and what looked like pieces of bone, and some salt and dirt. Sara went and stood beside Marie who was leaning over something on a long table at the end of the room.

"I cannot sleep sometimes, too," Marie said. "I am making what you would call a charm. We call it a gris-gris. A conjure bag."

Sara recognized some of the material on the table, now cut into circles.

"Those are for Thérèse," Marie said. "Extra protection. I will put inside each a feather of inspiration, a piece of a used candle for her passion, a stone for protection from the earth, and a shell for the blessings of Mami-Wata. And my incantations. I will make her a love gris-gris too, so that her man never leaves her. Tonight I am making one for a white woman. Her husband is not faithful to her. She has paid me a great deal of money." Marie shrugged. "I cannot subvert the man's will. He will do what he will do. But I can make her seem more alluring. If I could control men, I would control my own man, no? Sew those two circles together so that when I turn them inside out they will make a little pouch."

Sara picked up the already threaded needle and the two pieces of cloth. On the cloth, Marie had written symbols Sara didn't recognize. She stood next to Marie and began sewing. She whispered, "May you know love, may you know love, may you know love as the dove knows the air. May you know love as the trees know the earth. May you know love as the sun knows heat. May you know love as the fishes know water. May you know love."

"You have a way with the invisibles," Marie said. "They listen to you. They are all around you, waiting for your songs. For your creations. They love beauty."

"I'm not sure I see beauty any more," Sara said. "And I don't hear the invisibles. I don't hear the faeries. I don't hear anything except the roar in my ears and the heartbreak of my soul. And that is a sad sound."

Sara bit her lips. She shouldn't have said that. It sounded too much like she was feeling sorry for herself. She knew she was surrounded by the beauty of this house, but she didn't really see it. She knew the city was probably beautiful, but she could hardly bear to be out in it. She broke out in a sweat every time she had to go away from the house. Everyone had noticed it, she knew, but no one said a word. They had stopped asking her to run any errands. "Pierre is better at it anyway," Renaud told her. "He knows where everything is."

When Sara finished sewing the pouch, she handed it to Marie. Marie had several piles of what looked like spices or herbs in front of her. Marie began putting a little of each into the pouch. She spoke French as she dropped each ingredient into the bag. Sara heard the whispers again and she looked around the room. She saw no one but Marie. The air moved around her. Marie spit on the pouch, lightly. Still whispering, she ran it through a candle flame. Then she dipped her hand in a dish of water and flicked it at the pouch. She sprinkled dirt over it.

"Finis!" she said. "Madame Delvaux will be very joyful!"

"You said you couldn't subvert the man's will," Sara said. "You could. I know that my will was subverted by the enchantment that befell me."

"Is that what happened to you?" Marie asked. "I suspected as much."

"I've broken the enchantment," Sara said. "As far as I can tell."

"But it follows you around still," Marie said. "Like a ghost that can't find its way home. Yes, my young Sara, I could bend the man's will to this woman. But that kind of magic can return on a person if they're not careful. And who am I to decide what is good for another person—unless those persons are my children, of course." She laughed. "I've seen too many people call upon the loas for no good. I won't do that. I have been tempted many times. It is not easy for my family in this place. Visible and invisible harm is always being directed at them. I try to protect them."

"Who wants to hurt them?" Sara asked.

"Many jealous white people," Marie said. "But mostly Monsieur's white wife. She is jealous of us."

"It must be difficult for her, though," Sara said. "For him to have . . . another family."

Marie looked at her. "Difficult for her?" She shook her head.

"I'm sorry," Sara said. She didn't know what was wrong with her tonight. She kept saying things she shouldn't be saying. "I don't know what I'm talking about."

"It is difficult," Marie said, "but it is most difficult for us. I have been with Monsieur Fontenau since I was fifteen years old. Madeleine and Renaud were already born when he married . . . her. She has given birth to three daughters and she is pregnant again.

She wants a son, so she is jealous of Renaud. She sends people to spy on Renaud. I am afraid she will send someone to harm him one day." Marie shrugged. "Monsieur Fontenau has done what he can. My children will inherit. And he will take care of me all of my life. But I have my own money now. He could leave me and I could continue as I am. I would miss him, of course. I have loved him many years." Marie sighed. "These are things best left unsaid. The spirits must have wanted us to meet tonight and tell each other secrets. I knew as soon as Renaud brought you home that you would be a blessing for this household."

"What made you think that?"

"I had a dream that *La Sirène* was coming," Marie said. "And then there you were! *La Sirène* comes to us in our dreams. It is how she makes herself known to us."

"Lately I only have nightmares," Sara said. "If *La Sirène* or anyone else is trying to communicate with me, I'm not under-standing."

Marie nodded. "You're tired. You've had a difficult time of it."

"Madame Broussard," Sara said, "I found out something that has disturbed me. I thought you owned my contract, but I found out your husband does. I would feel much better if it was yours. I just come out of a situation where I was beholden to a man and he was cruel to me. I know Monsieur Fontenau isn't that way, but I would feel safer if it was you."

Marie nodded. "I understand. And Monsieur Fontenau is a good man, but he is a man. This may be something I can do. But now it is time for me to finish these gris-gris. You should go to sleep."

"I'm not sleepy," Sara said. "I can keep helping, if you like."

THIRTEEN

On the Sunday before Thérèse left Marie's, Madeleine came into the kitchen where Polly and Sara sat drinking tea.

"Renaud and I are taking Thérèse out since it's her last Sunday with us," Madeleine said. "And we need a chaperone. We thought you might come with us." She was looking at Sara.

Polly laughed. "When have you ever needed a chaperone?" she asked. "No, wait. I said that wrong. When have you ever taken a chaperone with you anywhere?"

"I'm changing my ways," Madeleine said. She grinned.

"You're going out to the square," Polly said, "and you know your ma doesn't like you out there."

"Sara has never seen it," Madeleine said. "It might help lift your spirits."

"I have no spirits that need lifting," Sara said. "What is this square you're talking about?"

"I didn't think white people could go," Polly said. "She might not be safe."

"They'd just think she was one of the black Irish," Madeleine said. "Besides, it's dark out. No one will know."

Sara shook her head. "I'm staying right here."

"Please," Madeleine said. "It would mean a great deal to Thérèse."

Sara rolled her eyes. "That girl wouldn't recognize me if I was standing right in front of her. She doesn't care about me."

"I care about you," Madeleine said. "You can't spend the rest of your life afraid of people."

Sara looked up at her. "I'm not afraid of no one."

Madeleine put her hands on her hips. "You're lying to me now or you're lying to yourself." She tried to imitate Sara's accent.

Sara laughed.

"Renaud is coming," Madeleine said. "We will protect you. It's gonna be a fine night."

"Please stop trying to talk like me," Sara said. "It's hurting my ears."

"You sound like an old woman," Madeleine said, "and we're the same age."

"Go with her," Polly said. "It might do ya some good. Don't let any of the soulless get you."

"The soulless?" Sara said. "And what is that?"

"The living dead," Madeleine said. "Polly! You don't believe that superstitious nonsense, do you?"

Polly shrugged. "I've lived in this city a long while. I believe in almost anything."

Madeleine and Thérèse put on white dresses and white kerchiefs. Madeleine brought a white dress to Sara's room.

"I found it at the market," Madeleine said. "It'll fit. Here's a kerchief to go with it." Sara took off her dress and slipped on the muslin dress. Then Madeleine put a necklace of cowrie shells around her neck.

"Just like mine!" Madeleine said. "Now we're twins."

"Yes, no one will be able to tell us apart now," Sara said. She laughed.

Waiting for them in the sitting room was Renaud, dressed in black.

"Where did you tell Mameau we were going?" Madeleine asked.

"I said we were going to the Place Publique," Renaud. "Where else? I won't lie to Mameau."

Madeleine looked at him.

He shrugged. "I said we were going for a walk. Which is true."

"Why doesn't Mameau want you to go wherever we're going?" Sara asked.

"Because it is where the slaves go," Thérèse said. "And we are not slaves." Thérèse always enunciated every word she said when she spoke to Sara, as though Sara was the stupidest person in the world.

Madeleine looked at Sara and smiled, as though to say, "Forgive her. It's only Thérèse."

They went outside. The day was sinking into night. Renaud and Madeleine walked on either side of Sara, and Thérèse walked ahead of them all. Sara felt strangely protected by the three children of Madame Marie.

She felt the music before she heard it as vibrations coming up from the ground. And then she heard it: the sound of drums. Only they sounded different from any drums Sara had heard before. She could feel the music in her chest. Renaud and Madeleine hurried across the road. Thérèse held back a bit. And then Sara saw a mass of people, many of them dressed in white, dancing to the beat of the drums and other instruments Sara didn't recognize.

Sara stopped. Thérèse looked back at her.

"Are you coming?"

Sara shook her head. Thérèse hesitated, and then she kept walking. Sara looked behind her. She wasn't certain she knew how to get back to the house. Before her were hundreds of people, maybe even thousands. She heard her heart in her ears.

Madeleine came running back to her.

"I thought you were right behind me," she said. "Come on." She took Sara's hand. Madeleine had never touched her before. None of them had. Hardly anyone had touched her since she and Murphy had made love the night Cormac raped her.

"It's all right," Madeleine said. "You're safe here. I promise. We'll stay on the edge of the crowd here and dance. Or we can go shopping. Over there—" She pointed. "—they're selling jewelry. Some gris-gris bags, no doubt. Candles. Other things."

Sara let Madeleine lead her into the edge of the crowd. Sara felt the beat of the drums through her feet. Madeleine let go of her hand and began dancing. Renaud and Thérèse stood nearby. Sara closed her eyes. She remembered dancing on the hills near her home, around a fire, to the beat of the drums. She swayed to the music. She could smell the earth of home, could feel the sea spray on her cheeks. The memory of it made her knees wobble. She almost dropped to the ground and wept. She kept dancing, dancing. Swaying. Calling out as the others around her called out.

And then she heard someone wailing. Howling. Like one of the wolves at home. She felt water on her cheeks. She licked her lips. "Laugh or cry, we swim in your tears," she heard.

Sara opened her eyes. A sea of people danced around her. And two white girls danced close to her. They held hands and danced and sang. They looked into each other's eyes and sang. Then they looked at her and waved. "Hello, mama!" They smiled, turned, and ran into the crowd.

Sara put her hand on her belly. So that was why she was a bit bigger than she had been last time. She was having twins.

She leaned her head back and laughed.

Sara sang all the way back to the house. Renaud and Madeleine tried to sing with her. Thérèse shook her head and said, "She's gone a little crazy."

"No," Madeleine said. "She's being herself. Free!"

"I am hardly free," Sara said. "I've got this debt and I've got two little babies to birth."

"Two?" Renaud said. "So you figured it out."

"What do you mean?" Sara asked.

"Mameau said you would have twins," Renaud said. "She knows these things."

"Mameau knows everything," Thérèse said. "She knows that I will be happy forever!"

Madeleine put her arm through Thérèse's. "There's still time to run away. If Renaud gets this commission we can all travel together to this place called Wayward. We'll make our own new life together."

Thérèse snorted. "I can see you and Renaud digging in the dirt like field slaves," she said. "That's all that's out there. Dirt and poverty. You would not last a week."

"I will be painting," Renaud said. "Not digging in the dirt as you say."

"You should find yourself a gentlemen, Maddy," Thérèse said, "and you should find yourself a woman, Rey. But since I know neither of you will do this, I tell you I love you just the same. And I can hardly bear to wait to begin my new life." She twirled. "I will be the happiest of us all. You will see."

Thérèse opened the door to the house and went inside. Sara started to follow.

"We'll be back later," Madeleine said.

Thérèse stopped and looked back at them. "Where are you going at this hour?"

Renaud did a little dance. "To find some happiness." He grinned. "Good night, fair princesses!" Renaud began running down the street.

Sara suddenly felt sick to her stomach. She put her hand out to steady herself. Madeleine ran up to her.

"Are you unwell?" she asked.

"I don't know," Sara said. "I-I think you and Renaud should stay home tonight." As she said it, her stomach began to settle.

"Renaud!" Madeleine called.

"I will meet you," he shouted.

"No! Come back!" Madeleine shouted. "He didn't hear me. I'll go get him and bring him home."

"Stay here," Sara said.

"Have you had some kind of premonition?" Madeleine asked.

"What is all this noise?" Mameau came to the door. Sara stood up straight. The nausea was gone.

"Sara thought Renaud and I should stay home," Madeleine said.

"As you should," Mameau said. "Your sister is leaving to-morrow."

"I think she had a vision or something," Madeleine said.

Sara shook her head. "No. I heard a whisper and got sick to my stomach and I felt very worried about Madeleine and Renaud."

Marie looked out into the night.

"I can go get him," Madeleine said. "I know where he's go-ing."

"You shall do no such thing," she said. "Come. All of you. I will send Pierre after him."

They all stepped inside the house. The mother and two daughters went upstairs to finish Thérèse's packing. Sara went into the sewing room and put the last touches on the red dress. She wished she hadn't said anything—wished she hadn't told Madeleine she thought something was going to happen. She never had premonitions. She had just gotten nauseated. That was it. She was pregnant, after all.

When Sara was finished with the dress, she took it upstairs to Thérèse's room. She laid the dress across the sofa. The women gasped. It was red with shell-shaped bits of lace stitched over the bottom half of the dress.

Sara helped Thérèse put the dress on. It fit her snugly and then flowed out a bit below her hips, where the lace started.

"Oh, you are beautiful!" Marie said.

"You look like *La Sirène,*" Madeleine said.

"I wish you would quit calling us that," Thérèse said. "It is a derogatory term."

Marie smoothed the dress at Thérèse's shoulders. "No, I do not see it that way. I think the name speaks of our connection to the great spirits of the waters of our homeland. We are the daughters of Mami-Wata, of Yemaya."

"I live here," Thérèse said. "Not in the water. Not on the islands. Not on the dark continent." She looked at herself in the mirror. "It is very beautiful, Sara. I will save this for a special occasion."

Sara left the family and went to her room and tried to sleep. Every time she heard a noise, she sat up and listened to see if it was Renaud. She could hear Madeleine and Marie talking in the parlor, their French words floating through the house like dust motes in sunlight.

She must have fallen asleep because she awakened to screaming. She sat up. She heard nothing but silence. Maybe she had dreamed it. She got out of bed and hurried out of her room. She ran across the courtyard and into the parlor. Thomas and William were carrying Renaud up the stairs. Marie was talking to Pierre.

"*Vite! Vite!*" she said.

Pierre ran out of the house. Marie saw Sara. "It is awful! Renaud has been beaten within an inch of his life. Pierre has gone for the doctor. I can help him some. And you? I don't know if he will live, *ma chère!*" She hurried away from Sara.

Sara ran back to her room and got her treasure box. She didn't have time to stop and make healing soup. Maybe something in the box could help. She carried the box up the stairs and went into Renaud's room.

He lay across his bed. His two sisters and mother leaned over him. His face was swollen and distorted. One eye had swelled shut. His lips were broken and bleeding.

Marie and Madeleine carefully took off his clothes. Renaud moaned and sobbed.

"He's conscious," Sara said. "That's good."

Marie nodded. Polly came into the room with a basin of water and a cloth which she put on the stand near the bed. Then she washed his face. Marie gently pressed his stomach and then put her hands on his kidneys. She lightly pressed on his ribs. He didn't cry out.

"I don't think anything is broken," she said. "The doctor is coming, Renaud. Have no fear. We will take care of you."

Sara opened the treasure box. She heard a "whoosh," as though wind had suddenly blown into the room. No one else seemed to notice it. Murphy's shell was on top. She brushed it aside and picked up the jars. She got a glass of water from the nightstand and dropped a few grains of the dirt and a few crystals of salt into it. "Upon my will," Sara whispered, "this brew shall heal. I call on the fey to fix my friend Rey on this very day."

"I put a little something in it from home," Sara said.

Marie nodded. "Renaud, you need to sit up a bit and drink this potion Sara has spirited for you," she said. Renaud moaned.

Thérèse was crying. Madeleine and Marie helped him up. Sara held the glass to his lips and he drank some.

"Mameau," he whispered. "They wanted to kill me. Why, Mameau?"

"Do you know us?" Mameau asked.

Renaud opened one eye. "Thérèse, Polly, Maddie, Mameau, Sister Sara. *Oui,* I know you all."

Marie left the room. Sara crouched next to Renaud and put one hand on Renaud's head and the other on his arm. She closed her eyes. She could smell the sea. She could feel the rocking of the ocean waves as she swam with her sea sisters. "Pain and injury," she said, "come out of the marrow and into the bones and out of the bones and into the blood and out of the blood and into the flesh and out of the flesh and into the skin and out of the skin and into Renaud's hair and out of his hair and into the deep blue sea as sure as the tide comes in every day and goes out again." Sara's fingers throbbed; they felt as though they were stuck to Renaud. She repeated the chant twice more. She swam deeper into the auld sea. Up ahead of her, she could see her daughter swimming with the auld ma.

"Sara." Someone was shaking her. She opened her eyes. It was Madeleine. Sara looked at Renaud. He was sleeping. Marie was putting salve on his face.

"The swelling has gone down already," Marie said. "And he's fallen to sleep. *Merci,* Sara. Madeleine, take her to bed. She looks exhausted."

Sara squeezed Renaud's hand as she stood. She picked up her treasure box and went with Madeleine. She didn't feel tired. She felt more energized than she had in weeks.

"What was that?" Madeleine asked.

"What do you mean?" Sara asked. "It was a healing chant. I don't know where I remembered it from. It just came to me."

"The whole room vibrated," Madeleine said. "The candles

flickered and pieces of flame broke off and flew around the room. Mameau said the spirits were everywhere, especially in you. You had your hands on Renaud for a long time."

"No," Sara said. "It was only a minute or two."

They passed Polly and a strange man coming up the stairs.

"That's the doctor," Madeleine said.

"Go on back to Renaud," Sara said. "I'm fine on me own."

Madeleine nodded. Then she left Sara alone.

Sara went to her room and lay down on her bed with the treasure box next to her. After a minute or two, she opened the box. It was too dark to see inside it, but she could feel the scratchiness of the yarn, the cool steel of the scissors, the softness of the cloth covering the tiny jars. It all reminded her of home.

She picked up the tiny sea shell Murphy had given her. She hoped wherever he was he was safe and happy. She imagined him sitting near a sandy beach with a drink in one hand and a woman on his lap with his other hand on her waist. She smiled. She put the shell back and picked up the shell her mother had given her. She held it up to her ear. She could hear the auld sea. It was calling to her. Singing to her. She began to cry, and the children in her womb began rocking gently. After a while, all three of them fell to sleep and dreamed.

FOURTEEN

The next day, Thérèse was supposed to leave for her new home and her new life. They had planned a big family breakfast. When Sara awakened, she heard people up and about already. She got dressed and went to the kitchen where Polly was preparing a meal.

"Madame Broussard wants pastries and coffee for breakfast," Polly said. "Monsieur Fontenau is here, as planned, but they've been arguing since dawn."

"How is Renaud?" Sara asked. "May I go up and see him?"

"Yes, of course," Polly said. "You did a good thing last night. Renaud is a good boy."

Sara went upstairs to Renaud's room. She knocked on the closed door.

"If you have something beautiful to say you may enter."

Sara smiled, glad to hear Renaud's voice. She went into the room. He was sitting up in bed in his maroon-colored pajamas. Both eyes were open now.

"Sister Sara!" he said. "Come sit with me."

Sara closed the door and sat in the chair next to the bed.

"You look better than you did last night," she said.

"I have you to thank, I hear," he said. "I dreamed I was swimming in the ocean. At first I thought I was drowning, but then I saw you. Only you were *La Sirène* and you were taking me to the promised land. Or the promised sea. A little girl was swimming with us."

Sara smiled. "I'm glad you weren't hurt worse," she said. "What happened?"

"I was out with others like me," Renaud said. "Two of us were outside. It was hot inside and too smoky. I wanted to breathe some fresh air. And we started kissing. These two men jumped us. They let my friend go, but they kept beating me. I thought I was dead. But Pierre came with some other men and they pulled them off me. That's all I remember until I got here."

"Why would those men beat you?"

Renaud shrugged. "For many reasons. I am not always as discreet as I should be. Mameau has warned me for years. As more Americans come here, it has gotten worse. Maybe it was because I was with a man. Maybe it was because the man was white. No one but people like us ever goes to that place. It is our place. Mameau thinks Papa's wife sent men after me. She thinks Madame Fontenau wants to hurt me."

Madeleine came into the room, grinning. She plopped down on the bed.

"You'll never guess what," she said. "They had most of Thérèse's things loaded into the wagons. The carriage is almost ready to take her. She is so pretty in the brown dress you made her, Sara. And then someone comes to the door. We thought it was one of Monsieur LeFevre's men here to escort Thérèse to her new house. But it was some strange young white man."

166

Sara and Renaud looked at her. She lay back on the bed and laughed.

"Please, I am an injured man," Renaud said. "Tell us what has happened."

"Renaud, it was your young white man," Madeleine said. "He came to see if you were all right. Papa looked like he was going to have a stroke. You didn't tell me he was rich, Renaud. He told Papa that he was willing to set you up in a house, like Thérèse, and take care of you." Renaud gasped. "Mameau had to keep Papa from striking him. He finally left."

"He loves me!" Renaud said. "He truly loves me." He leaned back against the pillow. "It was almost worth it to have him come here. It is so romantic!"

"How is you both almost getting killed romantic?" Sara asked. "You have to be careful, Renaud. I don't know this city or your world, but you almost died last night."

"There are worse things than dying," Renaud said. "You of all people should understand that. You have been loved before and you know you would have done anything to protect that love, to have it go on and on."

Sara rubbed her forehead. "Yes, I would have done anything. I tried to do everything I could. But it was all taken away from me. Maybe if I'd been more aware of the people around me, maybe I could have done something to stop it." She got up. "I'm sorry, Renaud. I didn't mean to be cross. I'm glad you're all right."

"Don't go, Sara," Renaud said. "I am not angry with you. I know that you understand."

"I do," she said. She thought of the night she had run away from Cormac and stayed with Murphy. She was fortunate they hadn't been caught. Both of them could have been killed.

"Of course I understand." Tears filled Sara's eyes. She leaned over and kissed Renaud's forehead lightly. "I hope you both find all the love you deserve."

Sara left the room. She heard Madeleine talking to her brother in French. She suddenly ached for home. She wanted to return to her old life more than anything in this world. When would she stop feeling this ache? When would the grief go away? She sighed. She put one foot in front of the other and went down the stairs.

The servants all lined up to say good-bye to Thérèse. She looked beautiful in her cinnamon-colored dress and her black velvet bonnet. Her hands were together inside a brown muff. Madeleine and Marie cried. Monsieur LeFevre smiled kindly.

Monsieur Fontenau said, "You'll see her tomorrow. All this crying for nothing! Adieu, adieu! We're leaving."

Monsieur LeFevre stepped out of the house first. The footmen opened the carriage door and LeFevre helped Thérèse inside. Then he got in. Monsieur Fontenau got on his horse.

Then Thérèse was gone. Marie shut the front door.

"Now if I can only get the rest of you settled and safe," she said.

"I'm going up to see Renaud," Madeleine said. She ran up the stairs.

"I told you she wanted to harm my children," Mameau said to Sara, "and now she has. I will not let this pass." Her hands were trembling. "If you had not been here, I don't know what would have happened. I don't know that I could have saved him. The doctor said it was fortunate his skull wasn't fractured. They kicked him! If Pierre hadn't come." She shook her head. "And we only sent him after Renaud because of you. You saved his life, Sara. *La Sirène* did send you to us. I cannot thank you enough."

"You are welcome, Madam," Sara said.

Sara went to the kitchen to help Polly. The look she had seen in Mameau's eyes troubled her. She wanted revenge—just as Sara had wanted vengeance against Ian and Aine.

By nightfall, Renaud was up and about. Marie forbade him

168

to leave the premises. He and Madeleine sat up in his room and played cards. Monsieur Fontenau returned to the house and he and Marie argued. He was still shouting when he left the house.

A few minutes later, Sara heard the familiar swish of Marie's satin skirts as she went past the sewing room and into her conjure room. Sara breathed deeply. She poked the needle through the cloth in her lap and pulled it through to the other side. She listened. Poked the needle through the cloth again. The house quavered. Or the air did. It reminded Sara of a tiny pebble dropped into the middle of a huge pond. The ripples were barely discernible unless you paid close enough attention. The air felt warmer, too.

Sara knew what was happening. Marie was calling on the spirits to wreak her vengeance. Sara put her sewing down and got out of the chair. She hesitated and then she went toward the conjure room. A sweet scent wafted out under the closed door. Sara heard whispers.

"Good neighbors," she said softly, "if you could protect me here, I wouldn't mind it. In fact, I'd appreciate it."

She knocked on the door. The air felt heavy and too fragrant, like when incense was burning in a church. Sara had never liked incense. Or churches.

Marie didn't answer. Sara opened the door anyway.

She saw a room transformed. The shelves, tables, jars, and altar were there, but the walls had dissolved and a sea roared all around. In this sea were forests and animals and the spirits of all of those who had come and gone and those that were gone all listened to Marie's powerful voice that they knew so well. And at that moment, she was about to call upon them that could to strike down Madame Fontenau.

But Sara walked into the room and the candles wavered and the walls returned or became visible again. Or maybe they had never been gone in the first place.

Marie turned around. Tears streamed down her cheeks.

"You can't do this, madame," Sara said.

"I will do it," she said.

"You don't know that she caused you harm," Sara said. "Not for certain. You don't know."

"I know in my heart," Marie said.

"Our hearts can be wrong," Sara said, "especially when we're hurt. I was in love and pregnant and then a man stole my soul and wouldn't give it back. And I had to live with him. I had to be his wife. One night I found my lover, the father of my child, having sex with my sister. I saw that. That image lives in my memory as though it happened today. I was so angry at them and at him for deserting me that I called upon the powers of the auld sea. I called upon all the powers that be to avenge me. And a storm came. It destroyed my whole village—and it killed my lover and my sister. Nothing could be worse than that. I'd rather have them alive and with each other than dead at the bottom of the sea. The people of my village were innocent. Some of them died. I beg you not to do this."

A breeze blew through the enclosed room and all the candles went out. Marie and Sara stood in the darkness together. Sara listened to Marie's breathing. It was quick and ragged at first, but then it began to slow.

A few minutes later, the candle on the altar sputtered and came alive again.

"All is well," Marie said. "I have come to my senses. The spirits will forgive me for calling them out. I will make amends. Stay with me, Sara, if you will."

Sara stayed beside Marie that evening. They dressed candles together. That was what Marie called it when they anointed the candles with her special oils. She drew symbols and wrote words on them.

"This is for good health," Marie said. "And this one is for prosperity. This one is for invisibility. This one is for happiness."

They filled gris-gris bags together. Finally Marie said, "I am exhausted." She took the ring of keys off her belt and handed them to Sara. "Lock the door. I may change my mind before morning."

The following day, Madeleine and Marie went to visit Thérèse. While they were gone, the young white man visited the house again. Renaud sat with him in the parlor. After the man left, Renaud went into the sewing room to work on the painting.

"George—that's his name—George found out who beat me up," Renaud said. "It was his old paramour. Apparently he didn't like him being with a man with my skin color." Renaud shook his head. "People, they can be so *stupide!*" He dipped his paintbrush in water. "At least Mameau won't have to curse Madame Fontenau. That would not have made for a happy life!"

A few days later, Renaud found Sara in the kitchen. He led her to the entrance of the sewing room and told her to close her eyes. Then he brought her into the room. "Now you can see," Renaud said. "I stayed up all night to finish it."

Sara opened her eyes and could hardly believe what she saw. Tears burned her eyes. He had painted the hills of Ireland. They sloped down to the sea, just as they did at home. He had even painted a tiny village between the hills. The sea filled up most of the wall. Mermaids, mermen, and all sorts of sea creatures swam in the great auld sea.

"It's the nicest thing anyone has ever done for me," Sara said. "Thank you."

Renaud shrugged. "Not any nicer than you saving my life."

Days passed in Madame Broussard's household. Madeleine and Renaud stayed with Sara in the sewing room for part of the days. Sometimes they all sat in the courtyard together. Renaud didn't want to leave the house.

"Now I have two of you who are afraid to leave the house,"

Madeleine said as they sat in the courtyard one afternoon. "How will I ever get out of here?"

"I'm not afraid," Sara said. She was repairing a pair of Renaud's breeches. "It's just safer here."

"Safe? Hah! What a word. Safe is like being dead."

"No, trust me," Sara said. "Dead is dead. When I dropped my baby into the great auld sea, she was dead. And it wasn't because she was too safe."

Madeleine and Renaud looked at one another.

"We don't know quite how to respond when you say something like that," Renaud said.

"Say that I'm right," Sara said. "Because I am."

Just then they heard the raised voices of Monsieur Fontenau and Madame Broussard.

"When did Papa get here?" Renaud asked.

A few moments later, Marie and Monsieur Fontenau walked into the courtyard. Sara stood. Monsieur Fontenau waved her down.

"Papa has some news," Marie said. She twisted a handkerchief between her hands.

"I have gotten a letter from Monsieur Jackson," Fontenau said, speaking in English.

Renaud jumped up. "He has written?"

"We have been in correspondence," Fontenau said. "I told you if he sent the money for the commission then I would know he was serious. He has sent the money with his representative. The man has been here for a week or so, but I wanted to find out more about Monsieur Jackson before I told you."

Renaud clapped, then hugged his sister.

"You will allow me to go then?" Renaud said.

"I had reservations," Fontenau said, "but things have not been good lately." He glanced at Marie. "Your mother and I think it will be good for you to get away."

"It will be very different there," Marie said. "It is a desert. They live away from civilization. I'm not certain how you will like it."

"Jackson has arranged transportation," Fontenau said. "His man will take you west to this Wayward Ranch."

"Papa, I want to go, too," Madeleine said.

"We thought you would," Marie said. "And we would like you to chaperone your brother and see that he doesn't get into any trouble."

"I will send my representative, too," Fontenau said. "Someone who will not be swayed by either of your charms."

"Gabriel," Madeleine and Renaud said at once.

"When will we leave?" Renaud asked.

"Do you think you could be ready in a week?" Fontenau asked.

"Oh Papa! I could leave now!" Renaud said.

Fontenau put his arm across his son's shoulders. "Come. Both of you. We will get supplies. I am not certain what you'll need for a place called Wayward, but we'll take Jackson's agent with us. Juan Alvarez. He might know."

Fontenau and his children left the courtyard. Sara's heart began racing. Wayward. She suddenly remembered that Murphy had said his place in the desert was south of a place called Wayward.

"Sara," Marie said. "I have a surprise for you, too. Monsieur Fontenau has given me your debt."

"I am so relieved," she said. "Madame, I-I don't know how to ask this, but I must go with your son and daughter."

"Sara, you are pregnant," Marie said. "You're going to have twins. It is a long journey to this Wayward place."

"I'm hardly showing," Sara said. "I will work hard and pay off the debt. I promise. You liked the quilt. I could make you many quilts like it, only better. I could make you dresses and send them to you. Madame Broussard, I am supposed to meet the father of my babies in a place south of Wayward. A place in the desert. He found a mermaid spring. That's what he called it. It is where I can find home again, I believe. Don't you think the spirits must have opened the door for this, for me to be here and now?"

Marie sighed. "I did so like having you here," she said. "You mustn't tell Monsieur Fontenau you are leaving to look for this mermaid spring. It will be our little secret. But he will have to approve you going with them. He will think it is very foolish, as do I. Why not wait until the children are born and grown up a little bit? Then you can take them. But I understand. And you can look after my children on this trip. You and I will conjure and weave a spell so that the journey will be safe and you'll get to where you're going in one piece."

Madeleine and Renaud were happy to have Sara along for the trip. Monsieur Fontenau and Gabriel were a bit harder to convince. Marie said she would feel better if Sara was along. Fontenau asked Sara if she had ever ridden a horse. Sara swore she had ridden them all the time when she was a girl. She had gotten so good at lying she didn't even cringe when she said it. Besides, she had ridden bareback a few times when she was younger. How difficult could it be with a saddle? They were taking a wagon that looked like a very strong carriage, plus several riding horses. Two of them would be in the wagon at a time and three would ride.

The night before they were to depart, Marie and Sara stayed up and made gris-gris bags and talked to the faeries and the spirits the whole time. Madeleine and Renaud said the house hummed that evening and into the morning and they dreamed of tropical islands and the desert sun.

In the morning, Sara stood in the sewing room one last time.

"Thank you, room," she said. "You've been wonderful." She pressed her hand against the painting Renaud had made for her.

Then she went into the courtyard and looked at the mermaids. "Goodbye, sea sisters."

Then she hugged Polly goodbye.

Marie stood in the front doorway. Renaud, Madeleine, and Gabriel were all on horses. Monsieur Fontenau, too. He was going to ride with them for a time. Madeleine looked beautiful in her riding pants and jacket. Renaud grinned. He was completely recovered from his injuries, and he looked equally as handsome in his shirt and riding pants.

Renaud and Madeleine had no idea what it was like to travel a long distance, Sara knew. It would not all be pretty. Perhaps Marie's talk with her spirits and Sara's chants to the good folk would keep them on the right path.

Gabriel—Sara didn't know his whole name because everyone just called him Gabriel—sat straight and tall in the saddle without any expression on his face. Juan Alvarez sat in the wagon holding the reins of the horses loosely in his hands. The wagon was already packed with Madeleine and Renaud's luggage. Sara stood on the steps, holding her small bag close to her. She looked over at Marie next to her and smiled.

"I added something for you in all those bags of my children's," Marie said. "You might be able to use it at your new place." She handed Sara an envelope. "That's your contract. I've said it's paid in full and I've put a letter in there that you can give Gabriel if he gives you any problem. I trust you will send me what you can to pay off the debt, but as far as I'm concerned, the debt was paid when you saved my son."

"I thank you, Madame Broussard," she said. "I don't know what will happen or where I'll be. But you're always welcome there or anywhere else I live."

The two women embraced.

Sara waved to Polly who stood just inside the house and then she walked down the steps to the wagon. Juan Alvarez reached for her hand and helped her up. She sat next to him.

"Good day to you," Sara said. "My name is Sara O'Broin."

"Sorrow?" he asked.

Sara shook her head. "No, Sara."

"Sara," he said. He said the word carefully.

"I am Juan Alvarez," he said. "I am pleased to meet you." Sara liked the singsong of his words—it was different from Madeleine and Renaud's accent, yet the same in some ways. He was different-looking from anyone she had seen before. He was brown-skinned and his nose and face were angular. She squinted. That wasn't what was different about him. It was that he did not belong in this city.

Monsieur Fontenau kicked his horse forward. The other horse-back riders followed him. Juan slapped the reins and the horses jerked the wagon forward.

Sara did not look back. Those that were paying attention said later that a whole string of invisibles followed the wagon. Some recognized the good people—the faeries—and others said some of the loa followed. Whoever and whatever they were, they all danced. What a ruckus they made.

Those that weren't paying attention didn't hear or see a thing, except for Irish Sara riding in the wagon with a Mexican-Indian, following two light-skinned black people and two very light-skinned Frenchmen. They didn't even see the horses or their bridles covered in faery bells.

FIFTEEN

At first, they encountered little more than dragons. Juan was good at steering them around these long-limbed creatures that curled up in trees, along shorelines, around hills. No one seemed to notice besides Sara and Juan, and they said nothing to one another, only glanced at each other when it was time to make another detour.

River maidens stared up at Sara from their watery homes. When Juan stood beside her and saw them, too, she knew he was a kindred spirit.

She said, "You can always tell a river maiden from a human woman. If some piece of a woman's clothing is almost always wet, then she is most likely born of the sea or the river or the lake."

Juan touched her sleeve. His fingers came away wet. "You mean like this?" he asked.

"Aye," she answered.

After a time, the dragons gave way to wolves who ran beside

them sometimes as men, sometimes as women. Sara ached to run with them. When Gabriel raised his gun to kill one of them, Renaud shouted, "Don't kill beauty, Gabriel. It will come back to haunt you."

Later a bear man asked to join them for dinner. Juan said it would be impolite to refuse. So they sat around the fire together while the bear man told them stories.

The next morning, only Juan and Sara remembered the bear man or the stories.

Sometimes monsters came in the form of men with shotguns. Once they tried to buy Renaud. Madeleine would have killed them if a crow hadn't called out. Gabriel made the men go away. Sara thought that one day she would need to learn how to take care of monster men the way Gabriel did.

Gradually the land began to change. Or maybe it happened overnight. Sara was never certain. One day they were surrounded by green. And then they weren't. Various types of cacti pushed up through the dry ground here and there. When they saw the first one, Sara had to get out of the wagon and look at it.

"You could use these as sewing needles they're so sharp," she said.

The cactus didn't answer her.

The air was dry. At night, coyotes howled at the stars or the moon. Or each other. One night, Juan began howling along with them. Madeleine followed his lead and howled. Soon Renaud and Sara were calling out to the coyotes, too. Gabriel watched them. Soon the coyotes stopped yipping.

The humans all laughed. Except Gabriel.

"I think we confused them," Sara said.

"They don't understand our accents," Juan said.

Sara liked the desert immediately. It was familiar in a way she did not quite understand. The silence throbbed in her ears like a distant ocean. In the forests and on the plains they had crossed, Sara had heard and sometimes seen coyotes, but the ones in this desert were different from those. These ones were leaner, more curious. They stopped and watched Sara and the others, seemed to be contemplating whether they wanted to stay and chat for a while.

The flora was strange and wonderful. Not only the cactus but the bushes and trees. Some of them smelled so sharp that Sara's nose crinkled. Some of them were so dark and gnarled with roots that spread out across the desert. And under nearly every tree and bush and cacti of a certain size, other trees, bushes, and cacti grew, taking advantage of what little shade there was.

Sara watched the mountains in the distance come and go. The mountains watched them too. Sara felt their gaze. They were old and wrinkled and they slouched into the earth like children at the beach dug themselves into the sand. Ahhhh. What a life that must be.

One day, Sara saw a giant green cactus man walking slowly through the desert. She jumped out of the wagon and ran toward it. It was taller than three of her, with thick arms raised to the sky. A tiny owl looked out of a hole in the trunk.

"Good morning to ya, Mr. Cactus Man," she said. "I have been looking for you. Can you point me to where I need to be going?"

"I think she's finally gone crazy," Madeleine said as she rode her horse up beside Sara. "She's talking to the plant life."

Sara clapped her hands. "Juan!" she shouted. "We're almost there, aren't we?"

"We are near the Vasquez Hacienda where *mi madre* works," Juan said, "and where I was raised. We will be there by night-fall."

And they were. Before the sun set, the group from New Orleans arrived at the Vasquez Hacienda.

Legend has it that when Vasquez first heard strangers had come onto his land he rejoiced: This was what he had prayed for, he was certain. He hadn't prayed to the Christian god because that god had not protected his two sons when they went off to war. No, he had prayed to the spirits of the land. He had prayed to the ancestors of the place. He knew he should not have ever let his boys leave this land, but like their mother, they had considered Spain home. Off they had gone to seek their own fame and fortune. They had died and now Vasquez lived alone in the New Spain countryside with his many servants and workers. Only they kept leaving, too. So he had gone out into the desert and fallen onto his knees and asked for something to happen to take away his pain. "Kill me or heal me," he pleaded. When he opened his eyes, he saw the eyes of a jaguar looking back at him from underneath a palo verde tree. The tree was all green, and this particular jaguar was all black. Vasquez closed his eyes again and waited for death. Nothing happened. When he opened his eyes, the jaguar was gone.

That first evening, as the horses pulled the wagon toward the shadowy building ahead of them, Sara wondered if this was the place she had been looking for.

Men with lanterns hurried out of the building as they pulled up. Someone shouted in Spanish. Other people ran to the horses. What a commotion they were making for them, Sara thought. She could see arches and a huge wooden door that opened into a kind of courtyard. Inside, light blazed.

Sara glanced over at Juan. He smiled. "They will take care of you now," he said.

"You're coming with us?" she asked. She had grown accustomed to his presence. She loved Renaud and Madeleine, but they were not steady. Juan was steady. She liked that.

"I'll visit with my mother," Juan said. "And then I will see you soon."

Before Sara knew it, she was out of the wagon, walking alongside Madeleine, Gabriel, and Renaud. They followed a man with a lantern under the huge stone arches into a courtyard lit by torches. Tall fronds cast even taller shadows. A bird called out. Sara smelled flowers.

They walked down a portico. At regular intervals, the man with the lanterns stopped and opened a door and told Gabriel in Spanish that this room was for the señorita or the señor until they each had a room of their own. Sara went into her room, looked around, and then peeked out her entrance again. Madeleine was looking out, too.

"My room is huge," Madeleine said. "I cannot believe it." She ran over to Sara and together they went into Sara's room. They both sat on her bed.

"I would say this is the biggest bed in the world," Madeleine said, "only mine is the same."

The room also contained a wardrobe, desk, chair, and wash basin. Sara went over to the basin. Steam rose from the water.

"It's hot," Sara said.

Madeleine jumped off the bed. "I am going to my room to wash then!"

Sara washed her face, neck, hands and arms. Someone brought her bag to the room. The person came and went so quickly that Sara was not sure if it was a man or woman. She took out her quilt and folded it up at the end of the bed. Then she put her treasure box on the desk.

A few minutes later, Madeleine opened the door separating their rooms and came into Sara's. She was wearing a dress.

"What have you done, darlin'?" Sara asked.

"This place makes me feel like wearing a dress," she said. "Just for tonight. Señor Vasquez has invited us all to dinner. Would you like to wear one of my dresses?"

Sara laughed. "I am now quite distinctly pregnant." She put her hands on her belly. The children had been quiet for days. Now one of them kicked her. Sara smiled. "But I will change out of this into something clean. Am I to eat with you?"

Sara pulled off her dress and put on a blue frock.

"The woman who came said everyone was expected for dinner," Madeleine said. "I think. I couldn't understand her very well."

Sara heard Renaud's voice on the other side of the door on the opposite side of the room. "May two gentlemen come into your room?"

"I don't know about gentlemen," Sara said. "But you are welcome."

The door swung open and Renaud and Gabriel walked into the room. Renaud held out his arm to Sara.

"Shall I escort you to dinner?" he asked.

"Couldn't ask for better company," Sara said as she took his arm.

The four of them went outside again and walked across the courtyard. They went through another door to a large dimly-lit foyer. A small dark woman was waiting for them. She held a single candle. The candle wavered as the four newcomers came inside and a shadow moved across the woman's face.

"*Bonjour*," Madeleine said.

The woman nodded and motioned them to follow her. Madeleine glanced at Sara. Sara shrugged. They followed the woman into a large room with a long wooden dining table at the center of it. Golden light from two candelabras near the ends of the table glinted off the plates, silverware, and glasses. Above them, the ceiling vaulted into darkness.

"This must be a mistake," Sara whispered. "The gentleman could not have meant me to be here, too." She started to pull her hand away from Renaud, but he stopped her.

"Stay," he said. "When Vasquez sees us, he may decide he is mistaken about all of us."

At the opposite end of the room, a door opened and a man strode through the door and into the room. He was tall with thick wavy black hair streaked here and there with strands of gray.

"Micaela!" he said. "You didn't offer my guests any wine?" His English was almost without accent.

Sara looked behind her and realized the small woman was still there. Her shoulders were hunched, as though she was in distress.

"We just got here," Sara said. "She didn't have a chance to do anything."

The man stood at the head of the table and looked at Sara. He had the darkest eyes she had ever seen. They seemed kind and hard at the same time. His forehead was lined with age or heartache. As he looked at Sara, he shifted—or trembled. Sara was not quite certain what happened—but a look of recognition passed over his face.

"Please, sit," he said. He looked away from Sara. "You are all welcome guests. Rodrico, serve the wine please."

Sara glanced behind her again. The woman was gone. A young man moved toward the table. Renaud held out a chair for Sara. She wasn't sure why, but she sat in it. Gabriel did the same for Madeleine.

"I am Javier de la Vasquez at your service." He sat down last.

"I have the pleasure of introducing Mademoiselle Madeleine Fontenau and Monsieur Renaud Fontenau," Gabriel said.

Vasquez nodded to the Fontenaus. Then his gaze rested on Sara. Gabriel cleared his throat, then said, "This is Sara O'Broin. She is in service to Madame Broussard."

"*Was* in service," Sara said. She hadn't meant to say it, but she did. Now everyone was looking at her. "My debt is paid in full. I have the paper to prove it. I am a free woman."

Renaud clapped. The sound rang out in silence. He stopped.

"This is a grand dinner, I'm sure, Mr. Vasquez," Sara said, "and I thank you for the invitation, but I'm guessing you want me to eat with the other servants."

Sara pushed her chair back and stood up from the table.

"But you told us all that you are not a servant," Vasquez said. "And I want you to stay and eat with us. I'm sure you have great stories to tell."

"Most of them aren't fit for company," Sara said.

Vasquez laughed. "Your words are like music," he said. "Where is it you come from?"

"From far away," Sara said. "From the auld sea."

"That is far indeed," Vasquez said. "You will find, Señora O'Broin, that I am not like most Spanish men. I care nothing for the church, for instance. I say that out loud even though it could have gotten me killed years ago. I care little about Spain or her rules. I care little for countries! This is the land I live on. It is the land I care about. If my children had stayed on this land, they would be alive today. They are dead and buried in Spain with their mother. I can only grieve for them. But I will not leave this place."

Rodrico finished pouring the wine. Vasquez raised his glass. "But enough sad talk," he said. "To my company, to those from New Orleans and those from the sea. You are all welcome to stay as long as you like."

They all raised their glasses. Vasquez looked at Sara. Then he brought the wine to his lips.

Sara hesitated. She had been told since she was a child that if she ever ended up in the land of the good folk—if she ever stumbled into the land of the fey—she shouldn't drink or eat the food; otherwise she would never be able to come back home.

She was not quite sure where she had landed this time, but it felt peculiarly comfortable.

She brought the wine up to her lips and took a sip. She could never go back home now, anyway. Perhaps this place was her new home.

SIXTEEN

The meal was delicious. Sara ate more than she was used to and she fell into her bed full and contented. She was almost asleep when Madeleine came into the room and got into bed with her.

"May I sleep with you?" Madeleine asked. "It is frightening in my room. This is not a good place, *ma chère*. We cannot stay here for long."

"You can sleep here, of course," Sara said. "But what are you afraid of?"

Madeleine curled up under the covers. "I don't know," she said. "I know it is a bad place."

"Places aren't bad," Sara said. "Or good. They are only places."

"This from someone who cries at night in bed alone for her long last homeland? You who have crossed half the country to come to a desert you've never been to because a man named

186

Murphy told you it was wonderful? I think I can disagree with you based on your own words to me."

Sara laughed. "I cannot fault your logic since I don't understand it."

A few minutes later, Renaud knocked and then came into the room. He lay down on the end of the bed, on top of the quilt.

"I knew one day you two would get together!" he said.

"Ah, she would never have me," Madeleine said sleepily. "What are you doing here, Rey? Have you fallen in love with Sara, too, and are going to tell her finally?"

"I am trying to sleep," Sara said. "Remember: I am sleeping for three."

"I, too, do not consider myself good enough for Sara," Renaud said. "I could not sleep. This place is haunted. I don't think we should linger here long."

"It is not haunted," Sara said. "I think it's lovely."

"Lovely?" Madeleine tried to imitate Sara's accent. "Didn't you notice how rundown it is? The walls are filthy. The tile is chipped. And his clothes tattered."

Sara turned over so she was lying on her back. The children didn't like that, so she shifted positions again. "I didn't see any of that," Sara said.

"It's no wonder," Renaud said. "You must be smitten, too."

"What are you two talking about?"

Madeleine sat up. "You must have noticed the master of this dungeon—"

"Dungeon!" Sara sat up. "This is no dungeon. It's more of a palace. The whole place sings. Can't you hear it?"

"Those are the whispers of the people haunting it," Renaud said. "I think Monsieur Vasquez has enchanted you. I think he called you forth from the old sea, and now that he has you, he's not letting you go."

"You are both daft," she said. "For one thing, I'm pregnant

187

with two children. No man is gonna want me. For another thing, the man is old enough to be my grandfather. Or my father at least. You've never seen anyone treat me as an equal before this, and you don't know what to do with yourselves."

"We treat you like an equal!" Renaud said.

"Oh darlins!" Sara said, laughing. "You don't treat anyone as an equal. You wouldn't know how."

"She's right," Madeleine said. "But you're wrong about Vasquez."

"I'm going to sleep," Sara said. "If you're staying, please be quiet."

Sara dreamed she was swimming in the deep auld sea and Javier de la Vasquez swam with her. Up ahead of them, her three children swam.

In the morning, Sara awakened to the sound of Gabriel gasping. She had never heard him gasp or exclaim. He was standing in the middle of the room staring at the bed. Sara slowly sat up. She moved Madeleine's arm off of her hip. Renaud was stretched out on the end of the bed.

Renaud opened his eyes and yawned. He saw Gabriel and said, "Would you care to join us."

Gabriel turned red. He opened his mouth to say something and nothing came out. Finally he turned and left the room.

Señor de la Vasquez gave the travelers a tour of the hacienda. He seemed most proud of the vegetable garden and the fruit trees. As Sara walked beside Madeleine and listened to Señor Vasquez, she noticed that the garden looked dilapidated. It needed weeding, and the fruit trees needed pruning. Inside the big house, cracks ran up dirty walls. Paintings hung askew. The corridors echoed with a strange kind of emptiness. The kitchen was cramped and small.

Away from the big house were the stables, a granary, smithy, and other buildings. All seemed half-empty or unused. Still, many people worked at the hacienda.

"This place used to be like a bustling city," Vasquez said. "And then when my sons died, I lost interest, I suppose. Or maybe it's me growing old. We've had a drought so we can't grow as much. And cattle are such boring creatures. Who wants to run cattle?"

"You must be very wealthy then," Madeleine said, "if you don't have to make certain the ranch makes you a living."

Vasquez shrugged. "What are monetary riches when those you love are gone?"

The four of them ate with Señor Vasquez at every meal. The food was as good at Sara remembered from the first night, but she felt something was missing. She could not quite put her finger on what it was. Still, she enjoyed sitting and eating with Señor Vasquez around the big table or out on the patio—that's what he called the courtyard. After a few days, Renaud and Madeleine seemed to relax some, especially after Vasquez urged Juan to take them out for a ride. Vasquez had four black horses. Sara had never seen animals so black, as though the black came from another world. And their coats were shiny, as though they had been curried by the faeries because no mortal horse could look as fine. Their manes and tails were long and wavy. They pranced when they walked.

"They have the same sire," Vasquez said, "and four different brood mares. The blood will out, every time."

Sara didn't know what he meant, but the horses were beautiful. And feisty. They snapped and kicked at one another. Renaud looked a little frightened of them.

"They'll settle down once they're out in the desert," Vasquez said. "They can't be fighting one another when they're watching out for jaguars."

Juan's stallion was still beneath him. Sara smiled at him. On a horse was when Juan seemed most like himself—and the horse seemed most like itself.

The horses and riders trotted out into the desert, away from the hacienda.

Sara looked at Vasquez. "Jaguars? I've heard of them. Are they up here, then?"

"They're spotted every once in a while," Vasquez said. "I saw one three times in my lifetime. Once before I got married. Before I learned my sons had been killed. And once before you arrived—before your party arrived."

"What do you suppose it means?" Sara asked.

"I think it means you were destined to come here," he said. "I believe you have come to save me."

Sara shook her head. "I don't know what you mean, sir," she said. "I have no means to save anyone, and I don't believe in destiny. It's been too cruel to me."

"Something brought you here," he said.

"A man told me about a place in the desert where I can find peace," Sara said. "So I came here."

"You can find that peace here," he said. "I asked Gabriel about you. He said that Madame Broussard thought very highly of you. You are a great seamstress. He says there are rumors you are also a great curandera. You have a way with the spirits."

"I am not a 'great' anything," Sara said. "Maybe you could say I'm great at getting pregnant because I've been pregnant twice now in the space of only a few months. Usually the women of my clan have more control over these things, but I had an enchantment over me, so I couldn't control anything." She glanced at Vasquez. He looked puzzled.

"You can see this place is falling apart," he said. "I haven't the heart or the inclination to do anything about it. These people rely on me for their livelihood. Maybe if my house was livable again, I would feel as though I was livable again. I would ask you to stay just to stay, but I have a feeling you would say no to that. So I'm offering you a position. I would like you to manage my household. I will pay you a good salary and you can live anywhere in the house you like. You can raise your two children here."

She looked around until her gaze settled on Vasquez. "I will do this, but you must promise me something. You must swear this to me on that which you hold most dear."

"Anything," he said.

"I will be a servant in your house, but that doesn't mean you have any right over my body. You cannot touch me."

"You will not be a servant," he said. "You will be in charge of my house! You will be my sister. On my word as a gentlemen, I promise I will not touch you without your consent."

"I have heard such promises before and they were broken," she said.

"I am an old man," he said.

Sara smiled slightly. They stood a few feet apart, but she could feel the heat coming from his body. She knew he was as virile as he had been when he was nineteen.

"Does that mean your word is even more valuable, then, because you are old?" Sara asked.

Vasquez laughed. "That *is* what it means! But I will assuage your concerns further. I will give you the keys to the house. They are the only set. You can lock any door you like. Then you know you will always be protected from any wolves at the door. And that wolf will never be me."

"I will consider this seriously," Sara said.

Vasquez nodded. "That is all I can ask."

One day, when Sara was alone in the garden, Juan came up to her and held out his hand to her. Sara shook it.

"You look well," Juan said. "Are you enjoying your stay?"

"I am," Sara said.

"I wanted to introduce you to my mother," he said. Sara followed him into the house. They walked down a long cool corridor to the kitchen. Inside Micaela sat on a bench drinking coffee in the tiny kitchen.

"This is *mi madre*, Micaela."

Sara put out her hand and Micaela took it and held it. She smiled as though this was the first time she had ever seen Sara.

"The patron has told her to rest," Juan said, "and not work so hard, but she doesn't know what to do with herself. I told her she could play with her grandchildren."

"You have children then?" Sara asked.

"My two sisters have children," Juan said. "They live near. I told her she could come live with me at Wayward. She won't." He kissed his mother. "*Adios,* mama." Then he and Sara walked down the corridor away from the kitchen.

"Juan, I don't think I'm going to Wayward. I haven't told Renaud and Madeleine yet. Señor Vasquez has asked me to manage his house."

Juan looked startled.

"I love it here," Sara said. "I think I could make it into a beautiful place again. It doesn't need much."

"I'm sure Señor Vasquez and his house would benefit from you," Juan said. "But how does it help you find your mermaid springs?"

"I will look for it," she said. "But I'm going to get bigger and bigger, at least until the children are born. This seems a good place to stop for a while."

"The Wayward Ranch is a good place, too," he said. "They will welcome you and take care of you."

"I don't need anyone to take care of me," she said.

Juan shook his head. "We all need that," he said. "I am worried."

"Why?" Sara said. "Isn't this where you grew up? Weren't you happy here?"

"I was happy," Juan said, "and I was miserable. My father was not good to me or *mi madre*."

"Señor Vasquez seems to need someone right now," Sara said. "He seems lost. If I stay here I can help him and he'll pay me a salary. I'll be able to figure out what to do with my life now."

Juan nodded. "Mama has told me Señor Vasquez sees you as an angel sent from heaven," he said. "Or from the land or sea. He has been more patient since you came."

"What do you mean?"

"When his sons were killed," Juan said, "it was as though a very bad storm came through here. He was cruel to many people. It was his grief. You've been a good influence on him."

"I will miss you," Sara said. "And Renaud and Madeleine. I might even miss Gabriel. But staying here will give me purpose. Promise me you will come to visit me regularly."

Juan smiled. "This is a promise I will make."

Renaud and Madeleine did not react well to Sara's decision to stay behind in "casa grande spirits," Madeleine's nickname for the big house.

"He's going to eat you up one night," Madeleine said. "You wait and see."

"He has given me his word," Sara said. Of course, Cormac had given his word, too. "Plus I have the keys." She held up an iron circle of keys. "No one will eat me up."

Sara and Señor Vasquez stood outside as the four travelers prepared to leave. Gabriel, Juan, and Renaud rode horses; Madeleine sat in the wagon and held the reins. She was dressed once again in trousers.

"I had them put Mameau's gift in your room," Madeleine said. "We will see you soon. *Je t'aime!*"

"We will write to you every day!" Renaud called.

Sara shook her head. "No you won't."

"I will write sometimes," Renaud said. "Especially to tell

you all about the painting." He winked. "You will have to come up and see it all."

Then they galloped away. People who were at the hacienda that day said Señor Vasquez and Señora Sara looked like an old married couple standing side by side. Sara rested her hand on her belly. Señor Vasquez waved. Then the two of them turned to go back to the main house. Señor Vasquez touched Sara's back, lightly, with his hand as they went forward. Then, as though he remembered that they were not man and wife, he dropped his hand. Above them, three ravens called out. Sara nodded in acknowledgement. Then she walked into the house of ghosts.

SEVENTEEN

Marie Broussard's gift to Sara was several bolts of colorful cloth along with a box of spools of thread. Sara kept them in her room until she could create her own sewing room.

The first thing Sara decided the big house needed was a big cleaning. She asked Micaela to hire extra help, and then they began cleaning and scrubbing the house. Sara worked right alongside them. The soap and water took off years of smoke, dirt, and dust. Room by room the house began to lighten. Some walls had delicate paintings beneath the dirt—usually decorative flowers or birds flying across the arches.

Vasquez watched from afar. He warned Sara not to do much of the labor herself.

"You want the workers to respect you," he said. "You tell them what to do and then you watch them do it."

"But Señor Vasquez," Sara said, "I wouldn't respect someone who stood around and didn't do any work."

Señor Vasquez laughed. "It is work to stand around watching others work."

Sara picked a room with light yellow walls that overlooked the gardens as her sewing room. Rodrico found a shelving unit in one of the storage buildings. He cleaned it and brought it into the room. Sara set the bolts of cloth on them. Once she had a chair in the room—a chair that faced the window so she could look out into the courtyard—she felt as though she was almost ready to sew.

"Now I need Renaud to paint the walls," she said.

Rodrico found workers to help in the garden. Sara didn't know what would grow in this part of the world, so she had to rely on the advice of others. Gardeners came and pulled out the weeds and began planting beans, squash, tomatoes, and some greens at one end of the garden where it got shade in the morning and evening.

Señor Vasquez was happy to help Sara with all the decisions. The more changes Sara wanted to make, the happier Vasquez seemed. She told him she was only bringing the house back to what it had once been.

"No, it has always been a sad house," Vasquez said. "Even when I was growing up. And later, my wife, who came from a fine Spanish family, she was sad here."

"You grew up here?" Sara said. "I thought you were Spanish."

"Yes, I am Spanish," he said. "But I was born here. My wife always thought she married beneath her. So you, Sara, you change anything you want to make this a happy place. Once the children are born, this will feel like a home again."

"You never have any people here except your servants," Sara said. "Don't you have family or friends who visit?"

"No," he said. "No one. But once it is beautiful again, we will have a great fiesta!"

Sara brought in workers to expand and change the kitchen.

"Food coming from that cramped and hot place will taste cramped and hot," she told Vasquez. "You want an airy kitchen. A huge kitchen! Then all of life will taste good."

Since Micaela still did most of the cooking, Sara asked her what kind of kitchen she wanted. She opened her arms wide. "Grand!" she said.

Sara nodded. "Yes, that's exactly what you will get."

Señor Vasquez expected Sara to eat most of her meals with him—except breakfast. He ate breakfast alone in his room. Sara relished this time in the morning. She usually sat on the patio near the servants' rooms. She ate what they called frijoles, often with eggs, and peppers or tomatoes. She liked being with the other servants, even though Vasquez insisted she was not a servant. Often Sara and the others didn't understand each other. Micaela's English was not very good, and Sara hardly knew any Spanish. Rodrico and David knew a great deal of English, but they didn't always understand Sara's accent. Alicia was one of the women who had come in to clean and she helped Micaela with the cooking. She seemed to understand everything everyone said. Or maybe she just nodded so that they would finish talking and she could start talking. She had stories to tell about everyone.

"This place has what they call a curse on it," Alicia told Sara. "Do they say that in Irish? The Spanish stole this land from the Native people and the Natives cursed them."

Micaela made a noise. "I never heard a thing like that. My people come from this land and they never cursed anyone."

Alicia nodded. "The curse is real. Why do you think no one will work here?"

"I thought the place got rundown after Vasquez's sons died," Sara said.

Rodrico shook his head. "It has been getting worse for years."

"It's because of Señor Vasquez," Alicia said. She leaned forward and whispered. "His whole family. They say they all turn into animals too much. You do that, it's hard to come back." She nodded again.

The others shrugged.

"I don't understand," Sara said.

"Don't you have a—" Alicia turned to the others and they talked amongst themselves, trying to figure out a word to use. "We all have a kind of spirit animal when we're born. Some say it's like a guardian angel, only it's an animal."

"Only the old people believe this," David said.

"No, I've seen them walking in the arroyos right out here," Alicia said. "You can tell they are really spirit animals because they will talk to you."

"Like I said," David said. "Only old people believe this."

"Señor Vasquez's animal is the jaguar," Alicia said. "His mother told me before she died. She was afraid one day the jaguar would come after him and kill him. I told her I never heard of that happening. The spirit animal protects. It doesn't kill. But you see, if you are too much of the animal then you become like an animal. A man who is an animal."

"Why would that be a bad thing?" Sara asked. "Animals are never cruel. They don't murder or rape. They kill when they are hungry."

"But a man is meant to be a man," Alicia said, "not something else."

"Sometimes we are more than one thing," Sara said. "That's the way of the world. We all change into one thing or another."

Rodrico nodded. "Like the arroyos. Sometimes they are dry, like the desert, and you can walk in them forever."

"As long as you watch out for the woman in white," Alicia said. "She'll snatch you from the arroyos."

"And other times they are flooded with water," Rodrico

said. "They are rivers flowing so full and so violently that you can't imagine they were ever dry or that they will every be dry again."

David nodded. "And the things that swim in those new rivers you wouldn't believe. My mother swears she sees mermaids in the new river out here during the monsoons every year. I thought I saw them one year, too. If you catch one, they will grant you three wishes."

Rodrico said, "I thought they had to marry you if you caught them."

"Maybe that's it."

"Like you two could ever get your hands on a mermaid," Alicia said. "One of them is smarter than the two of you put together. They would slip out of your hands before you'd have time to give them a kiss."

The men and Alicia laughed. Sara glanced at Micaela. She was looking out into the desert.

"What about you, Micaela," Sara asked. "Have you seen a mermaid?"

"I've seen everything," she said. "Including this mess you are all making. Help me clean it up."

The meals Sara spent with Señor Vasquez were very different from the ones she had with the servants. Sometimes he talked about the places he had been in the world and the people he had known. Mostly he talked about the land. He talked about the way the desert smelled after a rain, especially when the day had been very hot. He talked about the mountain lion he had followed for days once when he was a boy. His intention had been to shoot him, but then the lion turned and looked at him, and he couldn't do it. His father beat him until he bled—told him he would never be a real man. But he was always glad he had not killed the lion.

"Of course I went on to kill many more creatures," he said

with a wave of his hand. "There was no other way. But I tried to honor each animal. Everything has a time to die."

He also talked about books he had read. He took Sara into his library one day. Books filled every shelf and the shelves went to the ceiling. He showed her where the English books were. She took several back to her room and practiced reading.

Sometimes she took a book out to the wash, and she sat in the dirt and read. That never lasted long. She would feel a breeze on her cheek and look up to see a bird standing on top of a saguaro looking at the world. Or maybe she would hear a hisssss and she'd glance around for a snake and wonder if she could call it to her. Sometimes a coyote showed up in the wash and watched her. Sara always whispered, "Are you man or beast?"

Sara's mother had told her long ago that those who learned to read could no longer converse with the good folk. They could no longer understand the language of the birds, trees, and weather spirits. She feared her mother might be right. She didn't hear many whispers these days, only the sound of the air beneath the raven's wings or the wind rattling the dry leaves of the palm tree. Sometimes she heard whistling in the house and wondered if the goddess Brigit was calling to her, but it usually turned out to be Rodrico or David.

When she could get away from the house, Sara wandered out into the desert. Vasquez warned her not to leave the hacienda, but she went anyway. She most liked walking in the wash near the hacienda. Her feet slipped in the loose sand like they had on the ocean beaches near home. She imagined she was walking on the bottom of a deep river—and she supposed she was. The river bottom happened to be empty of water right now. She liked stopping in the middle of it, far from the house, and listening to the world. To the birds. To her own breathing. She wondered what animals watched her. She knew there were many: She followed their footsteps in the wash. She wondered if they followed behind her and looked at her footprints and wondered what she was.

The spring rains came and went. The arroyo ran with water for a few days. Vasquez had David hitch up a buggy to one of the horses and he took Sara to a place far out into the desert until they were looking down at a field of purple.

"What is it?" Sara asked.

Vasquez smiled. "It is the desert in bloom," he said. "Once the desert gets water, it becomes hopeful and blooms again. It is like a man who has been without hope until a young woman comes into his life and makes his world beautiful again."

A few nights later, the saguaro bloomed. Vasquez had told Sara they bloomed at night and the blossom only stayed for a short while. She was sleeping when she heard whispers. She opened her eyes. The giant cacti men and women were speaking to her. She got out of bed, put on her shoes, and went outside of the main house. The moon was high in the sky and illuminated David and Rodrico standing on the patio near their quarters.

They turned to her.

"You can't be out at night," David said. "It is dangerous."

"I heard the flowers open," Sara said. "I want to see them."

"We will take you," Rodrico said. "Be careful."

"You two are as fussy as old men," Sara said.

They walked a bit away from the main house until they were standing near several saguaros. Bats flew all around. The moonlight made the flowers on top of the cacti people look almost black.

"It smells like candy," Sara said. She breathed deeply and held up her arms. Bats flew between her hands and up to the saguaros.

David and Rodrico glanced back at her. She knew they smelled nothing except the dry desert air.

"What are you doing?"

The three of them jumped at the loud and harsh voice and quickly turned around. Vasquez stood behind them. His hair was disheveled and his robe hung loosely around him.

"Sir," Sara said. "Are you unwell?"

"Oh, it's you," Vasquez said. His tone softened. "You must not be out here. The desert is dangerous at night. Rattlesnakes and jaguars. Lost men. Come back inside." He said something to David and Rodrico in Spanish. They nodded and walked back toward the patio.

"Take my arm," Vasquez said. "I don't want you falling."

"Sir, it is as bright as noon out here," she said. "I won't fall."

"Please," he said. He held out his arm. Sara hesitated and then slipped her arm through his. She felt a spark of heat coming through the cloth. Sara looked up at Vasquez. He didn't seem to notice the spark. He patted her arm. "There. Now isn't that much better?"

Together they walked back to the house. Vasquez left her at her room. Sara listened to him walk away. Then she took out the keys as she did every night, and she locked herself inside her room.

Soon the desert grew hot. Sara had never known a place could get so hot. Before the sun came up, when the night was as cool as it would be, Micaela went through the house and opened up all of the doors. She knocked softly on Sara's door each night. Sara would get up and open all of her doors.

It soon got too hot to close her doors at night. They kept the main doors and gates closed and locked at night to keep out the wild animals, but otherwise the doors between the rooms remained open. By mid-morning, they boarded up the side of the house that got the most sun.

Everyone tried to work around the heat. The workmen came in before first light to complete the new kitchen which was when the repairmen who were fixing the cracked walls showed up. When Sara got up, she often saw the gardeners digging in the dirt.

One day Madeleine and Renaud returned with Juan for a visit. Sara went outside to greet them as soon as she heard they had come. She shook Juan's hand first.

"You look well," Juan said.

"I look like I'm three people," Sara said. "Which I am. Your mother will be glad to see you."

Juan carried Madeleine's and Renaud's luggage into the big house, and then he left the three of them alone. Sara took them around the big house to show them the renovations.

"I can't believe it," Madeleine said. "It's beautiful."

"Mostly it needed a good cleaning," Sara said. "And maybe we'll bring in some art work. I've found there are quite a few artisans in the area. Many of them used to work here, but a lot of them avoid the hacienda. I am to understand that Señor Vasquez wasn't always kind to his servants. I need to convince people that he's changed. He's been very kind to me."

"He's not come after you in the night?" Madeleine asked.

"No," Sara said. "No one has come after me. Do you still feel the presence of any ghosts?"

Madeleine pursed her lips. "Yes, but they are much better dressed and much happier."

Sara put her arm around Renaud's waist.

"So how goes the painting?"

He smiled. "It is the most amazing place, Sara! You must come live with us. There are so many beautiful men. And women. And colors. And we all live together." Then he whispered, "And some of us sleep together. Madeleine is in love."

Madeleine shrugged. "It is good to be in love, no?"

"And the painting I have been doing is wonderful!" he said. "The walls are my canvas! Everyone is very impressed with me. They want to be with me because they think I am a great artist."

Sara laughed. "I'm so glad you're here."

"You look like you're going to burst any second," Madeleine said. "And in this heat. It must be awful."

"So far I don't mind the heat," Sara said. "And the house stays cool."

"We've been told it will only get hotter," Madeleine said. "I think it is already too hot, but it's not like back home. It is a much dustier heat. See how much we love you that we were willing to come out in this horrible heat. We wanted to see how you are and how Señor Vasquez is behaving."

Renaud and Madeleine joined Vasquez and Sara for dinner. Vasquez was charming and gracious. Sara watched him and wondered if she would ever see the other side of him. It was difficult for her to understand how someone could be one way one minute and completely different the next—even though she had witnessed Cormac's erratic mood changes daily for weeks. Vasquez was nothing like Cormac. Vasquez was a changed man, a good man. Circumstances of life could change anyone. She had changed. She had once been bold and carefree. Now she felt more hesitant and fearful.

She wished she could go back to her old self.

"Perhaps you can convince your friend Sara to leave this hot desert for a while," Vasquez said near the end of dinner. "At this time of the year, I go south to attend to business. I have a house where it is cooler. Sara should come with me. She will be more comfortable. It is closer to the city so she will have a fine doctor."

"Why would I need a doctor?" Sara asked. "Women have been birthing babies before men were even born."

Vasquez laughed. "This is true," he said. "But you would be more comfortable where it is cooler."

"These cottonwood trees give the house shade. And the little fountain on the patio cools it off some."

"Why don't you want to leave?" he asked. "The work on the house is almost finished for now. You don't have to worry about that. The kitchen will be complete when you come back."

"I appreciate your offer," Sara said. "But I've been traveling for so many months. I want to settle in here more. I want to feather my nest, so to speak."

He nodded. "I think I understand," he said. "I want to be here when the babies are born. I could wait."

"If you want to leave this heat," Sara said, "please don't wait on my account. I have no idea if the babies will make an appearance in two days or in two months. I've been told twins often come early, but maybe they will stay late. Go on your business trip. Renaud and Madeleine will be here for a while at least."

Vasquez shrugged. "As you wish. I will leave within the week."

EIGHTEEN

Sara put Renaud to work. First he painted a seascape in her sewing room. Madeleine sat in the room with them while Renaud painted. She read and Sara worked on a quilt she was making to send to Madame Broussard. A breeze came in off the patio and Sara and Madeleine turned their heads to take advantage of it.

"Ah, wind," Madeleine said. "I do long for it. But then when it comes in the desert it stirs up so much dust."

"Are you missing home?" Sara asked.

"I miss the place," she said. "But here I can be who I want to be. No one bothers me. It is live and let live."

"Unless someone gets angry at you and then it is die and let die," Renaud said. "Some of these cowpokes—or *vaqueros*—have a temper. They get cranky out there on the range all alone, I guess. There was a gunfight in Wayward a few weeks ago. Not on the ranch. We missed the entire spectacle. I'm glad for that."

"And you, Sister Sara?" Madeleine asked.

"I am ready to birth these children," she said. "That is all I care about right now."

"Have you found the mermaid springs?" Renaud asked.

"I haven't looked," Sara said. "Honestly, I had forgotten about them."

Madeleine gasped in mock horror.

"Leave her alone," Renaud said. "Wait until you are pregnant. You will forget everything too."

"I will never be pregnant," Madeleine said. She shuddered. "That would mean I would have to let a man get close enough to me to impregnate me. That would be horrible."

Sara laughed at the way she said "horrible." She remembered Murphy's hands on her body. That had not been horrible. What had happened earlier that evening, with Cormac, that had been monstrous.

A few nights after they arrived at the hacienda, Renaud and Madeleine both came into Sara's room after they had all retired for the evening.

Sara sat up in bed. "What is it?" she asked.

"We keep hearing strange noises," Madeleine said. "Like something growling or snarling."

Sara listened. She heard nothing.

"There," Madeleine whispered. "Did you hear that?"

Sara shook her head.

"I believe someone has put a spell on you," Madeleine said, "so that everything about this place seems wonderful to you."

"Stay here with me if you like," Sara said. "Renaud, you too. Renaud?"

He stood at the open door facing the patio.

"I think in this desert you can be whatever you want to be," he said. "And someone is being wild tonight."

"There it is again," Madeleine said.

Sara did hear something. It sounded like someone was crying.

"Please, can we close the doors," Madeleine said, "and use your keys to lock them?"

"If that will put your fears to rest," Sara said, "I'll do it."

Sara got out of bed and closed all the doors. She put the key in each and locked them. Then she pulled the boards across the window. It was pitch dark in the room.

She felt her way back to the bed. Renaud sat on the end of it. Sara reached out and felt Madeleine's hand reaching for her. She got onto the bed next to her. Sara listened to the darkness. She heard only their breathing.

"I can't hear it any longer," Madeleine said. "Good. But it is too hot to sleep. Sara, we are worried about you."

"Why?"

"This man Vasquez," she said. "There is something not right about him."

"He is still in grief over his sons," Sara said. "But he is getting better."

"It is more than that," Madeleine said. "It is the way he looks at you."

"He treats me like a daughter," Sara said.

"I am glad my father didn't look at me that way," Madeleine said.

"Maddy," Renaud said. "Maybe it is a cultural thing. Spanish men do love women."

"He's got her locked up here away from everyone," Madeleine said.

"I am not locked up," Sara said. "And there are people everywhere."

"Have you ever heard the story about *la Belle et la Bête?*" Madeleine asked.

"I don't know," Sara said.

"This father sells his daughter to a beast," Madeleine said. "The father stole a rose and the beast was going to kill him because of the theft of this silly rose. He said 'I will kill you unless you give me one of your daughters.' This papa was not a man of honor, as you can tell from him stealing the rose."

"It was a flower," Renaud said. "Was that worth someone's head?"

"So he sends his youngest and most beautiful daughter," Madeleine said. "And he tells her she must obey the beast and live with him. So she does. The beast isn't especially nice to her, but they spend a great deal of time together in this dark old mansion. He has a library with many books. They eat good simple meals together. He wants to marry her, but she refuses. And then one day she consents. Who knows why? Once she professes her love he turns into a beautiful prince and they get married and have many children."

"If that was supposed to be a cautionary tale," Sara said, "it wasn't a very good one."

"She transforms the beast into a prince," Madeleine said. "But what does she get? She has to live in that dark old place and give birth to baby after baby."

"I think you meant to tell her the story about Bluebeard," Renaud said. "When you were talking about this earlier, you mentioned Bluebeard."

"Do you know Bluebeard?" Madeleine asked. "He was an ugly old man and no one in town wanted anything to do with him. His wives kept disappearing. But one young stupid woman agreed to marry him. She was happy away from everyone, living in his big mansion. He had to go away on business so he gave her his keys and said she could use any key except this one tiny key. Of course as soon as he left, the young wife put the tiny key in the door and opened it. Inside was a chamber of horrors. Blood everywhere. He had killed all of his former wives and now she was going to be next."

"Shhh," Renaud said. "I hear something."

Sara felt cold. She reached for the quilt. It did sound like something was outside. Or someone.

The door rattled. Someone was trying to open it. Madeleine gasped. The three of them huddled together.

The rattling stopped. A moment later, the door that adjoined Sara's room with Madeleine's shook. This time the door rattled louder, as though someone on the other side was trying harder to open it.

Sara heard her heart in her ears. The rattling stopped.

A minute later, the door between Sara's and Renaud's rooms shook.

"This is ridiculous," Sara said. "Who's out there? What do you want?"

The door rattled again.

And then silence.

"Do you think it was him?" Madeleine whispered.

"What are you talking about?" Sara asked.

"Vasquez," she said. "Maybe he was trying to get in."

"Vasquez is not Bluebeard," Sara said.

"He did give you the keys," Renaud said.

"And not one of them did he forbid me to use," Sara said. "Now go back to your own rooms and let me sleep."

"We can't go back now," Renaud said. "What if whatever it is is still there?"

"Maybe the faeries wanted to see if we were still here," Sara said, "so they were givin' us a little fright. You can stay here, but me and my babies need some sleep."

In the morning, Sara ate breakfast with Madeleine and Renaud in the dining room. Since they had arrived at the house, Vasquez had been coming down to eat with them every morning. This morning he was absent from the table.

Sara asked Rodrico where he was.

"He left this morning," Rodrico said.

"Without saying anything to me?" Sara asked.

"He was in an accident last night," Rodrico said. "We had to call the doctor in. Looked like he had been mauled, but he wouldn't say. We tried to wake you up, but we couldn't and the door was locked."

Sara looked at Renaud and Madeleine. Madeleine shrugged. Renaud smiled sheepishly. "So that was what the rattling was at the doors last night."

"It was early this morning," Rodrico said, "before light. I didn't rattle the door, I don't think. I did knock and call your name. The patron said not to disturb you, but I thought I should let you know. He did say he'd be back in a few weeks."

Later in the day, Sara sought out Micaela and asked her what had happened to Vasquez.

"It was the anniversary of the deaths of two of his sons," she said. "He has a difficult time every year. Sometimes he goes out into the desert. It isn't safe there at night."

"Will he be all right?" Sara asked.

"Señor Vasquez is a powerful man," Micaela said. "He can take care of himself."

With Vasquez gone, Sara relaxed the rules of the house. Soon everyone was eating on the patio together—the servants, workers, and Sara, Renaud, and Madeleine. When it was too hot to work, they played games or told stories. Juan even joined them a few times. When it got too hot to move, they ate hot peppers and listened to the insects buzz.

Sara began dreaming of the sea again. She swam with her sisters, her mother, the auld ma, and her daughters.

She grew restless.

All the women she had known wanted to stay still in the last weeks of their pregnancies. Sara wanted to move. It was difficult to move. She was small and her two babies were big. She missed going out into the desert. She liked the silence. She even liked the danger of it. Or the closeness of life and death. If she were left alone in the desert for even a few hours during the summer months, she knew she would die. And any number of creatures would help facilitate that death.

Still, she felt what was underneath it all. The memory of the ocean. And the presence of the desert. Tomorrow mountains could push up through it and it would be changed again. And yet, it seemed unchanging.

She liked that she had to pay attention to her surroundings every second she was in the desert. She couldn't get lost in her thoughts—or in the past.

One day she asked Juan to take her out into the desert. He seemed glad for something to do. They left as the day grayed into morning. Micaela packed them a lunch and plenty of water even though they planned to be back in a couple of hours.

Monsoon clouds rode the ridge of the mountains. Juan told Sara that meant they might get drenched, but if that happened, the day wouldn't be quite as hot as it had been. The horse carefully picked its way down a kind of dirt path, rocking them back and forth as it went.

"*Mi madre* was angry with me for agreeing to take you out," Juan said. "She said the babies will be born any minute."

Sara shrugged. "Then you can help me, although I doubt I'll need much help."

Juan laughed. Sara leaned back and watched the world go slowly by them.

"Why do you hate being at the hacienda so much?" Sara asked.

"I don't hate it," Juan said. "I grew up there. I grew up here. I love the desert."

"But not the house," Sara said.

"You have done a good job with the house," Juan said. "Everything is better there. Even Señor Vasquez."

"That doesn't really answer my question," Sara said.

"There are more houses on the land," Juan said. "Did you know that? Most are falling into ruin. There's one I used to like to play in when I was a boy."

"What did you like about it?" Sara asked.

"It seemed more a part of the land than the big house," he said. "The spirits of the place spoke to me there."

"Can you take me?" she asked.

"It might take an hour or more to get there," he said. He looked up at the sky. "We'll need to stay away from the arroyo." He shook his head. "*Mi madre* will take me out and drown me like La Llorona herself if anything happens to you."

"I've never seen a grown man so afraid of his mother."

"I'm not afraid of her," he said. "I respect and honor her wishes."

Sara laughed. "Whatever you say, Juan," she said.

They travelled for some time over the old road. After a while, Sara could see a line of cottonwoods and birches up ahead.

"Is that where the river is?" she asked.

Juan nodded. "When it's running." He pointed. "And near those trees is the old house."

In the distance, lightning flashed out of black clouds. A moment later, Sara heard thunder.

As they drew closer to the house, Sara could see it was a kind of reddish adobe building that looked like it was sinking into the pink earth. When they pulled up to the house, Sara realized it was bigger than she had thought at first. From the main part of the house, the building extended on each side of it, with arched porticos on each wing. Tall cottonwoods shaded most of the house. It was almost cool. Cool and humid. It felt as though it would rain any minute.

Juan helped Sara out of the buggy. He tied up the horse and then went to look for water. Sara stretched and then cringed. One day soon she would be able to stretch again. To breathe again. She went to the back of the buggy and pulled out the leather pouch. She took it over to the horse and let him drink some. Then she put the pouch back.

She stood looking at the house. The wind through the cottonwoods whispered to her. She breathed.

"This feels like a sanctuary," Sara whispered.

She walked toward the house. She could see where once there had been a garden. And over there was the patio. She put her hand on her back. She had to sit down. She kept walking until she reached a massive wooden door which she pushed open. The door creaked uneasily and kicked up dust. Dust swirled around Sara and became hands that propelled her gently forward into the house. A deer with a huge set of antlers trotted past her and down the hall. It turned and looked at her and then disappeared around a corner. Then a jackrabbit ran past her. It had the longest legs she had ever seen and the biggest ears. She laughed. Murphy had been right. They could leap over mountains with those legs. It ran around another corner. She blinked and walked further into the house.

Except for the dust—and the animals—the house appeared empty. She listened to the whispers as she went around the same corner the jackrabbit had taken. She walked down a short corridor and then into a huge room. She could smell peppers, tomatoes, bread, beans. A long wooden table with a bench on either long side rested in the middle of the room. Several broken tiles lay on the table. Sara walked over to it and looked at the tiles. She moved the pieces until they formed two whole tiles. One tile was green with a blue bird on it, another was yellow with a green tomato at the center. Sara put her hand on the table.

She felt dizzy for a moment. Then she heard murmuring. She took her hand away. The voices stopped.

She walked around the room. At the other end was an old stove.

This had been the kitchen, and it was almost at the center of the house. She liked that.

She left the kitchen and headed in the direction the deer had taken. She went down a couple of steps into a huge empty room. The walls were bare except for some kind of stenciling around the great fireplace. She crossed the room and walked down a long corridor. She opened some of the doors on either side of the corridor. Some of the rooms looked out at the portico. She could see the horse and Juan through the slats in the wood covering the windows. On the other side, the rooms looked out at the desert and half walls that had probably once been part of the building.

She kept walking down the corridor. It sloped down and then opened into a huge room with shelves against two of the walls. Long wooden tables stood in front of the shelves. The floor was covered in dust. No hoof prints or paw prints.

"The faeries of this place must be fooling with me," Sara said.

She walked across the room and opened the door. The house fell away into ruins here and was open to the elements.

Away from the house on a kind of ridge were what looked like more ruins—or at least a part of a building. On the path leading to the ruins a jackrabbit stood looking at her.

"That's the biggest jackrabbit I've ever seen," Juan said as he came up behind her.

"You see it too then?" Sara asked.

Juan laughed. "Yes, I can see him. He's going up to the wall. I'd forgotten all about that place. We used to go up there when we were kids and sit on the wall and look down at the river when the water was running."

"Will you help me so I can go up there?" she asked.

Juan stepped out of the house first and then he helped Sara down. He kept a hold of her hand as they stepped over the broken pieces of stone and wood. Once they were on the path, the jack-rabbit hopped up the path and Juan let go of Sara's hand.

"This is a beautiful place," Sara said. "Who used to live here?"

"Vasquez's mother came here after he got married," Juan said. "She and the daughter-in-law didn't get along. After she died, no one lived here."

"Seems like such a waste," Sara said.

They reached the wall. The jackrabbit was gone. The half wall curved slightly as though it had been part of a circle. Plants Sara didn't recognize grew up around the stone. She ran her fingers along the cool gray surface as she walked all the way around it. Then she looked beyond the wall. About a hundred feet from where she stood, the earth dropped away into a rocky ridge and Sara could see an arroyo—only now it was a creek. Water ran swiftly through it.

"I think that means we're about to get rain," Juan said. "We better go back to the house."

"What was this place?" Sara asked.

"I don't know," he said. "Someone told me it had been a chapel once, but I don't know. There's so little left of it."

"Did the weather get it?" she asked.

"Or people hauled it away," he said.

"Maybe the faeries used it to build themselves a desert house."

Sara sat at the long table in the place she believed had once been the kitchen while Juan brought everything from the buggy into the house. Then he undid the horse from the buggy and took the horse around the back where part of the stable still stood. When he returned, Juan and Sara sat together at the table and looked out at the desert as it began to rain. Soon the rain was so heavy they could not see beyond the cottonwood tree.

It rained so hard that day that many people claimed all the rivers, creeks, and washes flowed over their banks and made the desert the Old Sea again. As Sara watched the storm, the rain covered the windows. Or maybe the water rose and covered the whole house. Salmon swam past the house. Mermaids, too. There was the auld ma, motioning to her.

"The Old Mermaid is calling me," Sara said.

And just then her water broke. Her daughters were attempting to swim out of their own ocean and into this world.

At least that was what she told Juan. He put the blanket and pillow his mother had insisted he bring on the floor. Sara placed the pillow against the wall and then she half-sat half-lay across it.

Nobody is really certain what happened that day. When Sara talked about it later, she said it began to rain and then she began to have the pain. And then two children were born. When Juan talked about it, he said it rained for many hours and he was afraid something was going to happen. And then a strange kind of light filled the house, as though it had been hit by lightning and Sara said, "My girls are swimmin' out of my ocean into this one. We've got to help them get here alive." Those who know and those who don't say the creatures and spirits from the desert and the sea came into the house that day. Sara called on them. Madame Broussard called on them. Sara's ma back home called on them.

The first baby was born easy enough. She was tiny, but she was bawling. Her head was covered in black hair. Juan wiped her off and wrapped her in his shirt that he had torn in half. Then he handed the baby to Sara.

"She looks like her da," she said. "His name is Termain Mur-

217

phy. This one will be Em, after her da's last name. And we'll call her Emmy."

Thunder and lightning shook the earth then and the contractions started again. These ones were harder. Sara felt as though the baby was holding onto her womb for dear life.

"Come on, baby girl," Sara said. "You got to go with the flow of it."

The house shook again and the second baby girl was born. This one was a little bigger than her sister. She wailed and wailed. Juan wiped her off and wrapped her in the second half of his torn shirt. Then he handed her to Sara. This baby had curly blond hair. Her face was rounder than her sister's and her complexion was lighter. Sara bit her lip as she looked at the baby. The baby opened her eyes and looked directly at Sara. Sara knew those eyes.

"Cormac," Sara whispered.

She gave the baby to Juan.

"Have you named her Cormac?" Juan asked.

She shook her head.

The second baby kept crying.

"Help me out of this dress," Sara said. "I have to feed Emmy."

Juan took the dress gently off of Sara. She sat on the floor half-naked and didn't care. She pulled her top down on the right side and put Emmy on her breast. Sara felt the tug on her nipple.

"What about the other baby?" Juan said. She was still crying.

"No," Sara said. "I won't feed her."

"I don't understand," Juan said. "You must feed her. She will die if you don't."

"She will be fine until we find a wet nurse," she said.

"Sara, we're in the middle of the desert," he said. "In the middle of a monsoon. We can't get to anyone for a while."

"That is the daughter of the man who raped me," Sara said.

"She is the daughter of the man who stole my life from me. She is bad, like her father."

"Sara, she is your daughter," Juan pleaded. "She came from you. She grew inside you. What did that man contribute to this child? She is your child."

Sara shook her head. "You don't know what I've been through. You don't know how much I hate her father."

"What is a father?" Juan asked. "The man who had sex with my mother was not a good man. He did not treat her well. The man who raised me was a good man. Am I a bad man because of the man who had sex with my mother?"

The baby had stopped crying.

"Sara," Juan said.

Sara shook her head. She looked down at Emmy.

"I will feed her this one time," Sara said. "And then I will find someone else to do it."

She handed Emmy to Juan. He took her and gently laid her in his lap. Then he handed the other baby to Sara. She reluctantly put the baby to her breast. For a moment, the baby didn't nurse. But then she hiccupped and began sucking. Tears streamed down Sara's face. Juan sat against the wall, relieved. Sara reached for the other baby. Soon the twins were nursing. Sara looked from one to the other. She had no idea which baby belonged to which father. Well, she had some idea.

But how could it matter?

She could not let it matter.

Sara fell to sleep then, with the two babies on her breasts. They stayed like this all night and into the next morning. Sara didn't say a word. She nursed the babies when they were hungry and then she fell back to sleep.

Juan took the placentas outside and buried them near the cottonwood tree by the house.

NINETEEN

The storm passed away midday the next day, and the sun came out. Juan went outside and walked up to the half wall, sat on it, and looked out at the river, now swollen over its edges. Someone on a raft went by. She was all alone. She looked like Sara. She turned and waved to him. And then she leapt into the water. Her green tail sparkled in the sunlight. The raft dissolved into seaweed. Juan was so surprised he fell backward off the wall.

That was when he saw what was on the wall. He started laughing, got up, and ran down the hill and into the house.

Sara was getting dressed. The babies lay on the blanket sleeping.

Juan reached for her hand.

"I have to show you something," he said.

"Can't it wait?" she asked. "I'm pretty certain I just gave birth to two full-grown children because I hurt like hell."

"My mother was up cooking fifteen minutes after I was born," he said. "You'll be glad."

Sara held onto Juan's hand and carefully picked her way over the rubble and walked up the path behind Juan. When they reached the wall, he stepped out of her way.

"The rain must have washed the dirt away," he said.

Sara walked closer to the wall. Then she sank to her knees. She reached out and touched the stone and the place on it where the black mermaid with the red tail swam. Next to her was a mermaid with red hair. And then another with brown skin and brown hair. One with green skin and yellow hair. And another and another. They were thin and small, tall and heavy.

"These are the Old Mermaids," Sara said. "It's the wall Murphy told me about." She started laughing. "This is the place." She sat on the ground.

"I've got to show my girls this. This is home, Juan. I know it. I can feel it. This is where Emmy and Juanita are going to grow up."

"Juanita?"

"Yes," Sara said. "I have named her after her father." She looked up at Juan. "Do you accept the challenge?"

"I do," he said.

Before they left the house and land later that day, Sara and Juan walked up to the ruins one more time. Juan carried Emmy and Sara held Juanita. They stood in front of the old mermaid wall.

"This is such an amazing place," Sara said. "It's an old mermaid sanctuary, that's what it is. Look, Juanita and Emmy! See the mermaids there in the new river. I hope you both always swim in the ocean of yourselves."

"When the river runs dry again," Juan said, "you can find thousands of seashells in the riverbed."

Sara nodded. "Yes. And every time you pick one up, Juanita," she said. "It'll mean that some mermaid has found what she lost and she is whole again."

Juan cleared his throat. "Sara, I don't think the patron will like that you named the baby Juanita."

Sara looked over at him. "Why not?"

"He won't like thinking of me having anything to do with you," he said.

"He doesn't own you or me. We can do what we like."

Juan shook his head. "I don't think you understand the way it is here."

"I don't understand?" Sara said. "I come from a place where there were all kinds of rules, spells, and enchantments to keep us in our place. Or in the place and space where others thought we should be."

"It is better for everyone if he is pleased," Juan said.

"He shouldn't have that much power," Sara said.

"But he does," Juan said.

"I think he is a good man and he won't care."

"Why do you think that?"

"Because he has been good to me," she said. "Because I have been safe and comfortable at the hacienda because of him."

"You could be wrong about him," he said. "Have you been wrong before about these kinds of things?"

"Do you mean about men?" Sara said. She had thought Ian would be with her until the end of her life—thought he would defend her with his own life. But he hadn't. She hadn't liked Cormac, but she had never suspected he could do what he had done to her. And Murphy left her after Cormac raped her. Couldn't he have figured out a way to stay with her? And Daniel Martin had handed her off to some greedy captain who sold her.

"I may have been wrong once or twice," she said. "I will tell him her name is Nita. Only you and I will know her real name."

"*Gracias,*" he said. "And the part about me being with you

when you gave birth." He shook his head. "We should keep that to ourselves too."

Sara laughed. "No! It's too good of a story. I want to tell people how you blushed purple when you saw naked parts of my body."

Juan looked away from her.

"I'm sorry," Sara said. "I didn't mean to embarrass you. I am happy. I'm happy to be here. I'm happy to be alive. I'm happy you saved my baby's life." She leaned over and kissed his cheek. "Thank you, Juan."

When they returned to the hacienda it seemed as though everyone in the world ran out to greet them. Madeleine screamed when she saw her. Renaud laughed and clapped. Micaela reached for one of the babies. Renaud took the other.

"Which one was named after me?" Renaud asked. He rocked Emmy in his arms.

"Neither," Sara said. "You have Emmy. And Micaela has Nita. They're both Irish names that mean 'love.'" She glanced at Juan. "Now I want to sleep for about ten years. Someone show me where my room is. I've forgotten everything."

Sara did sleep for many days. She woke up long enough to feed the babies. Then she went back to sleep. The babies slept on the big bed with her, always touching one another. They had been in her womb for so long together, Sara supposed, that they liked the world better when they were close to each other.

"You are not Murphy's child," Sara told them, "and you are not Cormac's child. You are not my children. You don't belong to anyone but yourselves. Remember that."

Sara left her bed just as they completed the kitchen remodel. And Renaud was finishing up a painting on the far wall that looked a lot like the one in his mother's kitchen in New Orleans, only he had different animals wandering in the woods and he had painted a cactus here and there.

Soon after, Madeleine, Renaud, and Juan packed up to leave. Sara embraced them all.

"Please come back soon," Sara told Juan.

"I will," he said.

Sara watched them ride away. Once they were gone, Micaela, David, and Rodrico led her to a room in the house she had never been to.

"Close your eyes," David said. She heard a door open. "Now you can look."

She was standing on the threshold of a large room. On one side of the room was a cradle next to a long dressing table. Next to the cradle were two small beds. The walls were painted in bright yellow. And on the yellow, Renaud had painted huge colorful blossoms, seashells, what looked like gris-gris bags, treasure chests, birds, dogs, and cats. In the center of the room was a rocking chair. Sara walked toward it. She could smell the freshly cut wood. Carved on the back of the chair—in the part she would lean her back against—were two mermaids holding hands, their tails entwined. Somehow the carver had made one mermaid appear darker than the other, even though she could detect no paint.

"Juan made it for you," Micaela said, "and Renaud and Micaela and Juan put the room together for you and the babies."

"It's beautiful," Sara said. She looked at the three of them. "And you helped them, didn't you?"

"We just moved things around," David said.

"And painted," Micaela said.

"That dog was my idea," Rodrico said.

Sara laughed and embraced them all. "I am a very fortunate woman."

Señor Vasquez soon returned to the house. Sara had never seen anyone so excited to see two babies. He held them and talked to them as if they were his own children. He loved the nursery and offered to buy anything else she needed. He began spending most of his time with the three of them. The house became a noisy place and Vasquez seemed to relax. He helped the babies sit up. He watched them start to crawl and encouraged them to crawl into his arms. He rocked them when they cried. And when they slept, he and Sara went out into the desert together.

One night they sat together after dinner in the sewing room. The babies were sleeping.

Vasquez cleared his throat. "Sara," he said. "I have never met anyone like you. You've come to this place as a stranger but you have made it your home. Nobody cherishes this land the way I do—except you. I would like you to have part of this land."

Sara looked over at him.

"Javier, what are you talking about?"

He had insisted she start calling him by his first name.

"Your children are like my own children," he said. "I want you to feel as though this is your home. I would like you to do me the honor of becoming my wife."

Sara couldn't move for a moment. Then she looked over at him.

"But Señor Vasquez," she said. "I don't think of you the way a woman thinks of a husband. I think of you like an uncle or a father. Only you have been kinder and more loving than my da ever was."

"I know," he said. "Still, I want you to inherit this place when I die. I want your children to have it. You have brought me such happiness."

"You will live forever," Sara said.

"If you will agree to marry me," he said. "I will give you half my property before the marriage. I will make certain it is all legal. Then if you're unhappy in the marriage you can go live on your part of the property any time."

Sara shook her head. "I don't understand," she said. "Why

would you want me to marry you if you know I don't love you that way?"

"You could change your mind," he said. "I would wait. I would wait a lifetime."

"I appreciate your offer," Sara said. "But I'm happy the way things are."

"I want to take legal responsibility for the girls," he said. "It would be beneficial for them."

"It wouldn't be fair to you," she said. "And I couldn't have you getting impatient and forcing yerself on me. I've had that happen before and I won't let it happen again."

"I have been an honorable man while you have been in my house."

"You have," Sara said. "But men change when they get married. They think of their wives as property and they think they have a right to sex whenever they want."

"I am not such a man," he said. "I swear to it. If I live out my life with us as a chaste married couple, I will still live a happy life, just as we are now. The benefit will be that I can show you all off and then when I die, you will get all of my wealth."

"I don't like you talking about dying," Sara said.

"Are you refusing my offer?" he asked.

She stared at him. It would be nice to stay here for the rest of her life. Her daughters could live out their lives happy and healthy—and rich. She didn't consider herself married any longer, since she had married Cormac against her will. She wondered if Vasquez would consider her married. The chapel had been destroyed in the storm. No record remained of her marriage to Cormac. It was as though it had never happened.

Besides, the enchantment had been broken. Her marriage was over.

"Let me sleep on it," she said.

That night she lay on one of the small beds next to the cradle where her daughters slept.

"Listen," she said, "if any of the good folk are out there, if my sea sisters are with me in this desert, let me know if I should take this step. I don't love him like a wife loves a husband, but I do love him. And even if Murphy came, what would we have? This has been like a gift from heaven, and I don't even believe in heaven. If you could send me a sign, I would appreciate it."

Sara did not dream that night. In the morning, she opened her eyes and the girls were looking at her. They laughed when she smiled at them.

"I'm gonna do it," she said. "You will have a better life than I could have ever dreamed."

At lunch, she told Javier.

"I accept your offer," Sara said. "But I have some conditions. First, I want you to know I love and respect you, but my judgement hasn't always been good when it comes to men. I will want Gabriel to look over the deed to the property and make certain it is all legal. And then you must swear to me that you will never try to force yourself on me. I will call upon all the magic I know and all the spirits who aid me and if you ever try to hurt me, it will all turn back on you before you can touch me. Do you understand all that?"

Vasquez smiled broadly. "I understand everything," he said. "I will have the papers drawn up. And I will send for Gabriel right away. We can be married before Christmas?"

Sara nodded. "Javier, there are things about my past that you don't know. It could make a difference in how you feel about me."

He waved his hand.

"No," he said. "There is nothing you could tell me that would change my mind. But I would like to know if the father of the girls has any legal claim on them."

"No," she said. "He is a sailor. He may come one day, but I am not married to him."

"That is all I need to know. Do you want a small wedding or a large one?"

"A small wedding," Sara said. "And later we can have a big fiesta."

"I like that idea," he said.

Sara sewed her wedding dress from the cream-colored fabric Madame Broussard had given her. She made it a simple dress that she could wear again, with lace covering the bodice. She sewed the girls little dresses out of the same fabric. With every stitch she made, she sewed in protection and good health. When Sara was finished, she lit a candle and burned some of the herbs her mother had given to her. She made three pouches from the faery yarn. She dropped herbs and dirt and a shiny stone from the arroyo into them. Then she chanted to all the spirits who were listening.

"To those in the auld sea," she said, "and those of the new desert. To the good folk and those beyond and here. I call to all those I hold dear. Protect my girls and me from all harm. I say this charm again and again to hold us away from harm. And if Javier de la Vasquez ever comes near us with violence in his heart, from us he will forever be apart."

Then the house trembled. The workers in the hacienda stopped and looked around. Micaela said a prayer. A wind blew through the house and snuffed out the flame on Sara's candle—a candle Madame Broussard had given her.

"And so this spell is done," Sara said, "and my will be done."

Gabriel rode to the house one day. He went into Vasquez's study. Sara sat on the other side of the door with her ear pressed to it. They spoke in Spanish so she could hardly understand a word they said.

Some time later, Vasquez opened the door and invited Sara in. She sat across from Vasquez's desk and next to Gabriel.

"I have looked over the contract and the deed," Gabriel said. "It is legal. You now own half of the property."

Vasquez handed Sara several pieces of paper. "I had it written up in English for you, too."

Sara read it to herself. Sara O'Broin was the owner of said property.

"What part of the land is it?" Sara asked.

"I split it in half," Vasquez said, "so that you have everything north, including the place where your girls were born."

"It's really mine?" She looked up at Vasquez. He smiled. Then she looked at Gabriel.

"Thank you for coming, Gabriel." She held out her hand to him.

He stood and shook it. He held onto it for a bit.

"Are you sure this is what you want?" he asked.

She nodded.

"Then I will take my leave," he said.

Later Sara slipped the deed into her treasure box. Then she put on her wedding dress. Vasquez picked up Nita and Sara held onto Emmy. They walked down the long corridor to the chapel.

"I'm not Christian, you know," Sara said.

"I don't believe any of it myself," Vasquez said. "But this is how it is done."

They went into the small chapel and walked up to the altar. The priest stood waiting for them. Micaela sat in the back as a witness. As the priest recited his words, Sara looked around the chapel. She imagined how beautiful it would be with Renaud's paintings all over it. She could see it in her mind's eye: mermaids swimming all around the chapel. The Old Mermaid Chapel. Emmy burped. Sara and Vasquez laughed.

And the next thing Sara knew, she and Vasquez were husband and wife.

They celebrated by having dinner out on the patio. The girls crawled on the ground near to them.

"Does it hurt them to put the dirt in their mouths like that?" Vasquez asked.

Sara shrugged. "It does all of us good to eat dirt every once in a while," she said.

That night, Vasquez kissed her on the top of the head as he did every night and wished her sweet dreams. Then he went to his room.

Sara slept in the nursery next to the twins. This night she closed the door but did not lock it.

"No one will hurt us," Sara said to the girls. "We are safe here."

TWENTY

And so the weeks passed. They planned a fiesta to celebrate their marriage with the community, but then they decided to wait until the spring, or summer. They enjoyed their life together, the four of them. Vasquez seemed happy and content, and Sara was, too. She got a letter from Madeleine and Renaud wishing her congratulations and promising to visit soon. Sara was surprised Juan didn't come to visit. He had been stopping by at least once a month to spend time with the twins. Now weeks went by and she didn't hear from him.

Then one day it was so still inside and outside that Sara felt as though the entire desert was waiting for something or someone. The coyotes howled at noon. A buzzard perched on the cross on the chapel roof.

And the sky had never been bluer.

Juan came to the big house riding on an appaloosa. They say when he left, he rode out on the same horse, only now it was a roan instead of an appaloosa. Everything had change by then, so why not his horse's color, too?

He found Sara in the flower garden near the fountain. The children slept beside her in a cradle. She was watching the bees on the new flowers.

"Juan!" Sara said. She jumped up and put her arms around his neck.

"It has been months," she said. "Where have you been?"

He took her arms down off his neck and said, "I have something to tell you, Sara. You might not want the girls to hear us."

The buzzard on the cross jumped into the air and flew slowly away.

"They're asleep," she said, "but they wouldn't understand you—although they both are talking a little bit, in English and Spanish. Madeleine and Renaud want to teach them French. What is it that is troubling you? Sit next to me."

He sat on the bench across from her, with his hat in his hands. He slowly turned the hat between his fingers.

"I got back to the ranch and heard about your marriage," he said. "We had some trouble at the ranch and I went to California to get some wagon parts. I had trouble returning. We hit avalanches, snow storms, rain storms, crippled up horses, Indian raids. This trip was not blessed like the trip we had coming here. It seemed to me that it was cursed. Or like someone was trying to keep me from getting here. But I'm here now."

"What is it, Juan?"

"What has the patron promised you?"

"What do you mean?" she asked. "As his wife, I get all of his property once he dies. But he has already gifted me half of the property, including the part with the house where the girls were born. I want to fix it up, Juan. I want people living in it again."

"You have the deed?"

"I have the deed," she said. "I had Gabriel look it over."

He nodded. "He told me that. Are you happy?"

"I am happier than I have ever been," Sara said. She thought for a moment. "Perhaps that is the wrong phrase. I am more contented than I have ever been. I have a home, my children, a loving husband."

"He has been good to you?" he asked.

"He has," she said.

Juan looked at her. She smiled. He so rarely actually looked into her eyes that she was startled by it. She looked away.

"Then maybe it is possible for people to change," he said. "Maybe the past is the past."

"Please tell me what this is all about," she said.

"I told you he didn't treat my mother well," Juan said. "Señor Vasquez—he is my father. He had sex with my mother and I was the result."

"What?" Sara said. Her stomach fluttered. "Did she consent to this?"

"Not the first time," he said. "She was engaged to my . . . father. After a while, she said yes, until she was very pregnant with me."

Sara felt like she was going to be sick. She remembered letting Cormac have sex with her—remembered teaching him how to do it better so it wouldn't hurt her so much.

She looked down at her sleeping girls.

"And he's kept her here all these years," Sara said. "I mean, she's stayed all this time."

"She needed to work," Juan said, "and he mostly left her alone after she got married."

"'Mostly'?"

Juan looked at the ground.

"Then this should be all yours," Sara said. "You should inherit it, not my girls."

"This land belongs to no person," Juan said. "The white people misunderstand that. Besides, I am not his eldest son."

"They died in the war," Sara said.

"They died," he said, "but I don't know in what war. Some people say they killed themselves. But I wasn't talking about them. Vasquez has other children. He has other daughters and sons. All over this region."

Sara shook her head.

"How many?" No, that wasn't the right question. "Who are they?" That wasn't it either. "How old is the youngest?"

Juan looked up at her again. "What difference does it make?"

"It makes a difference," Sara said. "I need to know if he's changed."

"His youngest is one year old," Juan said.

Sara wanted to scream. She put her hand over her mouth.

"And are all of them the result of rape?" Sara asked. "I mean has he forced himself on all these women?"

Juan nodded. "As far as I know."

"But he has been so good to me," she said. "He hasn't touched me. Juan, please watch the girls. I think I'm going to be sick."

Sara pushed herself up off the bench. She ran out of the patio and under the arches and out into the desert. She ran by the old saguaro and a tall palo verde tree and into the wash.

And then she fell to her knees and vomited. She pushed herself up again. Down the wash about twenty feet, a jaguar stood watching her.

She had never seen anything like it before, but she knew what it was.

"I thought you were a good man," she said to it. "I thought you would take care of my children. But you are no different from the man who raped me except you've done it to more women than he has. How could you do it to so many people? And how could you disown your own children?"

The jaguar opened his mouth and grunted.

Sara turned her back on the cat.

"I want nothing to do with you," she said.

When she looked again, the jaguar was gone.

Sara and Juan took the babies back to the nursery. She asked Micaela to look after them. She gave Micaela the keys and told her to lock the door after she left and only open it for her. Juan offered to go with her.

"No, this is between me and my husband," she said.

She went to Vasquez's office, knocked on the door, then opened it. Vasquez looked up from his work and smiled.

He stood. "Hello, my dear. What can I do for you?"

She stared at him. His smile seemed genuine. The wrinkles around his eyes were familiar to her. How could he be who Juan said he was?

"You must be a powerful sorcerer," she said, "to make me see you and this house as beautiful when all along people told me it was haunted. It is haunted by all the crimes you have committed."

"I don't know what you're talking about," he said. He sat back in his chair.

"All those women," she said. "And the children you fathered. You've left them penniless. You've left them fatherless."

"Nonsense," he said. "They are a part of me. I've given them my lineage. They will survive."

"Did you know that the father of my children raped me?" Sara said. "Cormac MacDougal. He was a boy from my village who wanted me and I didn't want him. It hurt, what he did to me. It was an awful experience that I continually dream about."

"You must move on," he said. "It happened in the past. You are a different person than you were then."

"I am," she said, "because of what he did. You changed all of those women you raped forever."

"I am sorry for what I did," he said. "I am trying to make up for it."

"I am taking my daughters and I am leaving you," she said.

"Where will you go?" he asked.

"I have the land," she said. "I will live in the house where the girls were born."

Vasquez pressed his hands against his eyes. Then he stood.

"Please, Sara," he said. "We have been so happy. I have kept my word to you. I haven't hurt you. What difference does it make what I did in the past? I won't ever do it again. If you like, I will give all the children a stipend. I could make Juan the mayordomo of the hacienda. Then you and I and the children could go south for a few months. Please, think about this."

Sara shook her head. "I have been so happy here," she said. "I never imagined you could be so cruel."

"I have never hurt you," he said, "or the children. And I never will."

Sara turned and left Vasquez alone. She went to the nursery. Micaela let her in and handed her the keys.

"I had no idea," Sara said. "I'm sorry he hurt you."

Micaela shook her head. "That was a long time ago. Juan should never have told you. The patron will do good by you."

"What about Juan?" she asked. "What about his other children?"

"That's the way it is," Micaela said. "I think he really changed this time."

Micaela left the nursery. Sara closed the door behind her. Then she locked it. She nursed her babies and then she sat alone in the rocking chair.

Some say the moon went dark that night. And the next night. And the one after that. It went dark for days, maybe even weeks. And Sara sat in the rocking chair Juan had made for her. She fed the babies when they cried. She played with them on the floor when they were awake. She opened the door and took food from Micaela when she knocked.

When Juan came to the door, she said nothing. She held her breath.

Vasquez came to the door every day and asked for her forgiveness.

One night she heard a growl. She closed her eyes and slept. She was walking in the wash with her girls. Ahead of her was a woman in white. The ocean flooded the wash and the white woman grew a tail and fangs. "Be careful," she said, "I will take your children and drown them."

She woke up. She knew it was time to return to her room. She kissed the girls, then left the room. She locked the door behind her. Then she went to her room and locked all the doors. She lay on her bed. This was it. She could forgive him. She knew she could. She did not like that about herself, but it was the truth. But he had to prove himself to her.

She closed her eyes. And opened them again when she heard a growl. Or maybe it was a cough.

"By all the powers of three times three," she whispered, "this spell bound round is and will be. All the hurt shall go back on he if he crosses that threshold to come after me."

The door opened.

Vasquez was his own light.

"You were correct, my dear," he said. "I am a powerful sorcerer."

"Recall my words, husband," she said. "If you try to hurt me, it will fall back on thee."

He strode toward her like a tiger about to take its prey. And then the ground beneath them shifted. Or the house did. Vasquez stopped. Sara heard whispers. Saw light and darkness rise up out of the night. Or felt it as something brushed her legs, like she had when she had stood in the lagoon surrounded by colored lights. Vasquez's eyes widened. He did not make another sound, not even when he sank to the floor.

Sara stood over him for a moment as the light seeped out of the room. Then she went around him and out onto the patio. She reached for the bell over the entrance and she began ringing it. The sound shattered the night into a million pieces that caused the stars to look like shards for a second.

David and Rodrico came running toward her.

"The patron is ill," she said. "You better get a doctor."

Then she walked back into the house and ran toward the nursery. It seemed to take forever to get there. It was darker than usual. She lost her way. It was as though the corridor had suddenly grown a new turn.

She finally got to the door and tried it. It was still locked. She took out the keys. Her hands were shaking.

"I'm coming, babies. I'm coming." They had to be safe. They had to be. Why had she left them alone? Her hands shook as she put the skeleton key in the lock and turned it. She pushed the door open and went inside. She could taste her heart in her throat.

"Let them be safe, let them be safe."

Where were they? Why couldn't she see?

She fumbled around in the darkness.

"Where are my babies?"

She began to weep.

And then in the darkness she heard two little voices whisper sleepily, "Mommy."

"I'm here," Sara said. "I'm right here."

Rodrico, David, and Juan carried Señor Vasquez up to his room. Sara asked Micaela to stay with the girls. She went upstairs to wait for the doctor. Vasquez was conscious, but he couldn't seem to move or speak. His eyes were open. He looked frightened.

"Take his clothes off and put him in his nightshirt, please," Sara said.

"What happened to him?" Juan asked.

"All the evil he has done just came back on him," Sara said. "Husband, can you hear me?"

Vasquez looked at her.

"Do you want some water?" His eyes stayed wide and frightened.

Sara took her kerchief and wiped his sweaty forehead.

"We will take good care of you, husband," she said. "Have no fear."

The doctor came and went. He believed Vasquez had had a stroke.

"He will never walk or talk again," he said. "He most likely has the mind of a child now. You must care for him as best you can."

Sara was surprised she did not feel sad or happy by what had happened to Javier. She saw flashes of life in his eyes, and she did not believe he had the mind of a child. She sat with him for many hours of the day and read to him. She brought the girls in and they played on the bed and crawled over him as they always had. She asked others to come and spend time with him, too. Juan was the first one to volunteer. He read Spanish books to him from Javier's library.

Sara exercised his arms and legs. One day he tried to sit up by himself and his arms moved.

"See, husband," she said. "You can get better."

He stared at her.

"I used to see love in those eyes," she said. "What is there now?" She shook her head. "You were foolish to try to force your way into my bed. I told you what would happen. If you had waited, old man, I probably would have come to you on my own."

Tears rolled down his cheeks. He cried a lot. Sara couldn't tell if he was actually crying or if it was some kind of automatic physical reaction.

Micaela and Sara bathed Vasquez and took care of his personal grooming. Micaela was especially gentle with him.

"How can you be so kind after all he did to you?" Sara asked. Vasquez watched them.

"It was a long time ago," Micaela said. "Look at him now. You are kind to him."

Sara shrugged. "It is easy. He was always kind to me. Until the very last moment."

Sara explained to Vasquez that she needed someone to take over his business affairs.

"That would be me," she said, "except I don't know a lot about your business. Juan has been the mayordomo at the Wayward Ranch and I have asked him to take on that position here. And I'm going to pay him a fair salary. I looked at what you pay everyone. How do you expect people to live off that? I am giving them all raises. And I'm going to start work on the house where my babies were born. I'm gonna live there with them. The spell has been broken, Javier. I feel the sadness in this place now. I can feel what you have done. It is getting better though. The ghosts are leaving. It could be a happy place if you made it that way."

After a time, Vasquez began to sit up on his own as he regained the use of his arms. Every day the men took him out of bed and put him in a chair. Someone sat with him and tried to get him to feed himself. He stared at them blankly but opened his mouth when the fork or spoon got close. He took the food, closed his mouth, and chewed. For a while, he started spitting his food out. Until Sara came. She would feed him and he would eat. If anyone else tried to feed him, he spit it out.

One morning Sara said, "I will feed you today, old man. And I may feed you again. But you won't keep me trapped here with your tantrums. If you want to starve, you are free to starve yourself."

She left the room.

Later someone came to feed him and he let them. Several days later, he began feeding himself. His arm and hand shook as he tried to pick up the fork and then put food on it and then bring it to his mouth. He wouldn't do it if anyone was watching. So they brought in the food and then left Vasquez alone.

Sara felt a sense of purpose she had not known before. Sara and Juan spent many days going through Javier's office and trying to figure out his business. She contacted business partners in town. They all came out and talked with her and Juan. And then they visited Javier, to see for themselves that he could not take care of his affairs. People in town started to say Javier de la Vasquez had been bewitched. Most of them believed it was about time.

Sara told Javier everything that they were doing.

"You said you wanted to give your daughters and sons a stipend," Sara told him one morning as they sat out on the patio together. Javier seemed to like looking out into the desert. "I was thinking it would be better to give them some land, but I won't take your land from you. I will give them a stipend. Do you want to give them each a lump sum or something yearly?"

Javier stared in front of him.

"They might think you're trying to buy them off," Sara said, "for the crimes you committed against their mothers. Or because you were a terrible father. Terrible because you were their father or because you were an absent father. I'm not certain which."

Sara drank her tea. "Do you have an opinion?"

Javier turned his head and looked at her. She put her hand on his chin and looked into his eyes. "Can you hear me, husband? Do you understand me?"

He spit in her face.

Sara let go of his chin and wiped her face.

"A simple yes or no would have sufficed," she said.

Sara began dreaming again. This time she was swimming in the auld sea as it dried up and she walked up into the new desert, near the Old Mermaid Sanctuary. Her children were running around the patio. The house was full of people. They laughed and sang and worked and played. And the cacti, palo verde, and mesquite moved and danced slowly to music only they could hear. Two desert faeries sat in the sand drinking tea. They looked up at her and invited Sara for a "spot a tea." Her girls called to her and she went running into their arms.

The next morning she told Juan that she wanted to give money away to Vasquez's children.

He shook his head. "Perhaps you want to wait on that," he said. "Maybe in the future you could give out land. But this doesn't feel right. I wouldn't have taken any money from him."

"But you're working for him," she said.

"I am working for you," he said.

"But this is all rightfully yours," she said.

"All of this isn't 'rightfully' anyone's," he said. "Wait on this."

"I want to make up for all the wrong he has done," she said.

"Why?" he said. "You didn't do it."

"But he has given me half of his land," she said. "How can I live on it and raise my children if it belongs to someone else, or should belong to someone else."

Juan laughed. "Live on it and be happy."

"I will give the land to you," she said. "You can buy it from me for a pittance. Then you can do with it what you will. That seems fair."

"I am not taking your land," he said. "You don't have to do anything now. You have time."

"That's not always true," Sara said. "I thought I had time for many things but in the last year and a half my life has been turned upside down many times. It's as though I'm in a wave that's rolling me into shore and then taking me out again. But now, right this minute, I feel as though I have some power. I want to do right by it. And first thing I want to do is rebuild the Old Mermaid Sanctuary. Make it a good house. A nourishing place. I want to care for the land. I want people to live there with me and the girls—I want them to feel as though it is a sanctuary for them, too. But it was your place before it was mine. Will you come live with us there? You can be a better father to the girls if you're there with them all the time."

Juan laughed. "I can't keep up with you, Sara."

"I can't keep up with me either," she said. "But you'll help me?"

"I will," he said.

Sara squeezed his hand.

"You're a good man," she said. She looked at him. "And a good friend. You are a good man, aren't you, Juan? Are there any dark secrets you've hidden from me?"

Juan shook his head. "No dark secrets. No light ones either."

"Now let me tell you how I see the house," she said. "There's beauty everywhere. Renaud will paint the walls. We'll have tile in the kitchen—and the kitchen will be big. Big enough to eat there. The kitchen will nourish the entire house. And there'll be a sewing room. It'll be huge, and women—and men—can come from all around and sew and weave and put together quilts. I've heard there's sheep north of here and we could buy their wool.

And the ironwork I've seen is beautiful. Can we do some of that there, too?"

"Sounds like you want to create your own hacienda," he said.

"Our own village," Sara said. "Only I don't want to own everything. I want us to be a community. Like back home, only better. I want it to be a true sanctuary—where everything within it is sanctified, holy. Not by the church. Where I came from, it was all holy—which meant it was whole. We were all part of the whole. We all came from the auld sea. We'll all be together in this new sea. Juan, the world is changing. You can feel it, too. I've heard David and Rodrico talking about revolution. Don't tell them I said so. I think they've got the right idea. Only I don't want the killin' and stuff." Sara laughed. "It's gonna be good, Juan. It will."

TWENTY-ONE

Javier de la Vasquez did not get back the use of his legs. He didn't speak either. But he could use his arms. He learned to get himself into and out of bed by himself, into and out of his chair. He mostly ate in his room by himself, although Sara offered to take him into the kitchen so he could eat with everyone else. He never responded one way or the other.

Work began on the Old Mermaid Sanctuary. Sara hired crafts people and workmen from all over the area. She, Juan, and the girls went to the house and stayed in whatever rooms weren't being worked on. Juan's niece, Rosarita, came with them to watch the twins when Juan and Sara were busy.

Sara loved being at the sanctuary. It was a little cooler there, probably because of the cottonwoods. And sometimes a hush fell over the place that caused everyone to stop what they were doing and listen. Breathe. And it was also a place where laughter was contagious. Sara watched the workmen and learned from them. Soon she was creating walls out of the dirt, straw, and water.

People came from all around to help. Juan introduced her to them and then told her later that many of them were Vasquez's children. They had learned what she wanted to do for them. Coming to help was their way of showing their appreciation.

At the end of each night, they all sat around a bonfire and drank and told stories. Nita and Emmy listened carefully, usually one of them sitting on Juan's lap while the other circled the fire. They were both talking now in a kind of mixture of four languages: Sara's, Juan's, Madeleine's, and Micaela's Native language.

The weeks and months went by. Sara went back to the hacienda often to check on Vasquez and bring the girls to see him. His eyes lit to up whenever they were near. Sara understood. Everyone loved the girls. They were special. She had to watch them—or someone did—all of the time. Now that they were walking, they kept wandering away, trying to walk out into the desert. They were particularly intrigued by the wash.

One day Sara sat outside with Vasquez as the children played in the garden. Sara watched them. They sat opposite one another holding hands and talking. But they didn't seem to be talking to one another. Nita was looking at a butterfly as she spoke, and Emmy was looking out at one of the invisibles, Sara supposed, because Sara couldn't see anything.

"I keep telling them they cannot wander off without me," Sara said, "but they do it anyway. I'm worried."

She had gone into the wash and talked to all the creatures visible and invisible and asked them to protect her children and let no harm come to them. She put the fath fith on the girls all the time.

"Everyone keeps telling me the old jaguar will eat them," Sara said. "Or the woman in white will kidnap them. The people here are even more superstitious than the people back home. Although back home we killed off so many things that we didn't have as much to fear, except other people. That's what got me. It wasn't some old wolf doing the killing and destroying."

"The old jaguar won't harm them," Vasquez said.

They were the first words he had spoken in a year.

"So you can talk then," Sara said. "And think. I'm happy for that. But how can you be so sure?"

"I am sure," he said.

"I need to tell you some things," Sara said. "The man who raped me, Cormac MacDougal, forced me to marry him. I didn't do it of my own free will but because an enchantment was put on me. The storm I brought into my village destroyed the chapel where we was married. And later I broke the enchantment. I didn't consider myself married to him any more. I should have told you this. It might have made a difference. I don't consider him my husband. You are. I don't love you like a wife loves a husband, but I think I would have grown to. Now I don't think I'll ever love anyone like that again. I loved Ian McLaughlin and I loved Murphy. I love your son Juan, too. But I've decided marriage isn't something that's good for a woman. At least not if she's marrying a man. I wanted to tell you all this and see what you have to say about it."

Javier looked away from her.

He didn't say another word for another year. They had finished work on the Old Mermaid Sanctuary by then, and Sara asked Javier if he wanted to come live with them.

His eyes filled with tears, and he shook his head.

"You'll bring the girls to visit me," he said.

"I will," she said. "And Juan will come often. He's training Rodrico to be the mayordomo here. I didn't know he was one of your sons, too. He's a good man."

The girls ran up to Javier and climbed up onto his lap. They kissed his cheeks.

"Papa Javier is fuzzy," Nita said.

"Like a rabbit," Emmy said.

Several tears spilled over his eyes and rolled down his cheeks.

"No," Sara said. "More like a jaguar." Javier looked up at her. "Right, Javier? Probably would be good if you'd have yourself a shave."

That day, Juan, Sara, and the girls walked into the Old Mermaid Sanctuary as if it was their first time. Sara stood at the wooden gate and ran her fingers over the hand-carved sign hanging there: Welcome to the Old Mermaid Sanctuary. On the side of the gate was an old bell. Juan picked up Nita so that she could ring it. She laughed and slapped her hand against it. Then Emmy did the same thing. Sara opened the gate and walked through it.

Before them was a lush garden surrounded by the curved arches of the three portals. At the center of the garden was a fountain. Two mermaids swam up out of the middle of the fountain. Their tails were entwined and they held hands. Water poured out of their hands.

The four of them walked up to the wide portals. Chairs and tables were scattered here and there, near to the many doors that opened out onto the portal. Nita and Emmy ran through the main entrance and into the house. Sara and Juan followed them into the kitchen where Micaela was cooking. Micaela came and kissed them all. She smiled and clapped her hands. She was a different woman from the one Sara had met when she first came to the hacienda. She seemed younger, more alive. And she was boss of the kitchen. She told everyone to sit down and she would feed them.

Soon the smell of food brought people from all over the house and sanctuary into the kitchen. They sat at the long table in the kitchen and the tables outside. They laughed and talked and ate.

Everyone agreed that the main house at the Old Mermaid

Sanctuary was alive. It seemed to have grown up out of the earth and then the sun and stars came inside and gave it light and color. In the kitchen, flowers and vegetables grew as paintings on the tiled walls. Renaud said he had painted some of them, along with his love Leonardo, but he swore some of them had grown on their own. The household plates were made by Seraphina and her husband Roberto. Each was its own design. They had let Nita and Emmy help them paint them. Some had flowers on them. Others had pictures of seashells. A few had mermaids. Many of them had jackrabbits and coyotes on them. Some of them were filled with colorful geometric designs.

Those were the plates everyone ate off of that first day at the Old Mermaid Sanctuary. It wasn't actually the first day, but it felt like it because Sara and the girls were not going back to the hacienda. And that night, Nita and Emmy slept in their room—the room they had helped paint. Their handprints went all around the bottom of the room. When Renaud had asked them what animals they wanted painted on their walls, they both cried, "Jack the Rabbit!" And so he had painted giant jackrabbits all over the walls, except right above the hand prints. There he had painted Old Mermaids swimming across the walls. Only he said he had painted four, one for each wall and over night they had multiplied into thirteen.

Sara had filled the shelves in the girls' room with books. Before they went to sleep that first night, they each said good night to the jackrabbits, the coyotes, the eagles, the auld sea, the auld mother, Papa Javier and Papa Juan and all the good folk, visible and invisible.

Sara kissed them good night and then left the room. She stood looking at their closed blue door. On it hung a little wooden sign that read "Emmy & Juanita's Room." The girls had written their names themselves. Sara wondered if other two and half year olds could do that.

Sara didn't sleep in her room that night. Instead she went to Juan's room. She got into bed with him.

"I'm not going to have your children," she said. "So if you need some, you should get yourself another woman. And if Termain Murphy ever shows up, there's no telling what will happen."

And then they made love to one another. A hush fell over the sanctuary, as it often did. The jackrabbits told the coyotes to serenade the lovers, and that they did. Everyone had sweet dreams that night.

People started coming to the sanctuary almost as soon as Sara and the girls made it their home. Some people came to look at the beauty of it. To marvel at the mermaid fountain: no one was quite sure where the water came from or how it flowed through the mermaids, not even the man who built it. Sara wondered if they had somehow tapped into the spring Murphy had said was near the mermaid wall. Sara had never found it.

She did hear the singing. Many people did. It was only on particular nights or particular days. When it was really cold or hot. Or when the sun was down or the sun was up. When the moon was dark or the moon was full. They all heard the mermaids singing. And they all agreed they weren't trying to lure them away from anything or to anything. It was a welcome home song.

Some people came to help Sara with the sewing. Weavers came too. They made their own yarn at the Old Mermaid Sanctuary. And they made clothes. Quilts and blankets too. They sold them to those who could pay for them and gave the rest away. Some women left their husbands and came to the sanctuary and sewed.

Others came and helped in the garden. Or in the kitchen. No man ever came after their wives into the Old Mermaid Sanctuary. A few came to the gate, but they never came through it if they were angry. Some heard the mermaids singing and they sat down and wept.

A few potters lived at the sanctuary for a time. All sorts of artists came. They carved and painted and left gifts around the sanctuary. Musicians came and played outside under the moon.

Animals of all kinds visited the sanctuary and Sara asked no one to harm any of them. Horses began showing up, too, and Juan took care of them. Some stayed on to be with the people, others moved on, like other visitors.

Renaud and Leonardo moved into the sanctuary. The Englishman had left the Wayward Ranch and sold it to Gabriel, who ran it much the way the Englishman did, except he had more fun and the food was better. Madeleine came and went.

The girls grew and flourished in the sanctuary. They collected rocks and seashells. They found seashells in the wash every spring after the river dried up. No one understood where the shells had come from, but everyone agreed they must be a gift from the auld ma and the auld sea for her dearest children.

Sara was happy. Yet sometimes in the night she lay in her room and wept. She missed her mother and sisters and the auld sea. She still felt like she wasn't quite herself.

She and the girls visited the hacienda. She made certain plenty of people worked at the hacienda and spent time with Vasquez, but she could see he was lonely. She asked him again and again to come live with them.

He refused. He didn't talk to her, but he did talk to the girls when she wasn't around. She often listened at the door to see what he said. Mostly he asked about their lives and how they were doing. The girls always told him everything and brought him seashells every visit.

They heard at the sanctuary that revolutionaries were going into haciendas and villages and burning what they could and taking over the homes of the rich. Juan told Sara that the villagers and others were still very angry with Vasquez and his treatment of them.

"He could be in danger," Juan said.

Sara had a dream one night that people were coming to destroy them. She saw the hacienda burn, saw only the stone left. And then they came for the Old Mermaid Sanctuary.

She awakened in a sweat.

She told Juan what she had dreamed.

"I had the same dream," he said.

In the morning, they found that nearly everyone had had the same dream.

Juan hitched a horse to the wagon, and he and Sara hurried to the hacienda.

No one came out to greet them when they reached the hacienda.

Sara jumped out of the cart and ran into the house. She called out but no one answered. She ran into Javier's room. He sat in his chair. Rodrico sat next to him.

"He wouldn't leave," Rodrico said. "I couldn't leave him here alone."

"You should have left," Sara said. "Don't sacrifice yourself for him. Old man, are you coming with us or not?"

He looked at her. Juan came into the room.

"The girls would be very sad if anything happened to you," she said.

"Get the papers in my office," Vasquez said. "The deeds for the land and other family papers."

"I know where they are," Juan said.

"And the seashells," he said. He looked at Sara. She nodded. "I don't need anything else."

They got Javier into the cart, and then they headed back to the Old Mermaid Sanctuary. They didn't talk much. Sara silently put the fath fith on them and hoped it would work. They reached the

Old Mermaid Sanctuary before dark. Sara closed the gate behind her and stood there while Rodrico and Juan took Javier into his room—they had saved one for him. She whispered the fath fith.

"Please, auld ma, keep us all safe," she said. And then she went into the house.

It could be that the revolutionaries came by the Old Mermaid Sanctuary and decided to spare it. It could be they weren't revolutionaries at all but bandits looking for silver or gold, and most people knew the sanctuary didn't house that kind of treasure. The story goes they did come to the hacienda and tried to burn it when they couldn't find the old man, but it wouldn't burn. The stone and rock kept blowing out the flames. But the men did their best to destroy what they could. They stayed for a time—a day, a week, several years—and then they went on their way as the hacienda began to crumble into dust.

The Old Mermaid Sanctuary was safe from harm. Javier Vasquez stayed at the sanctuary. Sometimes Sara thought he needed sanctuary more than anyone. No one ever treated him any differently than they did anyone else, even those people who had known him all their lives. Even those people who were his children. He may have minded, but he never said so. Mostly he spent time with the children, but he sometimes stayed up nights playing cards. He still barely spoke. If he lost at cards, he always paid his debts.

One day Juan said to Sara, "This is a sanctuary," he said, "and I think a sanctuary needs a church. A church of the Old Mermaids." He pointed up the path where the old mermaid wall was. "I think we should build it right there and make the wall part of it. And we'll paint the inside and fill it with old mermaids and the old sea."

Sara smiled at him. "You're doing this because you think I'm unhappy," she said. "I'm not. I'm sometimes sad for the sea and my ma."

He kissed her forehead. "Can I build it for you?"

She nodded. "You can."

And so he did. It was a tiny church. As round as can be, built mostly from stone. As far as Sara could tell, everyone from the sanctuary and everyone else they knew came and helped. Everyone of them went into the chapel and painted something: mermaids, seashells, fish, trees, lions, bears, coyotes, little girls with fish tails and wings on their hearts. And the old mermaid wall was part of it all. Juan left off the ceiling so that it was exposed to all the elements they loved.

When Sara stepped into it for the first time after they finished, she could hear the roar of the old sea.

"It's as if I'm inside a seashell," she whispered to Juan. "You did this? It's beautiful. I may never leave." She kissed him.

That night she slept in the tiny church of the old mermaids. In the morning, she heard the mermaids whispering to her. She got up and went outside. She followed the sound into the desert until she saw a spot of green. She went to it and discovered a tiny spring bubbling up from the earth. She smiled and bent over it.

Then she heard, "I thought I might find you here."

Sara turned around.

Murphy was standing before her, clear as day.

"Is it you then?" she asked. "Or am I dreaming?"

"It's no dream, luv," he said. He opened his arms, and she ran into them. They held each other for a long while. When they let each other go, flowers were blooming from the green and water was tickling their toes.

"I went to the sanctuary and asked about you," Murphy said. "This man looked at me and said, 'You must be Murphy.' When I allowed that I was, he said you were in the church. I went there and heard the singing, and I followed it. It's the same singing I've been following for years, trying to find ye."

"I can't believe it," Sara said. "You're really here."

"You came here," he said. "Of course I would come looking for you. You're the love of my life."

"You're not the love of my life," she said.

"That Ian fellow was," he said.

She shook her head.

"The man at the sanctuary?"

Sara laughed. "Come on."

Sara took Murphy's hand, and they went back to the sanctuary. Juan was sitting on the patio with Vasquez and the girls.

"The spring's come back," Sara said. "It's a little miracle. And this is Termain Murphy. Nita and Emmy." The girls jumped up and ran over to her. "This is your da," she said. "I've told you about him. This is Murphy."

The girls shrieked and threw their arms around Murphy's legs. Murphy looked startled, and then he laughed.

"Murphy, these are the loves of my life," she said.

"Daddy, let us show you everything," Nita said. She tugged on his hand.

"They are precocious, to say the least," Sara said. "This one here is a hundred years old and that one there is two hundred."

Emmy nodded. "That's right," she said. "We are auld mermaids."

They said "old" the way their mother did.

Emmy tugged on his other hand. "But we're fast mermaids," she said. "Come on Daddy!"

Sara sat at the table with Juan and Vasquez.

"I know what you're thinking, old man," she said. "I told you the father of the girls raped me. That was true. On the night the girls were conceived, Cormac MacDougal beat and raped me. But I didn't want to have his children. I went to Murphy that night and asked him to make love to me. I asked him to be the father of my baby. And then I gave birth to two babies. And they don't look anything alike. I know that. Juan knows why. Murphy knows why. Now you know why. Murphy is their father, and so is Juan. And so are you. That's all I have to say about it."

She got up from the table. She squeezed Juan's shoulder, and then she followed the girls and Murphy.

Things went on at the Old Mermaid Sanctuary as they had been before, only now Murphy was a part of it. Sara didn't go to Juan's bed and she didn't go to Murphy's bed. She figured that would work itself out. Mostly she stayed with the girls.

Juan returned to the hacienda with Rodrico to see if they could salvage anything. It was the middle of the summer and hardly anyone was at the sanctuary and those that were were very still.

One hot night, Murphy came to Sara's room. They lay together for a long time, talking, and then they made love. Sara lay on his shoulder afterward and cried. Then she got up and retrieved the treasure box and brought it to the bed. She opened it and took the tiny shell out and handed it to Murphy.

"I'm giving it back to you," she said. "As we agreed."

He smiled in the dark and took it.

"I was always sorry I left you," Murphy said. "I should have found a way. I knew I loved you. I knew I should stay. But I couldn't figure out how."

"I told you to go," Sara said. "I was afraid the enchantment would hurt you. Did it?"

"I have ached since I left ya," he said.

"I broke the enchantment," she said. "I broke it good. I'm no longer chained to him."

"Are you sure it's broken?" he asked. "You still look sad, even when you're laughing."

She told him all that had happened since she last saw him.

"You can see that by the blood," Sara said, "one of them has his and one of them has yours, but they were in my womb together, so I say you're the father of both, though I tell them they don't belong to anybody."

"I love 'em both the same," he said. "The instant I saw them, I was filled with love for 'em. You better be careful or I'll steal them from ya."

"You don't have to steal them," she said. "Live here with us. You can be with them all you want."

"What would Juan think of that?" he asked.

"I told him long ago that things would change if you came," she said. "And I suppose they have."

"I can't marry ya," he said. "You're already married to Cormac."

"And the old man," she said.

"And the old man," he said.

She shrugged. "What's one more husband?" She laughed. "I won't be marrying you or anyone else. As for you and Juan, you'll have to work it out yourselves. I love you both. But I trust Juan more than any man alive. He's been constant. I appreciate that."

Murphy nodded. "He would never run out on you?"

"Never," Sara said. "And he built that chapel for me, so I wouldn't feel so homesick. I think that's what brought you back to me, really."

"I will stay," Murphy said. "For now, if you'll let me be of some service."

"I'm sure there's something you can do," Sara said. "But stay out of the kitchen. Micaela would beat you bloody."

TWENTY-TWO

It seemed the auld sea was washing back into Sara's life again. Every night she dreamed of the sea. She dreamed she was swimming sometimes, drowning other times. Sometimes she couldn't find her daughters. Juan and Murphy tried to comfort her. The other women staying at the sanctuary tried to comfort her. It didn't work. She felt restless. She helped Juan and Murphy build the irrigation ditch by the spring—the *acequia madre*, the mother ditch, Juan called it. And she liked being out in the sun, sweating.

But she kept hearing the roar of the sea.

She watched the horizon.

She knew a storm was coming even though she couldn't see it.

One day Sara sat under the cottonwoods with Vasquez and the girls who lay on a blanket sleeping. Sara yawned. It was too hot to do anything. She felt like going inside and sleeping.

"I'm going in for some *limonada,*" she told Vasquez. "I'll bring you back some."

She got up and went through the open gate and into the house. She felt butterflies in her stomach. She poured the *limonada* into two glasses—she'd share hers with the girls—and she went out into the courtyard.

A tall jackrabbit stood next to the mermaid fountain.

"Momma," one of mermaids whispered.

She hurried outside. In a split second, she saw a man walking toward Vasquez, heard him say "Cormac MacDougal," saw the girls sitting up, saw Vasquez reaching for the rifle leaning against the tree—some traveller had left it while they went inside—and Sara ran or leapt like some giant jackrabbit out of one of Murphy's stories. She grabbed the gun from Vasquez and pointed it at Cormac.

"If anyone is gonna kill this man," she said, "it's gonna be me."

Cormac held his hands up. He looked old and battered, not like the young man she had left behind only a few short years ago.

Sara touched the trigger. She imagined the bullet piercing Cormac's body. Imagined him dropping to the ground, dead. Then she would be truly free.

Cormac stared at her. His eyes were sad.

She did not want to notice that his eyes were sad.

"Mommy?" Nita's and Emmy's voices in a chorus calling to her.

Sara turned and looked at them. The sisters held hands. They looked frightened. Murphy and Juan strode toward her. Vasquez reached for the girls.

Sara had to end this. One way or another She had to end this pain for all of them.

Wash it away.

This had been going on far too long.

"Take the girls and Vasquez inside," Sara said. "I will do this alone."

"Sorcha," Murphy said.

"It's all right," Sara said. "Go on."

She stared at Cormac and waited until they had all gone inside the house.

Then she dropped the gun to her side.

"What do you want?" Sara asked.

"I'm glad to see you," Cormac said.

"You create havoc wherever you go," Sara said. "How'd you find me?"

"Your mother," he said. "She got a letter from you and she gave it to me. I was able to figure it out."

"I had written to her," Sara said, "it's true. But she never wrote back. I figured she never got my letters. Why didn't she write me?"

"She did," Cormac said. "She told you that I'd come back to the village a changed man. The spell was off me, and I could see the wrong that I had done to you. I went to the priest and asked him to do something about the marriage because you had gone into it against your will. He wouldn't do it. Said something about it being God's will."

"As soon as the enchantment was broken," Sara said, "I figured we were divorced."

Cormac nodded.

"You came all this way to tell me this?" she asked.

"Your momma never heard back from you after she wrote," Cormac said, "so I thought it was my duty to come tell you myself."

"Tell me that the priest wouldn't divorce us?" she asked.

"No," he said. "I came to tell you your sister and Ian aren't dead."

"What are you talking about?"

"The storm took them out to sea," he said, "but they were able to get to an island. They stayed there until they were rescued, after we left."

Sara felt like she was going to fall over.

"You mean I didn't kill them?"

Cormac shook his head.

"No, you didn't kill them," he said. "You didn't cause the storm either. I called that storm down on the village. I went to the cave and saw you and Ian together—at least that's what I thought I saw. I was so angry. I wanted you both dead."

"That's why you were so surprised when you saw me that morning."

He nodded.

"I didn't do any of it?" she said. "None of it?"

"You didn't," he said. "And your sister, she got Ian drunk and said she was you. That was the only reason he was with her."

"My whole family is alive?" she asked.

"At least when I left," he said. "Ian did forgive your sister, and they got married. They have a child."

Sara sank to her knees. She couldn't help it. She heard Juan and Murphy start to come out to her, to call to her. But Sara heard Micaela tell them to stay away. She was a fierce woman now that she was herself.

"I am a changed man," Cormac said. "I wanted to come and let you see that truth, and to tell you that you did nothing wrong. I'm sorry I wrecked your life. I don't drink anymore. I have worked these last years helping the poor. I'm trying to make myself worthy. Not because I want anything from you."

"You do want something from me," Sara said. "You want my forgiveness." She had no tears. She had no more hate for him. She felt a strange kind of joy bubbling up inside of her.

"Mommy!"

Sara turned around. The girls had escaped the house and were running toward her. She sat on the ground and let them come.

"As you can see," Sara said, "you didn't wreck my life. You no longer have that kind of power over me."

Cormac knelt on the ground.

"Cormac MacDougal," Sara said, "these are my daughters Juanita and Emmy."

Cormac began crying.

"You say you're a changed man," Sara said. "I will know that only by your actions. I'm not a weak young woman any more. You can't cast an enchantment over me. Your magic is not more powerful than mine. If you doubt this, ask that old man in the chair who cannot walk and rarely speaks."

Sara looked up. Micaela, Juan, and Murphy were all behind her. Sara sighed. When Renaud and Madeleine returned, she would have quite a tale to tell them.

"Are you hungry?" Sara asked Cormac.

Cormac said, "What?"

"She asked if you wanted some food," Micaela said. "Enough talk. More food. Let's go. *Vamanos*!"

Cormac stayed on the sanctuary for the day. He spent most of his time with the girls. He told Sara he would like to stay in the area for a while.

"There's a sheep ranch a few hours from here," Sara said, "and they're always looking for help. There's land if you wanted to start your own ranch. We're always looking for good wool."

Cormac nodded.

"Juan can give you directions," she said. "He'll ride out with you a ways."

"Thank you," Cormac said. "Thank you for everything."

Sara watched Cormac and Juan leave.

Then she did a little dance in the dirt. A cardinal in the cottonwood watched her.

"It's fun," Sara told the bird. "You should try it."

Sara could feel herself unwinding. It was as though she had been bound in something so long that she hadn't even realized it until now—now, as the thread unraveled. She laughed more. She danced all the time. Most mornings she woke from her dreams laughing.

The days and nights grew hotter. One day someone brought news to the sanctuary that the old jaguar had been shot and killed in the wash near the old hacienda.

"Why would they kill him?" Sara asked. "He wasn't causing any harm."

Sara glanced at Vasquez. He didn't look at her.

"They killed it and then when they went to skin it," Juan said, "it was gone."

"There you are then," Sara said. "They never really killed it at all."

Juan shrugged. "They were pretty certain it was dead."

"I hope it got away," Sara said.

Javier looked at her. "I don't think it did," he said.

Renaud spent the hot days in the huge sewing room, painting. He liked being in a room where women were working or men were playing, he said. The women spun the wool and made dirty jokes when he was in the room to see if he would laugh.

Renaud was in the sewing room on the day when everything changed again.

Juan was checking on the horses, and Murphy was in the library looking for a particular book. Sara was in the kitchen with Micaela. She had just run into the house to check on something. Later she couldn't remember what it was. She had left Javier on the shore of the wash with the girls. They were looking for and finding many seashells.

"Look, Papa!" they would say each time they picked up a shell. "A mermaid found her tail."

It was a clear and blue day. Everyone thought the monsoons were gone for the year. The wash had been dry for a week or more.

And then Sara noticed a shadow fall over the patio. Both she and Micaela looked outside. Sara felt sick to her stomach. And Juan and Murphy felt something, too, or heard something. Renaud, too, and every woman in the sewing room. They all ran outside. To the north, huge black rain clouds were riding the mountains.

They all heard the roar. Sara ran faster than she had ever run in her life. Juan and Murphy were ahead of her. Sara screamed her daughters' names.

They all knew before they got there that the wash had flashed. It was a river again.

No one was ever certain what happened in those next seconds. Murphy and Juan reached the shore first. Sara looked out into the arroyo and saw the new river raging past them, only it looked like the auld sea to Sara. She didn't see the girls or Vasquez.

She saw Murphy climbing into the paloverde that grew down from the cliff and hung partly into the wash before growing up again. He was reaching for Nita who was perched in the tree like an old buzzard. She put her arms around his neck and then he climbed back and gave Nita to Juan. Sara ran to Juan and took Nita. Murphy went back for Emmy. Soon Sara was sitting on shore with her arms around both daughters. They all sobbed.

"How'd you get in the tree?" Sara asked.

"Papa," they said. "He put us there."

"How?" Sara asked.

The girls said they saw the water first as a trickle, and Papa called to them. Then it all happened so fast. They were in the water, and Papa was swimming out to them, and he grabbed them and threw them into the tree. The tree person caught them, the girls said, and told them to hold on tight.

"And Papa swam away," Nita said.

"Like an old mermaid," Emmy said.

"Only he didn't have a tail," Nita said.

"He did have a tail," Emmy said, "but it wasn't an old mermaid tail."

Later, others asked the girls what happened, and Sara asked them again. They told a similar story for a time, and then it seemed to recede from their memories like a dream. Soon, they said they didn't remember what had happened.

That day, as far as anyone could tell, Javier de la Vasquez disappeared from the face of the Earth. Some say he swam south for a long time until he found a jungle. Then he climbed out of the water, a whole man again, and lived out the rest of his natural life in some small town near that jungle.

Vasquez left a will. Everything went to the people he had loved most in his life, he wrote: his wife Sara O'Broin and his two daughters, Juanita and Emmy O'Broin. They inherited everything except for the money he left each and every one of his offspring. He listed each of their names, by order of birth. Sometime later, Sara offered to sell land to them, and many of them did buy land from her near the Old Mermaid Sanctuary. Rodrico kept the old house at the hacienda. He fixed it up and made it livable again.

Sara and her daughters held a memorial for Vasquez at the Old Mermaid Sanctuary.

Everyone took turns going into the chapel and listening to the sound of the auld sea. Sara went with her daughters. They listened for a long, long time.

"I think I hear Papa," Nita said.

Emmy nodded. "Yes, he says he loves us for all time."

Sara listened. She heard the sound of the old sea, but nothing more.

"Papa Javier wanted to be a good man," Sara told her daughters, "but he was bound by so many things he didn't understand. Now those of us who knew him can learn from his experience. We can live in love and joy."

Her daughters looked up at her. "We already do that, Momma," Nita said.

"Now it's your turn," Emmy said.

Later that day they had a fiesta at the Old Mermaid Sanctuary. People talked about this party for years afterward. Magic happened. The food served that night cured people of long standing illnesses. Estranged couples got back together. Children were conceived. Lovers met lovers. Wild animals walked calmly through the patio and house. Desert faeries danced with anyone who would. The music went on all night. The old mermaids came off the walls and joined in the festivities.

As the sun came up the next morning, Sara went into the girls' room to kiss them awake. They slept together on one of their twin beds. Peeking out from beneath their one pillow was something red.

Sara kissed both girls, and they opened their eyes.

"Good morning, loves," Sara said. "What's that under your pillow?"

The girls sat up. Emmy lifted the pillow, and Nita pulled out a red cap.

"We forgot," Emmy said. "That man Cormac gave it to us when he was here, and he said to give it to you. We kept forgetting."

Nita held the cap out to her mother.

Sara took it. The cap vibrated in her hand.

"Mommy," Emmy said. "We were up so late. Can we sleep some more?"

Sara nodded. "Go to sleep then," she said.

She balled the cap up in her hand and hurried outside. She ran up the hill to the Old Mermaid Chapel and went inside.

"I got it back," she whispered. "I've got it back."

She ran back outside again. She whirled around. She tossed the cap into the air and caught it again. She could go home now. She was free. She was free.

She was herself again.

She held the cap up to her face.

She could go home now.

She looked back at the Old Mermaid Sanctuary. She heard people talking as they woke up and others as they began going to sleep after the long party. She looked at the cottonwoods and listened to the birds. A jackrabbit loped across the wash. She could hear mermaids singing, too. A coyote watched her from his perch on a rock near the spring.

Sara looked up at the clear blue sky.

She pulled on a loose string on the red cap. She pulled and pulled. The cap unraveled in her hands. She began dancing around the desert. She tossed a thread up into the air and a cardinal snatched it away from her. She tossed another and a cactus wren took it. Another floated to the ground and the jackrabbit ran with it. The coyote snatched up the gold thread. It trailed behind him for miles.

Sara threw several threads into the arroyo. The Old Mermaids walked across the vast empty riverbed and found Sara's tossed threads after night fell again. The moon plucked out the silver threads. The sun wanted the green. The jaguar might have taken the orange and black. The wind sipped up some of the thread. The green cactus man made himself a new cap that bloomed like a flower.

Sara scattered the thread throughout the whole desert.

She didn't need to go home. She was home.

When all the threads were gone, Sara went back to the Old Mermaid Sanctuary to find out what Micaela was making for breakfast.

ABOUT THE AUTHOR

K im Antieau's novels include *Church of the Old Mermaids, The Blue Tail, The Jigsaw Woman, The Monster's Daughter, Her Frozen Wild, Ruby's Imagine, Broken Moon, Coyote Cowgirl,* and many others. Her books have twice been shortlisted for the James Tiptree Award. She lives in the Pacific Northwest. Learn more at www.kimantieau.com.